The
Wonder Bread
Summer

Also by Jessica Anya Blau

Drinking Closer to Home

The Summer of Naked Swim Parties

"A light-hearted, enthralling read that enables us to laugh at our own less-than-perfect families."   —*Bust*

"The sharpness of Jessica Anya Blau's voice and wit never ceases to amaze me. From the first page this surprising novel takes a classic tale—adult children going home again—and turns it on its head. An absorbing, heart-wrenching read."   —Katie Crouch, author of *Men and Dogs*

"Reminiscent of Jeannette Wall's *The Glass Castle*, Jessica Anya Blau's sophomore effort is a raging success. With incredible insight and endless imagination, Blau has created the über-dysfunctional family that survives cringe-worthy encounters, yet manages to forge ironclad bonds."
                                                —*New York Journal of Books*

"From painful humor to poignant scene-setting, [Blau] takes no prisoners in her candid look at an unconventional clan."   —*Booklist*

"The hilariously irreverent sibling triad in *Drinking Closer to Home* had me laughing so hard at their gallows humor that I didn't realize how devastated I was until I was fully under their spell. This unconventional joy ride of a novel is also an unexpectedly powerful and multilayered exploration of unbreakable family bonds."
                                          —Gina Frangello, author of *Slut Lullabies*

"Blau writes funny, often heartbreaking, and always relatable anecdotes . . . [Her] lifelike characters are such a joy to get to know that one feels sorry to leave them behind."   —*Publishers Weekly*

"*Drinking Closer to Home* is as raw and heartbreaking as it is tender. Jessica Anya Blau has written an honest, haunting portrayal of a beguiling yet maddening family who together come of age amid the shifting morals of a country on the cusp of tremendous cultural change. With humor, compassion, and a keen insight into the human psyche, *Drinking Closer to Home* proves that despite the best of intentions, where we come from and where we end up are even closer than we could ever imagine."
                                          —Robin Antalek, author of *The Summer We Fell Apart*

The Wonder Bread Summer

A NOVEL

JESSICA ANYA BLAU

HARPER ● PERENNIAL

NEW YORK ● LONDON ● TORONTO ● SYDNEY ● NEW DELHI ● AUCKLAND

HARPER ● PERENNIAL

An incarnation of the first chapter originally appeared in *New York Tyrant Magazine*.

This book is a work of fiction. References to real people, events, establishments, organizations, or locales are intended only to provide a sense of authenticity, and are used fictitiously. All other characters, and all incidents and dialogue, are drawn from the author's imagination and are not to be construed as real.

HarperCollins books may be purchased for educational, business, or sales promotional use. For information please e-mail the Special Markets Department at SPsales@harpercollins .com.

FIRST EDITION

Designed by Michael Correy

Library of Congress Cataloging-in-Publication Data is available upon request.

ISBN 978-0-06-219955-3

13 14 15 16 17 OV/RRD 10 9 8 7 6 5 4 3 2 1

For David Grossbach

1

1983

Allie was in a fitting room with a thirty-three-year-old man named Jonas, pulling pinches of cocaine out of a Wonder Bread bag that was more than three-quarters full. It was the first time she had tried coke. Her heart was rat-a-tat-tatting and her limbs were trembling like a small poodle's. Clearly, this had been a poor decision.

Her best friend, Beth, had been doing coke all year, particularly at the end of each semester as she and Allie studied for exams. Beth was a French major, too. She was fun, she was happy, and she didn't seem to mind that Allie stayed straight while Beth did any kind of drug that was handed to her. It was an ideal college friendship: the two girls balanced each other like a perfectly poised seesaw—and they laughed together at everything, no matter what their mental state.

Worse than the jitteriness from the coke was the fact that Jonas (who was perched on a little copper-footed stool exactly like the one on which Allie sat) was now holding out his bare dick, which was black as espresso, blacker than his face, and as thick as a pair of tube socks rolled up. "Ever see one like this?" Jonas asked. He seductively rolled his voice as if Allie should have been happy to view his offering.

"No," Allie said. This was true. Jonas's was only the second penis Allie had ever seen in her life (she'd never even seen her father with his shirt off). And although the general form was similar to the one penis she knew, Allie was shocked by it—as shocked as if Jonas had pulled out his small intestine and laid that on his palm.

Jonas owned Miss Shirley's Dress Shop on a shabby corner of Oakland that bordered Berkeley. Allie and Beth had met him three months earlier, after he approached them in Carlos Murphy's Eatery. Sitting up at the bar with her fake ID and her dark red curls blown out into a sheet of silk, Allie had thought that for the first time in her life she might be bordering on cool. Jonas sat down beside her, dressed like someone from the pages of *GQ*, with a slick black beeper attached to his belt, and said, "You're Allie, aren't you?" And then he offered her and Beth jobs right then and there, without even asking if they were qualified. Of course Allie said yes. She had been looking for a job for months and hadn't been able to find anything that was less than a forty-minute bus ride from her apartment.

At that moment, with a hot, flirty bartender calling her name and a summer job she could show up at the very next day, Allie thought her good luck was ramping up. But now, looking at Jonas's dick waggling out of his fly—half-up, as if it were being held by an invisible wire—Allie wondered if what little luck she had was starting to run out.

"I've gotta get outta here." Allie could hear the quaver in her voice.

"No, you don't," Jonas said, and he waved his dick from side to side, then pulled his balls out from his underpants—conjoined black kumquats.

"Yes, I do." Allie reminded herself to breathe. She wiped her nose with the base of her palm, then stood and pushed the fitting-room curtain aside.

"What the fuck?!" Jonas reached out from the stool and pulled the curtain closed again. "Someone could see us back here." It was a straight shot from the fitting room to the display window and glass door.

"So maybe we shouldn't be back here." Allie wished she could worm her fingers up her nose, down her sinuses, through the ventricles of her heart, and rub out all the coke she had done, like erasing chalk from a blackboard. She wished she could swirl her hands in the air and erase Jonas, too. "What if a customer comes in?" Her voice teetered on a precipice. It seemed like crying would make things worse, so she swallowed away her instinct to do just that.

"I locked the door." Jonas picked up the slouching bread bag from the floor, spun it shut, then fastened it with a wire twisty that he had pulled from his shirt pocket. "Now sit down. I won't touch you, I swear. I just want to look at you."

Allie sat, because she had yet to figure out how not to do what she'd been told. In fact, Allie assumed that it was her obedient nature that had kept her focused throughout high school, never going out or dating (not that her father would have allowed it), and doing more than what was expected in her classes so that she earned straight A's, and then a scholarship to the University of California, Berkeley.

"Why don't you take off your clothes and let me really see you?" Jonas's right hand was now lifting his dick up and down like a handshake.

"I can't." Allie looked toward the curtain so she wouldn't have to look at Jonas.

"Beth took off her clothes for me," Jonas said.

"No way." Allie tried to imagine Beth sitting naked on the delicate stool with the floral padded cushion. Beth's hair was long and shiny, as dark as Jonas's skin. Everyone said she looked like a young Elizabeth Taylor, or like Nastassja Kinski in the movie *Tess*. There were times when Allie found it hard to be out with Beth, because she was so pretty that no matter how good Allie felt she looked, she always concluded that her red hair and big butt, which men loved but women rarely envied, couldn't compare to Beth's sleek, polished beauty.

"Yeah, way." Jonas's handshake with his dick became a stroke. "And she sat right there where you are while I played with myself."

"I don't believe you," Allie whispered. She could barely speak—there was an apple in her throat.

"Believe it. I saw that mole just inside her thigh. I saw her dark brown nipples."

Allie tried not to gasp. Beth loved that mole. She called it her third eye and claimed it watched everything that went on between her legs.

"We've done it every time you've left work early," Jonas said. Often, if no one came into the shop all morning, Jonas sent one of the two girls home at lunch. Today, Allie worked alone, because Beth hadn't felt like going in and had told Jonas she was sick.

"That's crazy." Allie shut her eyes. The Earth felt like it was spinning in the wrong direction. She grasped the sides of the stool as if that would help her regain balance.

"Her nips are big. And they pop out like pencil erasers."

Allie forced herself to look at Jonas, to see what Beth had seen. She watched his hand, watched his dick, and tried to imagine that she was Beth.

Beth was rich. Really rich. She worked for fun. She worked because she didn't want to be left behind while Allie was at the dress shop, blasting the soundtrack from *Flashdance* and dancing in front of the mirrors. Beth could have bought the shop from underneath Jonas, so why would she have chosen instead to sit naked in it while he masturbated?

"Exactly how many times has she done it?" Allie turned her head away from Jonas, but her eyes kept flicking back to him. Was doing this *normal*, she wondered? Was every college girl sitting around and letting strange, grown men look at her while jacking off? Often Allie felt like she was five steps behind other people—as if the protocol for being twenty (and all other ages, too) had been whispered down from mothers to their daughters. And Allie, who hadn't seen her mother in two years, and hadn't lived with her since she was eight, was always at a disadvantage. It was like the coffee thing. Most of her friends had coffee pots in their rooms, or French presses. Allie would watch them make a pot, casually dumping in the damp-looking grounds as if they knew by instinct exactly how much to use. While Allie sipped the brewed cup that had been handed her, she'd wonder how they came to know how to make this so perfectly right.

"I guess Beth's done it, like, three times." Jonas made a little grunting sound in his throat.

"Oh," Allie said, because there were no other words that would come to her.

"But I'd rather look at you," Jonas said. "Beth's too white for me."

"You don't think I'm white?" When she was a little girl, Allie's grandmother, Wai Po, told her that if she pretended she was white, the whole world could be hers. Faking it took no effort on Allie's part, as most people proved to have little imagination. Until they met her black father (whose own father was white) or her Chinese mother (whose father was Jewish), everyone assumed Allie, with her loopy-curled hair, raindrop-splattered freckles, and light brown eyes that weren't slanted much more than some of the Mexican kids' eyes, was white.

Of course, Wai Po's *fake that you're white* advice had a little coda whispered in her granddaughter's ear: "But no matter what, marry Chinese." Only once (the year Wai Po died, when Allie was eight), was Allie brave enough to point out that Wai Po herself did not *marry Chinese*.

"This is true," Wai Po had whispered. "And look at your mother. She all trouble."

"I can tell you've got black in you." Jonas laughed. "And some Chinese, too!" His hand picked up the pace.

"Someone must have told you I'm black and Chinese," Allie said, although since neither of her parents had ever shown up at Berkeley, even to drop her off when she started school two years ago, no one in town knew her true racial identity. Maybe because he was black, Allie thought, Jonas could see it in her.

"Nobody told me nothin'," Jonas said, and he craned his neck out as if to look at Allie more closely.

Allie was wearing tight stone-washed jeans, pink Candie's mules, and a *Flashdance*-style off-the-shoulder pink shirt (it was Beth's) over a black tank-top. But she felt completely naked, or like she might as well have been naked. The feeling was revolting, terrifying, and yet there was a sense that something thrilling was happening. The fact that Jonas was doing what he was doing while looking at *her* gave Allie a small frisson of excitement. She was utterly ashamed, and yet compelled. There was a chance that if she moved too quickly, she might throw up.

"Just show me your tits," Jonas said. "Nothing more."

"No, I can't," Allie said, but she didn't get up from the stool.

"Be a good employee," Jonas said. "It's payday today."

A shimmering tremble ran through Allie's body. Jonas had

been claiming he was in the middle of financial restructuring and could pay Allie and Beth in cocaine each week, or with a lump sum once things had settled. Beth took the coke but Allie had been holding out and waiting for the cash. After two months of not having collected a paycheck, Allie saw her debts growing into a stone wall that was about to topple and squash her flat. She was behind in rent (she had been using the hundred dollars her father sent each month for food and bus fare, rather than putting it toward her $250 rent), but that was the least of it. More important, she was behind in her tuition payment. If Allie didn't pay last spring's tuition and this coming fall's tuition by August 16, five days from now, the University of California would drop her from their roster. All her hard work would add up to nothing. She knew she should blame herself for her troubles, but really, Allie wanted to blame her ex-boyfriend, Marc.

"Just take off your shirt and sit there in your bra," Jonas said. "No big deal. It's like wearing a bathing suit."

"I really need you to pay me today," Allie said. "If I don't give school at least half of what I owe, I'll be kicked out." Allie had thought about asking Beth for the money, but just couldn't bring herself to do it. All she could hear was Wai Po—who, when she wasn't whispering, only spoke in a shout—say, *NO MATTER WHAT, NEVER BORROW MONEY FROM FRIEND OR FAMILY.* Allie had first been told this at the age of six, when she had asked Wai Po if she could borrow eight dollars to buy a wooden croquet set at the garage sale next door to her grandmother's house.

"Why don't you get the money from your dad?" Jonas asked.

"He's not that kind of dad," Allie said. When she had told her father, Frank, that her boyfriend, Marc, had borrowed both her scholarship and her student loan money, then had broken up with her before paying her back, Frank had said, "If you're ignorant enough to give a man money then you better teach yourself real quick how to get it back." Frank was a firm believer in self-reliance, a skill he had pushed onto Allie over and over again as she spent her childhood navigating the impossibly slow and unreliable bus system in Los Angeles, getting herself to dentist's appointments, checkups, school, Camp Fire Girls meetings, and the Boys and Girls Club, where eventually she worked as a volunteer. He also, Allie knew, probably didn't have the cash.

"Take off your shirt, sit there for thirty seconds, and then, I swear, I'll pay you everything I owe you and you can even go home early."

Allie hesitated. "How early?"

"One o'clock, how's that?"

Allie glanced toward Jonas and saw that he was pumping his hand now, squeezing and releasing his dick as if it were attached to an air mattress that needed to be blown up.

"Okay, I'll count to thirty," Allie said, and she felt tears streaming down her cheeks. The initial, tiny, clandestine thrill that she had felt knowing that she could turn a man on like this had dissipated with each sleazy, coke-hyped moment. How did Beth do this?

"You can't start counting until your shirt is off," Jonas said.

"One," Allie said, and she flipped up both of her tops so they were over her face, revealing the last thing her mother had bought her: a delicate, sheer bra, with embroidered pansies over the nipples. "Two." Allie pretended she was alone in her bathroom and continued the count in her head.

"You can put your shirt down now," Jonas said, when Allie was only up to twenty-five.

Allie flipped down her shirts. What she saw then was so foreign she didn't have the wherewithal to look away. Jonas was holding a linen handkerchief near his dick and spasming into it. In all the time she'd been with Marc, Allie had never seen his penis in orgasm. It was always inside her, hidden, mysterious.

"I've gotta go." Allie felt breathless, like she had just witnessed a car crash, or a beating, or some other act of violence. She was nauseous with regret. She ran out of the fitting room to the glass front door. A woman stood outside waiting, a soft, patchwork leather purse hanging from her forearm. The key was dangling in the lock and Allie turned it, opened the door, and kicked down the doorstop. The woman silently passed Allie as she entered the store. Three more women were right behind her.

"How are you today?" Allie said, to the last one through the door.

"Just looking," the woman said, and she rushed toward the sale rack in the back where Jonas had hung a few poorly stitched madras frocks he had bought by the pound from a South American merchant who couldn't speak English. Although she always knew there was cocaine in the back, had seen people walk in then out after "visiting" Jonas, and knew Beth and Jonas did coke together, Allie hadn't understood *that* was the real business until the day that she'd witnessed Jonas buying dresses without regard to what they looked like.

Allie watched the customers for a moment, although she wasn't sure why. She placed herself behind the glass-top counter in her customary position, elbows down, butt waggling behind, in an effort to force her body to feel comfortable. Jonas sauntered out of the dressing room and stood before Allie on the other side of the counter. Allie's stomach bumped and recoiled.

"That was reaaaaaly fun," Jonas said, and he winked as if they'd shared a tender secret. "Ain't nothin' sweeter than a yummy little Jewish-Asian-black girl."

"How do you know I'm part Jewish?" Allie asked. It seemed impossible that Jonas could perceive this tiny bit of her.

"I can see it!" Jonas laughed. "Just like I saw the black and Asian."

Allie couldn't even fake a smile. "Okay, so you said you'd pay me and I could leave at one, remember?" Was the barbed-wire feeling in her veins from the coke or remorse? How long would it take for all this to wear off?

"Yeah, yeah," Jonas said, just as his beeper went off. He flipped the beeper up from his belt so he could see the number, then said, "I'll write you a check as soon as I finish some business in the back."

Jonas went to the stockroom, where his desk was. Two more women came in. It was unusual to have so many customers. Miss Shirley's was on a shady intersection with a liquor store across the street and a rib joint two doors over. No one would have driven there to buy a dress—the customers were mostly people who lived in the neighborhood, wandering in because they were curious, or bored, or because they didn't have the energy to go elsewhere. But that afternoon, Thursday, one followed the other in and out the door, keeping Allie busy while she tried to ignore her shaking hands, her heart beating in her stomach, and the stone of regret in her throat.

At one thirty, Allie was ringing up what would be the last sale of the day. Jonas still hadn't come out of the stockroom and Allie didn't want to go back there, where she might once again be alone with him. She made conversation with her final customer, a middle-aged, dreadlocked woman with the soft, pillowy body of TV grandmothers, in the hope she would stay until Allie had her paycheck in hand.

"So where do you plan on wearing the dress?" Allie asked.

"I don't know." Middle-aged-TV-grandmother smiled. "I hadn't really thought of that."

"What shoes do you have at home to wear with it?" Allie glanced toward the back. She worried about what Jonas might ask of her before handing over the check. Allie stared down at the register, opened it, and counted out, in twenties and one ten, the amount owed her for the past eight weeks: $1,530.00.

"I suppose I could wear sandals." The woman hesitated. She seemed startled by the sudden friendship. Or maybe she was surprised by the large sum of cash Allie had just removed from the till.

"Jonas!" Allie yelled to the back, "I'm leaving now, I paid myself from the register." How could he say no? The money was there now and he had promised to pay her.

Jonas rushed out and stood in front of Allie and middle-aged-TV-grandmother. He looked from one to the other.

"We're going," Allie said, pointing at middle-aged-TV-grandmother with her thumb. "I paid myself." Allie held up the thick wad of bills for Jonas to see. She was quivering so hard it looked like she was using the money for a fan.

Jonas snatched the cash, divided it in two, and shoved it down the front pockets of his gray slacks. "I said I'd write you a check," he said.

"Can you write it now?" Allie asked. "I have to pay at least part of my tuition or I'm going to be kicked out of school."

Middle-aged-TV-grandmother watched the conversation, wary.

"Come in the back with me and I'll give you a check." Jonas put his hand on Allie's upper arm and pulled her toward him.

"Will you wait for me?" Allie smiled at the woman.

"You want me to wait for you?" Middle-aged-TV-grandmother's brow furrowed in anxiety.

"You don't have to wait for her," Jonas said. "We're closing up early—I'll give her a ride home." He released Allie, walked to the other side of the counter, and stood by the door.

"But it should only take you a second to write the check," Allie said.

"Allie!" Jonas smiled real big. "Let the woman go!"

"Well, thanks so much," middle-aged-TV-grandmother said hastily, and she bundled her plastic shopping bag with her macramé purse, held them both against her chest, and went out the door, which Jonas shut behind her. As he was turning the bolt, she looked back through the glass and caught Allie's eye. *Save me*, Allie thought, but middle-aged-TV-grandmother didn't seem to understand; she turned and walked down the sidewalk.

"Who was that?" Jonas asked. "Your boyfriend's mother?"

"I don't have a boyfriend," Allie said.

"Marc," Jonas said.

"Who told you about Marc? Did Beth tell you about Marc?" Allie asked. Each time she said his name, Allie felt a finger jabbing the bruises on her heart—it was still tender, throbbing.

Marc and Allie had first seen each other in the outdoor courtyard of Café Roma during the first week of the fall semester. Allie was alone at a table, reading *Le Grand Meaulnes* in French.

"You can read that?" Marc had asked, peering in to look at the book from the table beside her. Something like a tidal wave had washed through Allie's head. She hadn't been able to hear, could barely see, felt numbness in her legs, and had to deliberately search inside her mouth for her tongue. First love at first sight.

Marc had a BA from Berkeley and an MBA from Stanford. He was tall, with broad shoulders and wide white teeth that lined up perfectly, like train cars. His eyes were brown, his hair was brown, his skin was like suede. He looked like someone out of a tuxedo catalog.

Impossibly, he seemed to like Allie. And he was impressed by her—her good grades, her fluency in French, the fact that she had never had alcohol or smoked pot, or cut a class, or had sex even. And so, Allie went on the second date of her life, the first having been senior prom with Blake Freid, who was a pimply genius. Unlike Blake after their evening, Marc asked Allie out again. And again. And again. At first Allie felt like she was in a dream where all she had to do was float, but eventually she relaxed and became her authentic self around Marc—she did goofy robot dances; she pulled up her pants to underneath her breasts, stuck her belly out, and pretended she was a middle-aged woman; she teased her hair out into a giant ball of frizzy red and laughed at herself in the mirror. And Marc seemed to like her even more.

In the beginning of October, in spite of his busy schedule (he was never able to see her two weekend nights in a row and could usually only get away one night during the week), Marc was officially Allie's boyfriend. That's when Allie's *trying* period began. She tried alcohol, got slightly drunk and discovered she liked the liquid feeling it gave her, the soupiness that ran through her veins and swirled in her head. Twice she tried pot, but smoking pot made her feel like she was shouting when she was whispering, so Allie decided that was the end of trying pot.

Eventually, and in spite of the fear that she would be irrevocably changed for the worse (slummier, less youthful and optimistic), she tried sex. The girls at school had told Allie that the first few times would be awkward and painful. It takes some time to figure out what you're doing, they said, and don't even think that you'll have an orgasm! Not so for Allie. It was great sex. Her body seemed to know just what went where. And Allie only felt changed for the better—like she moved better, danced better, walked taller. It was like discovering a country you never knew existed and finding that you already were familiar with the customs and could even speak the language. Sex was the highlight of Allie's year. If getting into Berkeley hadn't been so important to her, she might have said that sex was the highlight of her life.

When Christmas came, Allie went home to her father, Frank, in Los Angeles. She decorated a potted fig tree with tinsel and made a tinfoil star to put on the top. Frank made cocoa on Christmas morning and gave Allie a gift certificate to Berman's Office Supply so she could buy typing paper, typewriter ribbons, notebooks, and pens for school.

When Allie returned to Berkeley, Marc took her out to dinner, gave her two tickets for an Eddie Money concert, and asked to borrow $7,000 for the best business opportunity he'd seen since getting his MBA.

"It's a bar in San Leandro," Marc had explained. "A cash machine. The owner's in some trouble with his family—had an affair with his brother's wife or something—and has to leave town now."

"He slept with his brother's wife?!" Allie asked.

"No big deal," Marc said, and Allie should have known then that there were ways in which Marc would not be good for her.

"Kind of a big deal," Allie said.

"I'll pay you back in time for you to pay your spring tuition and I'll even give you five hundred dollars interest," Marc said.

It would be the quickest and easiest five hundred dollars Allie had ever made. It would be gourmet coffee money, snack money, or maybe she'd even take Beth out to a fancy dinner to repay her for all the food Allie ate from Beth's refrigerator. Beth's apartment was stocked like a real home. Not Allie's home in L.A., but like her high school friend Kathy Kruger's: Life cereal, milk, Oreos, Laughing Cow cheese, Triscuit crackers, oatmeal in packets, bags of oranges, bananas that went brown before you could eat them all.

The payback dinner with Beth never happened. Marc called Allie at Beth's (Allie herself didn't have a phone and so made and took calls at friends' houses) the day before she was to pay her tuition and explained that the bar had been broken into, the big-screen TV had been stolen, and without a TV there were no customers and no way for him to borrow against the equity. Three days after that, he broke up with her.

"Come back to the fitting room," Jonas said. "I'll tell you who told me about Marc, and then I'll write you a check."

"I'm not interested in the fitting room and I don't really care who told you about Marc." Allie hoped that at the end of her life, lifting up her shirt for Jonas would be the worst thing she'd ever done. If that were the case, she could take some joy in knowing it was behind her.

"Then forget about Marc and just come back to the fitting room." Jonas raised his eyebrows, then winked.

"I don't want to do what we did in there again," Allie said. And then, because it was almost impossible for her not to be polite, she added, "I'm sorry."

"Takes me less than thirty seconds—you know that!" Jonas slinked toward Allie in a slow shoulder-churning serpentine move.

"I'm really tired, Jonas," Allie said. Her voice was starting to quaver again. "I just want to get paid and go home." She pulled her pink satin purse out from under the register and dropped it on the counter. It was a sad-looking purse. The pink was turning gray with dirt.

"No reason to be tired with all the pick-me-up I've got in the stockroom," Jonas coaxed.

"I don't need any more pick-me-up." Allie tried to stand up straight, as she had read once that if you place your body in a position of control the feeling of control will come to you. *Take control, take control, take control*, she thought. "Jonas, you need to pay me right now."

"Stop worrying about your paycheck!" Jonas said.

"I quit. Pay me NOW." Allie splayed her hands on the counter, as if to exert some force.

"What do you mean you quit?" Jonas's face changed from rubber to stone.

"I was offered a job at that bagel place on Telegraph Avenue," Allie lied. She usually tried to be honest (*HALF LIE WILL RUIN WHOLE REPUTATION*, Wai Po had often said), but it seemed that a white lie was a necessary evil in this case.

"Why would you waste your time at some dumb-ass bagel place on Telegraph Avenue when you could be here, get paid, *and* get free blow whenever you want it!" Jonas thumped his hand on the counter as if to emphasize his last point.

"I can walk to the bagel place," Allie improvised, "and I'm sick of taking the bus—" She reached for her purse, but Jonas snatched it up first.

"Where do you think you're going?" Jonas held the purse behind his back.

Allie stood still as a cat. She tried to tally up everything that was in her purse. Maybe she didn't even need it. There were her IDs (school and driver's license); a dried, black Cover Girl mascara (she'd been meaning to throw it out); a tube of Lancôme lipstick (Beth gave it to her because she, Beth, didn't like the color); a pink comb (her only one); some Bic pens (accidentally stolen from the library at school, where she always borrowed a pen from one of the librarians); her quilted fabric wallet (empty save a few pennies and a dime); tampons (covers shredded, white cotton mice popping out of their cardboard inserters); rolling papers (Beth's); a miniature water pipe (Marc's, a souvenir, really); a Eurythmics cassette (useless, as she had no way to play it since her Walkman had died); a year-old index card with a phone number where she could allegedly reach her mother, Penny, in case of emergency (and in case Allie had enough money to make a long-distance call to area code 316, wherever that was); and the one-white, empty rabbit foot key chain Wai Po had given Allie on her sixth birthday.

Allie wanted the key chain. She had been carrying that rabbit foot, almost black and slightly bald now, for fourteen years. It brought her good luck, she believed, just like Wai Po had said, ensuring Allie's place in Berkeley, among other things. And, though she was loath to admit it to anyone, Allie hadn't spent a night without the rabbit foot nearby since the day her grandmother had handed it to her. Also, she wanted her mother's number. Penny may not have taken care of her in years, but Allie still held on to the thought that if she ever really were in trouble, her mother would bail her out. And without her student loan money, without her scholarship money, and now that it looked like she'd be without her paycheck, Allie was feeling like this might be the time.

"I have to meet the manager of the bagel place at two." Allie reached her hand around Jonas. He jerked to one side, laughing.

"What's the name of that bagel place?" Jonas was smiling so big, Allie could see the silver fillings on his molars.

"Sam's." Allie was glad the name came out easily. When she was nervous, she often forgot names.

"Sam's?" Jonas was grinning, walking backward toward the fitting rooms with Allie's purse in his hands.

"Yeah. Sam's." Allie marched toward him.

"Come back here." Jonas tore open the floral curtain. "Sit down, do a little toot, and let me look at you again. *Then* you can have your purse, I'll write you a check, and you can go meet the manager at Sam's."

"I'm really late," Allie said.

"I'll pay you a little extra for the time." Jonas winked. Allie imagined Wai Po watching this scene. She would have called Allie a *prossy-tute*, a word Allie had first heard when Wai Po caught Allie looking out the window of the car at a long-legged, skinny blond girl wearing a sequined bikini and white go-go boots on the corner of Sunset and Londonderry. *DON'T LOOK AT GIRL*, Wai Po had said. *A CHILD MIND IS LIKE PIECE OF PAPER WHERE EVERYONE LEAVE MARK. YOU DON'T WANT PROSSY-TUTE LEAVING MARK ON YOU.*

"Can I just have the purse and my paycheck? Please?" Allie stuck out her hand, then quickly hid it in her pocket before Jonas could see the tremor.

"Sit down. Do a toot and we'll talk about it." Jonas pointed with his palm at the gold-legged stools.

Allie sat. What else could she do? Jonas went to the stockroom and returned almost instantly with a Gerber baby-food jar full of coke. He sat on the other stool and handed Allie a plastic pointed pen cap. Allie knew what she was supposed to do with it; she had watched Beth use the slim, indented prong from a Bic cap to scoop out little piles of coke from origami envelopes. Jonas unscrewed the lid and held out the jar.

"I did enough today," Allie said. "It's not my thing."

"Do two capfuls and I promise I'll give you your paycheck," Jonas said.

"Please just give me my paycheck." Allie was afraid she'd start crying. In all her life, she had never felt such overwhelming powerlessness and frustration.

"Look how small the scoop is!" Jonas pointed at the pen cap in Allie's hand. Allie silently conceded (she wouldn't give Jonas the satisfaction of saying it) that it was tiny. "Two hits are like what a mouse would snort."

"Mice don't do coke except in laboratories where it's fed to them. Please, Jonas. I don't want to do drugs. Seriously. I'm not that type of person." Allie's entire back lifted and fell as she tried to breathe.

"Two mouse capfuls and then I swear on my godmother's life I'll give you your check and you never have to do drugs again in your life. Ever. I'll even swear on my dead mother." Jonas crossed himself with the baby-food jar.

Allie took the jar. She could see no other way out. And two capfuls would be a lot less than she had already done earlier—maybe she wouldn't even feel it.

With the tiny piece of plastic pinched between her first finger and her thumb, Allie dipped into the jar and pulled out the smallest anthill she thought she could get away with. She lifted it to one nostril and sniffed. She dipped again and did the other nostril.

"Good girl," Jonas said, and he leaned back on the stool and smiled at her.

Allie noticed that her purse was no longer in his hands. "Where's my purse?" she asked.

"In the stockroom. Don't worry about it." Jonas pulled the curtain shut then unlatched his gold belt buckle.

"Don't!" Allie said. "Keep your pants on. Please."

"Keep my pants on?" Jonas laughed. "Keep my pants on?!"

Allie felt the coke come alive in her head. It was like two loose wires had suddenly been connected in her brain and she was now pulsing enough electricity to light up the TransAmerica pyramid. "There's no time for that. I really need to get paid and go." The current jumped from Allie's head to her chest, then out the tips of her fingers and toes. She felt glowing, white-hot.

"Just show me your tits," Jonas said. "Come on!" He started to unbutton his slacks.

"No!" Allie said. "Don't do it yet."

"Yet?" Jonas smiled. He drummed his thick fingers on his fly. His fingernails looked like shiny nacreous seashells.

"Let's do more coke first," Allie said, stalling for time. She dipped, then lifted the pen cap and tried to fake a snort. Even though her hand was inches from her nostrils, she could feel freckles of powder sailing up her nose. The electricity tunneled into her bloodstream and was now jolting against the walls of her veins like a bolt of lightning trapped in a rabbit hole. The fitting room swelled upward and Jonas's gold belt buckle charged back and forth like the train in the *Soul Train* opening credits. "Is this the same stuff we did earlier?" Allie asked, and she placed the baby-food jar and the pen cap on the ground beside the stool for fear she'd drop them or electrically shoot them off her hands.

"It's cut with a little something special," Jonas said. His smile seemed to spread into the walls. "Now give me the tits and I'll take off my pants."

"Wait a minute," Allie said. "I've got an idea."

"You've got an idea?" Jonas laughed and Allie thought she felt vibrations from the *hahahaha* pricking at her cheeks.

"Yeah. Listen to this." Allie's words were bumping into each other with a rush. "I'm going to get totally and completely naked in the other room."

"Totally naked?" Jonas flicked his tongue around and shook

his head. Allie saw trails of his ears as if they were each a deck of cards splayed out on a table.

"Uh-huh. Naked except for my shoes." Allie lifted one spike-heeled Candie's mule, to show it to Jonas. Then she put a hand on the wall and pushed herself up. She reached for the curtain but couldn't move forward. She realized Jonas held her in place by the wrist.

"Just take your clothes off here," Jonas said.

"But if I do it in the other room—" Allie focused on her voice, she wanted to sound like someone who was calm, interested, horny—"imagine how I'll look when I open that curtain. It will be—"

"Fucking amazing," Jonas said, and he let go of her arm. "But if you run out on me or something, I'll send my man Vice Versa after you and Vice Versa will kill you." Jonas smiled big and winked.

"Vice Versa?" Allie asked. She felt her body jerking into yin-yang circles, the physical manifestation of the word *vice versa*.

"Go take those clothes off!" Jonas slapped Allie on the ass. "I'll tell you all about Vice Versa when we're done. He's a mean motherfucker. Scary as shit." Jonas laughed hard and gave Allie a little push.

Allie yanked the curtain shut behind herself, then wobbled into the stockroom. Her purse was sitting on a cantilevered metal shelf with the Wonder Bread bag of coke and a stack of white blouses that were supposed to be marked down that day.

"Hurry!" Jonas shouted. "My pants are already off!"

Allie snatched up the purse, shoved it onto her shoulder, and shouted, "I'm coming!"

The Wonder Bread bag was ballooning and shrinking like a lung. It was alarming, but Allie knew it wasn't real. She had heard enough stories about "bad trips" to know that she was experiencing one right now.

"Stop moving," Allie said to the bread bag.

Take me! the bread bag mewed. Or didn't, really.

It occurred to Allie that the coke in there was worth at least as much as the money Jonas owed her for her work. But there was no time to measure it out. Maybe she could take the bag home, remove the equivalent of her accrued pay, and then return the remainder somehow.

"You naked yet?!" Jonas shouted.

"Almost!" Allie called out. And then she leaned toward the bread bag and whispered, "I gotta go now."

Don't leave me here with him! the bread bag whispered back.

As if it were her desperate little companion, Allie reached out and grabbed the bag by the neck. And then she started running. Out of the stockroom. Past the fitting rooms. To the front door that she unlocked and opened in wobbly speed. Then down the street and around the corner. She didn't once look back.

2

Jonas didn't know where Beth lived. Beth had a car, she had never needed a ride home from Jonas like Allie often did. So that was where Allie planned to go to ration out the coke. She ran toward the Ashby BART station, her heart pumping like a machine gun, powering her along. She wasn't even winded as she clambered down the steps to the train, hoisting herself up and over the turnstile since she had no money, or time even, to buy a ticket. The train pulled in and Allie stepped on. She sat with her back to the station as they pulled away. If Jonas had followed her, she didn't want to know.

The man across the aisle stared at the Wonder Bread bag. He was middle-aged, nice-looking. There were cracks along his face that looked like they'd grown there from smiling, not scowling. Allie couldn't help but think that her life might be better if he were her father: he probably lived in a big house, threw dinner parties at home, saw his kids off to college, and sent them money when they needed it. She wouldn't have been working for Jonas if this man were her father. She wouldn't have lifted her top for him while he jacked off, or done the crazy-cut coke that was making her feel like her body was an alien organism and she was in a color-infused movie—everything burnt-red, turquoise-blue, and the yellow of a fully bloomed sunflower.

"Do you like Wonder Bread?" the man asked, and laughed.

"Yeah." Allie lifted the bag and looked at the perfectly formed color circles on the vanilla-white plastic. *Wonder* was spelled in big, ruler-sharp, thick letters. The bag didn't hang like a loaf of bread—there was weight, pull, a slightly rounded sag at the bottom. At that moment, Allie realized exactly what she had done. Her heart drum-rolled and her hand began to sweat so much she had to place the bag on her lap before it slipped loose.

Allie dropped her head back against the seat and shut her eyes. She could feel her ears. They were weighted, filled with sizzling blood. For a second, Allie feared her ears might start slipping down her cheeks, gliding the length of her neck. Then the BART train went suddenly silent. Or maybe Allie had lost her hearing. She pulled her head up and looked around.

"My wife won't let me buy Wonder Bread," the man said. (Relief! She could hear!) "Claims it's as good for you as a doughnut."

"My mother never bought it either," Allie said. Penny had never bought any food. Frank brought food home from his restaurant, or the family would go there and eat. Expensive gourmet hamburgers, French dip, onion soup au gratin, rice pilaf or fries. Allie had probably eaten enough salt to preserve herself. Upon her death, salt would take over and she'd become a giant piece of jerky.

The man lifted his hand. His lips parted slightly. Allie felt certain she knew he would speak soon. He was going to ask for a piece of bread.

The train pulled in to the North Berkeley station. Allie went to the doors and stood inches away from them. She felt as if her body might burst out and break the glass if the doors didn't open soon.

"You don't want to leave me a piece of Wonder Bread for my ride home?" the man asked, just as Allie had predicted.

"Sorry." Allie wished there were bread in the bag. Things would be so much easier if she had simply stolen a loaf of Wonder. The doors whooshed open and Allie stepped onto the platform.

She jogged up the steps and out of the station, and then she was running again.

Beth's apartment was on the second floor of a Spanish-style building, El Conquistador, which had a red-tiled roof, a sun-flooded tiled courtyard, and arched exterior walkways. Each upper-level apartment had a small half-circle balcony enclosed with a curved wrought-iron rail. El Conquistador even had one of the few parking garages in the city of Berkeley. If the building were a woman, it would be Princess Grace: calm, reserved, unpretentiously beautiful.

Allie ran up El Conquistador's painted-tile front steps, then down the exterior hallway. She knocked on the wooden-plank door to Beth's apartment.

Beth opened the door with her bare foot, her big toe pressing down on the cedilla-shaped handle. She was on the kitchen phone—the cord was stretched as far as it could go. Allie stared at Beth's foot. The toe turned into a hammer. Allie blinked and it was a toe again.

"Oh my god!" Beth said. "She just walked in the door!"

Allie's pulse throbbed in her feet—it felt like her toes were pushing out into giant sausages. She didn't speak. Her palm was growing more and more slick around the neck of the Wonder Bread bag.

"It's Jonas," Beth said. She backed up into the open kitchen counter so that the phone cord wasn't stretched, and held out the phone toward Allie.

"Tell him I don't want it all. Only what he owes me." Allie spoke quickly, so quickly she wasn't even sure she was speaking English.

Beth put the phone back against her ear. "Jonas heard you," she said, to Allie. "He said your future lover Vice Versa is on his way over to meet you." Beth placed the phone against her chest. "Like, you're going to go out with a guy named Vice Versa?"

Allie backed away toward the door, the bread bag still clasped in her hand. She knew that she should drop it there and run, but something—the coke she'd just done, her sense that Jonas *owed* her, her shame about the fitting-room encounter, and her regret over having given all her money to Marc—compelled her to tighten her fist around the bag.

"She, like, won't come to the phone?" Beth said to Jonas. She lifted her eyebrows and waved Allie toward her with one arm, then cupped a hand over the mouthpiece. "What is going on? What is he talking about?!" Allie could both see and hear Jonas's muffled voice coming through Beth's fingers. The words were the color of green smog. Allie shook her head *no* at Beth.

"Jonas," Beth said. "She just dropped off some shoes she borrowed and then left. Tell Vice Versa to call her back here later."

Allie moved her fist up and down slowly, miming a receiver being set in the cradle. She mouthed the words *HANG UP NOW.*

"Okay . . . okay . . . okay I'll tell her when I see her," Beth said. "But I swear I won't see her for, like, at least four or five hours . . . no, I live near Peet's Coffee . . . yeah, yeah . . . okay, good-bye." Beth hung up the phone.

"What'd he say?" Allie asked. She figured she had seven minutes before Jonas could make it to Beth's building. Floating in front of her face was a giant pocket watch ticking the seconds. It wasn't until she took a swipe at it that Allie realized the watch wasn't really there.

"He said his pal Vice Versa has a date with you and is going to pick you up no matter where you are and that you need to give Vice Versa the hundred K you took?" Beth said. "What is going on? Like, what hundred K is he talking about?!"

"Shit." Allie's heart rate increased, an engine revving in her chest. She looked at the bread bag. Could this much coke be worth a hundred thousand dollars? Even though Jonas dealt coke from the shop, Allie had no idea how much he charged, how much he made, or what people were paying for the little packets they walked out with.

"By the way, did you know that you've been evicted?" Beth asked.

"What do you mean I've been evicted? How do you know I've been evicted?!" Allie pressed the bread bag against her chest.

"I was walking by your place today, and then I remembered that jean skirt that you borrowed last week that I, like, totally wanted to wear tonight? And those chubby, dopey-looking twin guys let me in and I went up to your room and there was a bolt lock on your door and an eviction notice." Beth picked up the notice from the counter and handed it to Allie, who shoved it into her purse without reading it.

Allie lived in a grubby, shingled boardinghouse with a shared kitchen that always smelled like cooked beans and cabbage. She was more sorry that she was now the sort of person who got evicted for failure to pay rent than she was sorry that she was no longer legally able to live there. "I'm sorry you couldn't get your skirt. Does Jonas know where you live?"

"I didn't give him the address. He'll never find you." Beth peered into Allie's face. She tilted her head and Allie saw her as a parrot. "You totally don't look right," Beth-the-parrot said.

Allie closed her eyes. When she opened them, Beth had turned back into a person. "You aren't listed in the phone book, are you?" Allie had the presence of mind to ask.

Beth opened her mouth but didn't speak. She picked up the giant white pages from the kitchen counter and flipped through.

"Shit." She flashed her bottom teeth in a grimace. "Tell me what's going on! Like, what is this hundred K thingy, who is Vice Versa, and why are you so freaked out by a blind date?!"

"Vice Versa doesn't want to date me, he wants to kill me so he can get this coke!" Allie held up the bread bag.

"No way. There's coke in there?"

"Jonas still hasn't paid me, so I sort of borrowed this from him so I could pay myself what he owes me." Allie stared up at the floating pocket watch. It ticked louder now, as if someone had turned up the volume.

"Oh my god!" Beth took the bag from Allie's hand, removed the wire twisty, let it twirl open, peered inside, and laughed. "Oh my god," she said again. "You could exchange this coke for, like, a house in the flats!" Beth stuck a finger into the bag and shoved some coke up her nose. She dipped again and served the other nostril.

"I gotta get out of here." Allie took the bag, spun it shut, and tied it with the twisty.

"You need to give it back to Jonas. That's like, what's it called, grand theft larceny or something?"

"He needs to pay me!" Allie actually stomped her foot. Like a child.

"Take out the equivalent of what he owes you, and like, leave the bag here and I'll give it back to him." Beth seemed, Allie thought, remarkably unfazed by the situation.

"You think that will work?" Allie asked. "What if this Vice Versa guy really wants to murder me?" The pocket watch was thundering the seconds now. Allie took another swat at it to make it disappear.

Beth followed her hand, then stared down Allie's eyes. "No one's going to *kill* you. Just give back the coke." Beth put her hand on the bag. Allie pulled it in against her chest. Beth's delicate nose was starting to lengthen into a beak again.

Beth laughed. "You're, like, fucked up, aren't you?"

"I did that stuff Jonas keeps in a baby-food jar."

"The baby-jar coke?" Now Beth was cracking up. "No wonder you stole the hundred K bread bag! I had the tiniest toot of that the other day and, I swear, it made me crazy."

"Crazy? How?" Allie wanted to ask about Jonas masturbating, but she didn't. Her body was a quivery mess. It was hard enough just to speak.

"I don't know, he put on music and I was, like, dancing, and the walls were all, like, colorful, and Jonas was, like, watching me and I swear he wanted me to go into the dressing room and take off my clothes or something so he could jerk off and I was, like, no fucking way, there's no way I'm going to take my clothes off for some freaky guy like you! I mean, can you imagine? Who would do that? I mean what kind of pathetic loser would just sit there and let some guy totally jerk off while he's looking at her?!" Beth sniffed, wiped each nostril, and erased the beak.

Allie could feel twin snakes of regret in her bloodstream, moving in a double-helix rotation through her body. Regret was going to poison her if she didn't flush it out of her system soon. "So you just danced?" she asked.

"Yeah but I said some stupid shit. I told him about my third eye and my long nipples. Oh and I told him about Marc, too, and I swear that's, like, all he wanted to talk about the rest of the day." Beth stared into Allie's eyes again before her focus dropped down to the coke clasped against Allie's breasts.

The pocket watch bonged, like a grandfather clock. "I've gotta get outta here," Allie said. "Can I borrow your car?"

Beth reached into a ceramic bowl on the counter and plucked out her keys. She held them out to Allie. "Are you totally too messed up to drive?"

"Maybe," Allie said. "I'll put my rabbit foot on your keys and that will keep me safe." She placed the bread bag on the counter so she could dig through her purse for the rabbit foot. Allie believed in her rabbit-foot luck. It had kept her from getting pregnant that time the condom broke with Marc; and it was probably the thing that had prevented her from dying from whatever it was she had stupidly snorted out of that baby-food jar with Jonas. Wai Po often said, *IF LUCK COMES NOT, WHO COMES?*

The rabbit foot glowed up at Allie from the bottom of her bag. She thought she saw the tiny claws flickering back and forth just before she pulled it out. Allie opened the silver chain that looped through the top of the rabbit foot and attached it to the small ring that held Beth's keys. "Can you talk to Jonas or Vice Versa and try to work it all out? Negotiate a little, okay? Let him think we have the upper hand."

"Yeah, yeah, fine." Beth gave a little smile. The smile, Allie was relieved to see, dissolved the persistent bird beak that had started growing once more. "Come back in, like, two hours—I'll have it all settled by then."

"Okay. So tell him I'm just going to take out what he owes me." Allie was panting. She consciously shut her mouth and breathed in deeply through her nose.

"Yeah, I get it." Beth waved her hand. "Everything will be fine. Jonas is like a total pussycat at heart."

"He owes me!" It took tremendous force for Allie to say the words clearly and slowly. "Remind him of that. Marc owes me, too. I just want someone to pay me for once, okay?" There was an explosion of light in Allie's head—a crackling power surge.

"Allie, fucking relax! Now get out of here, go for a drive and come back in two hours."

"He owes me!" Allie said, and she walked out the door.

"WAIT!" Beth ran down the exterior hall after Allie. She put her hand on the bread bag. "Can I have another hit before you leave?"

Allie took off the twisty and let the bag spin until it unwound. She held it open toward Beth. Beth looked around to make sure no one was out, then stuck both her hands into the bag. Her fingers looked long and twisted, like licorice. When Beth pulled out two pinches of coke, her fingers had magically transformed again, now flickering back and forth between human fingers and lobster claws.

"Done?" Allie asked.

"Yeah. I'll see you in two hours," Beth said.

Beth had a brand-new 1983 Honda Prelude with a moon roof. It had power windows and locks, a tape player, air-conditioning, everything. It even had a license plate that Beth had picked out when she registered the car: CAL GRL. California Girl. Or Cal—the common moniker for the University of California, Berkeley—Girl. Allie almost thought she couldn't be friends with Beth after she had first seen that plate—the amount of attention it brought, the showiness, was too much. But eventually Allie saw that in spite of all the *things* Beth owned (all of which Allie would have gladly taken), she was not a thingy person. She had a nice car, but she'd let anyone borrow it. She had a nice apartment, but she'd let anyone crash on the couch. She wasn't a hoarder, and this, Allie believed, was a good quality in a friend.

Allie placed the Wonder Bread bag on the seat beside her. It appeared to be punching out sporadically as if there were a kitten in the sack. She shifted the car into reverse and backed out of the parking space slowly—her fear of bumping the cars on either side of her was equal to her fear of Vice Versa and Jonas.

The yellow wooden arm that would allow Allie to exit the garage seemed to take hours to lift (the pocket watch, now floating on the ceiling of the car, ticked off thousands of seconds). As it was rising, Allie examined the cassette that hung out of the player like a plastic white tongue, pushed it in, and changed the song seven times. Peter Gabriel. Beth loved Peter Gabriel. When she and Allie went to the Peter Gabriel concert at the Cow Palace in San Francisco, Beth started crying every third song. Allie had been bored senseless. She had tried to make the time pass quickly by entering into a daydream in which she was married to Billy Idol and they lived half the year (when he wasn't on tour) in a hillside villa in Cannes, France. She had been so immersed in the fantasy that she had been shocked when Peter Gabriel took his final encore bow. She and Billy Idol hadn't even finished decorating the villa.

Allie hit eject, threw the tape on the floor, and looked up to see where she was. Somehow she had managed to get herself down the street, toward University Avenue, near the freeway entrance. She popped open the glove box, reached in for a different tape, and blindly shoved it into the tape player.

The cassette turned out to be Prince. Much better. Prince was crooning about sex with a lady cab-driver as Allie pressed on the gas to propel the Prelude onto the 580 freeway toward a place she had yet to locate in her mind.

3

On the one hand, Allie felt like she had been sleeping for six hours—it was as if she had closed her eyes, opened them, and found herself awake on the San Diego Freeway in Los Angeles.

On the other hand, Allie felt like so much had happened in those six hours. She had memorized the entire Prince *1999* album. Every song. When she had messed up a word or two, she had rewound the tape and played the same section over and over until she had the right words, tone, notes, attitude even. Allie was convinced that her voice sounded exactly like Prince's, that no one, not even the most talented sound artist, would be able to tell them apart. She hadn't stopped to pee, or for gas, or directions. It was like the car had driven itself and she had been super-busy the entire time, making sure she didn't sing *got a time in my pock head and baby it's rarin' to roll*, which were the words she had been using the first time "Little Red Corvette" played. It wasn't until the third round of the A side of the tape that she realized how wrong she had been about those lyrics and so many others.

And now, on the San Diego Freeway at eight p.m. on a Saturday, Beth's Prelude was idling, the moon roof and windows were open, Prince was turned down low, and the baby-jar coke had worked its way out of Allie's system (no more timepieces floating in the air). Allie could actually think, focus, and figure out what she was doing and where she would go.

Yes, she had grown up in Los Angeles: Pasadena, for a time, while her parents were still together, and then apartments and condos everywhere from Santa Monica to the Valley. But in all those years of being a resident, Allie had never *driven* in Los Angeles. She got her license when she started dating Marc, and only then because he wanted to take her out to bars and restaurants where he hoped she'd have a glass or two of wine. Allie wasn't twenty-one yet, but Marc showed her how to use chalk and a pencil to change her birth year on the California license. The pencil color matched the print perfectly, so unless some ruthless bartender with a wet thumb rubbed his digit over the altered number, it was a pretty reliable fake ID.

Allie's father's restaurant was on Fairfax Avenue, so all she had to do was figure out how to get to Fairfax from the San Diego Freeway. She could hang out in the safety of her father's looming figure while she figured out where to go next. Hopefully, her father could help her locate her mother, Penny. Though Frank would disown Allie if he found out she was fraternizing with a drug dealer, Penny wouldn't be bothered by it. Her boyfriend, the faded rock-star Jet Blaster, was a former heroin addict. And, once, Allie had discovered in *People* magazine that her mother had been stopped at customs with "traces of cocaine on her luggage." Allie had been ten when she read that article while standing in a 7-Eleven waiting for her father to buy a pack of Juicy Fruit gum. With Wai Po's voice in her head (*WHAT IS TOLD INTO THE EAR OF MAN IS HEARD A HUNDRED MILES AWAY*), Allie swore she'd never reveal to a soul that her mother was involved in drugs. She hid all the copies of *People* behind *Life* and hoped that no one she knew at school read *People*. At the time, few things seemed more shameful. Now, Allie was almost grateful that her mother had a history and experience with drugs. Who better to help her out of this mess?

The glowing orange light in the center of the gas indicator flashed on. Growing up, Allie had seldom been in a car that showed when you were running out of gas. Her father had always driven an old, white cargo van that didn't have a working gas gauge. Frank had always said the van was part of the restaurant's fleet (although it was the *only* car in the fleet), something to haul cases of wine back from Napa Valley, or discount pots and pans from Mexico. And Penny had had an antique Triumph convertible that Allie rarely rode in. It was a two-seater car, something Penny used to go off on her own while Allie stayed home doing crossword puzzles and word searches with Wai Po.

Allie let the car glide off the freeway. There was an In-N-Out Burger on one side and a gas station on the other. She wished she had enough money, and gas, to use the drive-thru. In front of the In-N-Out Burger was a palm tree that appeared to have been blown halfway down by the wind. Allie was so busy staring at the palm tree that she almost missed the turn in for the gas station. She cranked the wheel to the left, pulled in too fast, and then hit the clutch and brake, stopping with a squeak. As she turned off the engine and pulled up the emergency brake, she realized a man was shouting at her. He was in a blue jumpsuit. Pale skin. A swoop of golden brown hair. Teeth whiter than the whites of his eyes.

"Yes?" Allie tilted her head out the open window. The guy approached.

"Your gas tank's on the other side," he said, and he smiled in a sly, almost bashful way.

"Oh, okay. Thanks." Allie started up the car and drove around to the other side.

"Fill it up?" the guy asked.

"Uh, yeah." Allie looked around and realized she was at the full-service pump. She was too embarrassed about the wrong-side-gas-tank mishap to undo the full-service mistake.

When the nozzle had clicked full, the guy unlatched it, then leaned toward Allie's window and said, "Eighteen dollars and sixty cents."

"Ah." Allie opened her mouth and smiled up at him. In her post-drug delirium, she had been aware that she had no money for In-N-Out Burger, but had somehow failed to understand that she had no money for gas, either. She lifted her butt off the seat and stuck her hand down the front pocket of her jeans to make a show of searching for money, although she knew the only thing in her pocket was her single house key.

"Just a sec," Allie said. She reached toward the floor, shifted aside the *Glamour* magazine that sat there, pulled up her grimy purse, and dropped it on her lap. Her wallet was tucked below the eviction notice. Allie opened it and rummaged through each empty pocket. She wasn't sure where this fake search would lead, but it certainly was buying time. Allie unzipped the change purse and looked at the pennies and a dime. She dumped them out in her palm. They felt sticky as if they had once been glued together.

With a hopeful grin, Allie held out the handful of coins.

"Do you have a credit card?" The guy flashed a closed-mouthed smile. Allie could see that this was as hard for him as it was for her.

"No. But . . ." Allie popped open the glove box in the hope that Beth kept a stash of cash there. Nothing. She glanced at the Wonder Bread bag. "Do you—" She broke off, not sure how to put it. Somehow, in the delusional drug-induced fantasy of paying herself by selling the coke, Allie had never thought about how to conduct an actual transaction.

"Do I?" The guy smiled again.

Allie was relieved to have an opening. "Do you want some coke in exchange for the gas?" It was almost shocking to hear the words come out of her mouth so smoothly. But, Allie told herself firmly, if she wanted to get out of the situation she had put herself in, she better get used to it.

"Coke? Cocaine?" The guy looked confused.

"Uh . . . yeah. You're not a cop, are you?"

He laughed. "Nah. I'm a student at UCLA. My uncle owns this station and I work here every summer."

"Cool! My best friend from high school, Kathy Kruger, goes to UCLA. Do you know her?! Sometimes she goes by Kat." Kathy Kruger was mellow. Allie had always wished she could be as mellow as Kathy. Kathy never seemed excited about anything and it made her seem wiser and more sophisticated than Allie.

"No. But, listen. If you have coke to sell, I know someone who would buy some. So, you could sell the coke and then you'd have the money to pay for the gas."

"Oh, okay!" Allie heard the excitement in her voice and took a deep breath. Mellow, like Kathy Kruger, she reminded herself. "I try not to do that kind of stuff."

"Yeah, me too." Or at least Allie *had been* the kind of person who tried not to do that kind of stuff. But who was she now? Now that she'd watched a man masturbate, done coke (coke and whatever it was cut with), and stolen enough drugs to buy a house in the Berkeley flats! For the first time, Allie was relieved that Wai Po wasn't alive. Her own shame compounded with Wai Po's disappointment would be too much for her to carry.

"Why don't you pull up there." The guy pointed toward the

little market attached to the gas station. "I'll call my friend and get him over here anon."

"Anon," Allie winced, as she started the car. *Anon* was a Marc word. He had even used it when she handed over her cashed-out student loan and scholarship money: "I'll pay you back anon!"

Allie spaced out, staring at nothing while waiting for the gas-station boy's friend to arrive. After such an intense high, she felt depleted and empty. In no time, she was asleep.

A knuckle rap on the window made her jerk awake. A guy was standing outside the car: blond, skin the color of browned butter, eyes like a doe. He had on a Mr. Zogg's Sex Wax T-shirt and was obviously a surfer. Allie turned the key in the ignition, pushed the button, and the window slid down.

"You the girl Jimmy told me about with the blow?" Sex Wax asked.

"Jimmy?" Allie asked.

"Jimmy." Sex Wax pointed to the gas-station guy with his thumb. He wasn't smiling. Allie wanted him to smile. She wanted him to flirt with her.

"Yeah." She said it slow. And she smiled.

"How much?" Still no smile. He was probably four or five years older than Allie. His body looked like it was made of hard rubber: smooth on the outside but dense as rock.

"How much do you usually pay?" Allie wished she had just once asked Beth how much she paid for the coke she loved to do. Although most of what Beth did was given to her by Jonas, so maybe even she didn't know the price.

Sex Wax cocked his head and narrowed his eyes. Allie could tell he was trying to figure out how and why *she* was dealing coke.

"It's my friend's," Allie said. "I told him I'd sell it for him and he wrote down a price list for me, but I lost it."

"He wrote down a price list for you?" Now Sex Wax smiled. He seemed incredulous. Allie's face burned. "What else you selling?"

"Just coke." Allie sat up straighter in the seat as if that would give her more authority.

"And he gave you a price list? Are you sure you have coke?" He leaned his forearms on the window ledge and peered in toward the backseat as if he were expecting someone with a billy club to be hiding there.

"I'll give you a taste," Allie said. "But shut your eyes."

"Shut my eyes? What are you talking about? Are you going to pull out a hidden price list?!"

"I don't want you to see where I keep it." Allie's heart was thumping the way it had when she'd done the coke.

"I'll turn around." He leaned against the car, the giant triangle of his torso filled the window in a perfect silhouette.

Allie unwound the Wonder Bread bag, took out a pinch of coke, and put it in the center of her left palm. She put the open bag on the floor in front of the passenger seat. "Okay."

Sex Wax turned around, looked at Allie's palm, and laughed. "You're the funniest fucking dealer I've ever met!" With his hands on the windowsill, he dipped down as if he were doing a push-up and snorted the line from Allie's palm. He straightened up, shook his head, and then bent down again and licked the dusty remains off the center of her palm. "Wow," he said. Even his eyes looked happy.

Allie felt like he had just licked her neck, or lips, or the inside of her forearm where she had liked to tickle herself into a semi–sexual trance when she was a young girl. "Good?"

"Fucking great. Where'd you get this? It feels like it isn't cut with anything. It feels like pure fucking coke."

"It is." Allie had no idea whether that was true, but why not?

"Fucking unreal!" He shifted his shoulders, almost as if he were dancing.

"Totally pure," Allie said, going with it. She watched him. He wasn't watching her. Allie knew this type. Since Marc broke up with her, as Allie willingly escorted Beth to bars, she had met many guys whose attraction to her appeared to be based solely on her appreciation of them. It was a smoothly paved one-way street—easy to cruise on as long as you didn't want to go in the other direction. Allie had stupidly kissed a few of these guys, thinking she might find a Marc replacement who would help mend her battered heart.

"So what about the price list?" Sex Wax grinned slow and wide.

"What are they charging down here in L.A.?" Allie asked as casually as possible.

"Usual," he said.

"Hundred?" Allie guessed. She knew coke was expensive and she remembered a group of four friends getting a hundred dollars together once in order to buy some for a Blondie concert. The trick would be to figure out *how much* for a hundred.

"For a gram of the good stuff," he said, and Allie nodded.

"That's exactly what I figured." Allie spoke confidently. She was starting to feel the part of the drug dealer.

"So you'll take a hundred a gram?" Sex Wax asked.

"No way," Allie said. "This isn't cut with anything." (Maybe.) "It's one twenty a gram." She felt fairly certain that a twenty-dollar increase over the usual price would be close enough to, and maybe even better than, what Jonas charged.

"Okay," Sex Wax said, surprising Allie, "I'll take three." He stood up straight and reached into his back pocket. His jeans were slung low and revealed the two channels running from each hip, tendons pointing down.

"Three what?"

Sex Wax laughed. "Grams."

"Oh, right!" Allie laughed, feeling a little panicked. She couldn't get too cocky. She had almost blown her cover.

"What's your name?" He leaned in the window, holding four hundred-dollar bills.

"Allie." She took the bills. "I don't have change."

"So give me three and a third."

"Sure." Allie stared at him with a small panic fluttering in her gut. She felt like she was in a play and hadn't yet memorized her lines.

"Do I have to turn around again?" Sex Wax smiled at Allie.

"Yeah. Can you go over by the pumps or something while I weigh it out?"

"Give me your keys." His open hand was sitting in front of Allie's face. For a second, she had an urge to lean down and lick his palm, the way he had licked hers. But she knew that was wrong. Gross, even.

"Why do you want my keys?" Allie asked.

"So you won't drive away with my cash!"

"Oh, yeah! Duh!" Allie pulled out the keys and placed them in his hand. Sex Wax closed his palm around Allie's lucky rabbit foot, then walked away.

"Wait! What's your name?!" Allie called out the window.

He paused, turned, and said, "Mike. And you're Allie."

"Right," she said. "Mike and Allie." And then she blushed, although if Mike had heard her, he gave no sign—he was walking back toward the gas station.

Allie leaned across the center divider and pulled up the *Glamour* magazine she had seen earlier. Paulina Porizkova was on the cover. Allie studied her beautifully square face for a moment and wondered what it would be like to be that pretty, if she would be in the mess she was in now if she were that pretty. Well, of course she wouldn't, she decided, she'd be modeling! Allie flipped the magazine open, tore out a page, set it in her lap, and tried to make an origami envelope. That was how Jonas packaged his coke. Allie had seen him in the stockroom one day with a *Penthouse* magazine open, picking out the most salient half-pages of photos and then folding them into tiny envelopes.

It wasn't as simple as Jonas made it look. Allie tried every combination of backward and forward and double folds on a half-page ad for Breck Shampoo, but nothing would hold its shape. Finally, she took the horoscope *(Things are heating up for Virgo gals this month, be sure to cool your jets before you fly off . . .)*, folded it in half, and set it on her lap. She lifted the Wonder Bread bag from the floor, stuck her hand in, pulled out a palm-full of coke, and dumped it into the fold of the magazine page.

Allie had no idea what three and a third grams would feel like (she couldn't even remember how many grams were in an ounce), but she lifted the magazine page and lowered it as if she were weighing it. Somehow pretending she knew what she was doing gave her a nice feeling of control. A shimmery layer of coke stuck to her hand and she wondered if Mike would want to lick it off. But of course it would seem bizarre if she offered up her palm. Allie wiped the remnants off on her jeans.

"Okaaaay," Allie whispered. "Got some of my paycheck!" She spun the Wonder Bread bag shut, tied the twisty around it, and stuck it under the front passenger seat. It seemed unsafe to get out of the car with the magazine page full of coke. Allie tapped on the horn a couple of times and looked into the rearview mirror. Mike was walking backward, talking to Jimmy as he inched his way toward the car. Then he turned and lightly jogged to the open window.

"Are you a hooker?"

"What? No. Why would you say that?" Allie looked down at herself, as if she were making sure she were still fully dressed.

"Your license plate says CALL GIRL."

"It says CAL GIRL. Like California girl," Allie said. Was Mike illiterate? He was so good-looking that it could make up for a lot of deficiencies, although maybe not illiteracy.

"Is that for me?" Mike glanced at the coke on Allie's lap.

Allie nodded and lifted the magazine page by the two sides. "Here you go." She moved it over to Mike, who started laughing.

"Shit! Wait! Put it back on your lap." Allie did as she was told. Mike ran around the car and got in the passenger side.

"Hey," Allie said, as he shut the door.

"Where's the magazine?"

Allie pointed to the floor. Mike reached down, brought the magazine up, tore out two pages, ripped each page in half, then did some folding. "Do you have a spoon or something?"

"No," Allie said. "I wasn't planning on selling coke. I came to pump gas but then realized I didn't have any money with me."

"What about the price sheet?" Mike asked, and he grinned. Allie shrugged. Mike laughed, then reached over, scooped up some of the coke with his right hand and dropped it into one of the folded squares. In what looked to Allie to be fast motion, he folded the magazine around the coke into a tight little package, which he dropped into the breast pocket of his T-shirt. He did this three more times. Then he picked up the dusty page from Allie's lap and licked it. Allie remembered the remnants she had dusted onto her jeans and regretted doing it. She could have gotten another lick.

"This stuff is fucking unreal," Mike said. "Where does your friend get it?"

"I don't know," Allie said. "He's in Berkeley. Or Oakland. Depending on what side of the street you're on."

"Oakland. Fuck. I gotta spend some time in Oakland." Mike paused, then looked over at her carefully. "So, if I go get some more cash, can you give me another three and a third grams just like this three and a third?"

Ah. Clearly she had overestimated her coke measurements, Allie realized. Good to know. "Well," she hedged, "yeah, but I'd have to stop off at my dad's restaurant and get my scale so I can really measure it out, you know?"

Mike smiled. "Okay. Cool."

"Okay then!" If Mike bought ten more grams, Allie calculated—real grams that she had weighed on her father's food scale—then Jonas's entire debt would be paid back.

"I'll follow you to the restaurant," Mike said, and he stepped out of the car and stuck his hand up for Jimmy, who was approaching. They high-fived, then Mike added a little fist-punch in the air.

Jimmy leaned in the window. "Can I get some money for the gas?" Allie could see he was a nicer guy than Mike, someone whose life was in order. He didn't do coke. He was a student at UCLA. He worked hard all summer. If he had been Chinese, Wai Po would have approved of him.

Allie handed out a hundred-dollar bill and Jimmy made change from the roll he had in his pocket, then ran off to help the orange Karmann Ghia that had just pulled up at the full-service pump.

"You know, I'm kind of lost," Allie said to Mike, out the window. "My dad's restaurant is on Fairfax. Can I follow you there?"

"You don't know how to get to Fairfax from here?" Mike asked. "And you're from here?"

"Direction deficit," Allie said. "I get lost in big buildings." It was true.

"I don't believe you're from here," Mike said. He reminded

Allie of Kathy Kruger's older brother, who offhandedly and somewhat charmingly dismissed whatever Kathy and Allie did— the music they listened to, the teachers they liked, the shows they watched on TV. Growing up, Allie had felt so alone that she often wished she had an older brother to bump up against and give her trouble. Her life at home consisted only of her parents, who were never around, and Wai Po. When Wai Po died, her mother left to be the tambourine girl in Jet Blaster's band, Mighty Zamboni. So, for most of her childhood, it was just Allie and Frank. And Frank never even asked about school and which teachers she liked.

"What? No. I mean, yes," Allie said. "I'm really from here."

"Yeah, right," Mike said, and he rolled his eyes, like a girl. "Where exactly is the restaurant on Fairfax?"

"Toward that street the museum is on. Toward the La Brea Tar Pits."

"Wilshire."

"Yeah, Wilshire, near the tar pits."

"The tar pits are on Wilshire. You don't know Wilshire?" Now there was an edge of cruelty in Mike's voice.

Allie smiled reflexively. "No, I know Wilshire. I said Wilshire."

"You said where the tar pits are as if you didn't know they were on Wilshire."

Allie imagined a wrench tightening a screw each time Mike spoke. It was as though he was ratcheting himself up into a clenched, angry fist. If he didn't shut up soon, her attraction toward him would evaporate.

"Well, I know they're on Wilshire. So let's go to Wilshire. Okay?" She smiled again.

"Great." Mike walked toward his red truck without looking back. A giant red toolbox spanned the width of the truck below the back window. Allie wondered if he were a carpenter or builder. Lately, she had been finding guys who worked with their hands sexy. Maybe it was a reaction to her broken heart; she was searching for the anti-Marc. Marc was all about ideas—his business plans, his MBA—and that certainly had done Allie no good.

Prince played in the cassette player as Allie followed Mike. Allie turned up the music so she could dim her thoughts. She knew she should call Beth and let her know where she was with the car, but at this point Beth, in Berkeley, felt connected to Jonas and Vice Versa, and Allie was enjoying the freedom of being hidden in an entirely different city. Also, Allie was worried about how she would explain herself—her presence, the Prelude—to her father when she saw him. The last time they had talked, he had lectured her on the value of hard work. Frank worked seven days a week at the restaurant. Allie didn't know anyone who worked harder than he did.

Instead of deciding on what to say to Beth when she finally did call, or what to tell her father (or even how she would get the food scale out of the kitchen to weigh the coke!), Allie thought about making out with Mike.

In high school, Allie had barely noticed boys. Kathy Kruger even asked her once if she was a lesbian. But then Marc came along and Allie discovered what it was like to have overwhelming feelings for someone. After Marc left, it was like she was ill, infected with a virus that gave her instantaneous unabashed desire that ran concurrent with her heartache. It was beyond reason, Allie knew, a hormonal-physiological impulse she couldn't will away. Every moment with another body (and she only ever went as far as kissing) seemed to rub out Allie's mental image of Marc, like a pencil drawing that was being slowly erased. And Mike, with his toolbox, surfer's tan, Sex Wax T-shirt, and swooping blond hair, would be an ideal eraser as long as he didn't get any meaner, any snappier, any more illiterate than he already was.

Once they turned onto Fairfax Avenue, Mike pulled over and motioned for Allie to pass him. Allie followed the familiar stores and restaurants until she got to the parking lot for Hamburger Hostel, Frank's place. It was empty. Allie looked at the clock on the dashboard. Eight forty. Was business even worse than Frank had intimated? The restaurant was usually packed by now—the old people would have eaten and gone and the first wave of teenagers, twenty-, and thirtysomethings would be filling the booths.

Allie pulled up the emergency break and got out of the Prelude. She clicked the lock button, loving the feeling she got from doing so. It made her feel rich. Fancy.

"Looks closed." Mike stepped out of the truck. Allie was startled again by how good-looking he was. Like one of those guys in a surf movie: belly as flat and hard as a surfboard, hair as bright as the sun, arms made of dense rope.

"Yeah, it's weird." Allie wandered toward the front door. The glass was tinted, so you couldn't see in. Allie hated that—it reminded her of drug dealers with their tinted car windows. She blushed at the thought that, in a way, she was a drug dealer now.

Mike tugged at the brass handle of the front door. It was locked. "You sure this is your dad's place?"

Allie felt a gurgly panic. Hamburger Hostel was her only stable point of reference. It was always there. Always open. Who was her father if not the man hovering over the employees at Hamburger Hostel? Was this why he had been totally unwilling to help her out financially? Did Frank need every penny he had in order to try to keep the restaurant open? Allie didn't want to look at the locked door. It made her queasy, like viewing a dead body.

"Your dad didn't tell you the place went out of business?"

Mike said. His eyes were narrowed, but he didn't look suspicious. If anything, he looked bored.

"No. This is a complete surprise," Allie said, and she pulled the door again as if it would suddenly open.

"Well, why don't you just measure out the coke with your hands like you did last time?" Mike asked.

"Let's go to a pay phone. I'll call my dad." Allie wouldn't let the transaction happen without a scale. She couldn't afford to give away more coke than the value of what she was owed. Besides, she needed to make sure her father was okay, still walking, still with a beating heart. The only way Frank's restaurant wouldn't be open would be if he were physically unable to get there or in complete financial ruin.

"Where's your mom?" Mike asked. "Didn't she tell you about the restaurant?"

"My mom's on the road with Mighty Zamboni. She's the tambourine girl." Allie started walking back toward the cars.

Mike laughed, following her. "No way."

"Way," Allie said. "She and Jet Blaster are a couple."

"I thought everyone from Mighty Zamboni was dead by now. Are you like a pathological liar?" The casual way Mike asked this made Allie wonder if he assumed lying to be a normal means of communication.

"They're still touring. None of them are dead."

Mike must have been as uninterested in Mighty Zamboni as Allie was, because he said, "My friends and I used to eat at your dad's place all the time in high school."

"Oh yeah?!" Allie looked at Mike and tried to spin her head out of the shock of the closed restaurant.

"Great fucking burgers."

"Yeah." Frank had always been proud of the burgers.

"Wait. This isn't your dad's place! The guy who owns this is some black dude. I remember seeing him at the cash register and checking on the tables all the time."

"That's my dad." Allie had never seen her father anywhere else within three hours of suppertime.

Mike took Allie's arm and turned her toward him. "You're black?!"

"Yeah. Half. Or a—" Allie was in the process of saying *a quarter* when Mike pulled her in and kissed her.

"That's so hot," Mike said, when he pulled up for air.

"It's the first thing I've said that you've believed." Allie laughed, then stopped laughing as Mike leaned into her and they went at it again. She could feel the four packs of coke pushing into her chest through Mike's T-shirt. She could feel his bones and muscle obliterating the worry about her father and his restaurant. And, yes, okay, so maybe he was only kissing her because he thought she was black (which she was), but there was no reason to think about that now.

Mike pulled off her again. "There's a pay phone at Tambor's. Wanna go there and call your dad for the scale?"

Tambor's was the deli down the street. Allie nodded.

In Tambor's, Mike walked with Allie to the alcove where the bathrooms and pay phones were. "I'm going to step into the men's room and do a little toot," he whispered. He backed into the door and winked before he disappeared into the bathroom.

Allie dropped a dime into the coin slot and dialed the number for her father's restaurant. The three harmonica-sounding notes of a misdial went off and then an echo-y, fuzzy recording said the number she had dialed was no longer in service. Allie felt hollow and sad, like she had just stumbled upon an obituary for a seldom-seen friend. Then she remembered the index card with her mother's number on it. She hit 0 and placed a collect, person-to-person, call to the number.

A voice that Allie imagined belonged to a white woman with a silk scarf knotted at her neck answered. After the operator asked if she'd accept the charges, the woman scoffed, "The queen's not here," and hung up. Allie was hit with a quick stab of rejection from the denied call, even though she didn't even know whose voice was on the phone. She tried to brush it aside.

Allie dropped another dime into the phone She tried 411 next. Her father changed apartments so often (always looking for the deals—free gym membership, free first-month's rent, free utilities for three months) that Allie had never had his home number. Besides, he was rarely home.

"There are seven Frank Dodgsons," the operator said.

"How about Franklin Lutwidge Dodgson," Allie said. Her heartbeat ramped up.

"I'm sorry," the operator said. "I have Frank G. Dodgson."

"Can you try the first one and then stay on the line until we find the right one?"

"It's against the rules," the operator said. "You'll just have to pick one."

Mike came out of the bathroom, rubbing his nose with the back of his hand. "There's no one in there," he said, and he pulled Allie's hips toward himself and started grinding into her.

"I'll try back later," Allie said, to the operator, and she hung up the phone. She wanted to forget about her current status as an orphan. Mike could help with that.

"Let's go in the bathroom together," Mike said, and he nipped the top of Allie's ear.

"The bathroom?" There was no way Allie would make out in a stall of the men's restroom.

"Yeah, go get some coke from your car." Mike stuck his hand

on Allie's crotch, over her jeans, and started rubbing. Allie pawed his hand away. "I'll rub it into your pussy," Mike purred.

Allie pulled her head back, shocked by the way he had used the word *pussy*. Even Marc, after months together, hadn't used that word. "Kissing's fine for me now," she temporized.

"What do you mean kissing's fine? We can't just spend the afternoon kissing." Mike leaned forward and sucked on Allie's earlobe. He was humming. "Do you have really dark nipples?" He reached for her breast. "That's the thing I love about black girls, those really dark nipples. Like eating melted chocolate."

Allie blocked him with her forearm. Desire was fizzing away like spilled water on a hot sidewalk. "Well, my mom's Chinese," she answered, "and I've got a white grandfather on either side, so I'm not that dark."

Mike squared his shoulders and leaned into her. "Are you black or not?" He had dropped the soothing purr.

Allie looked at Mike and wondered what was wrong with her that she had thought she was interested in him.

Before she could say anything, Mike said, "You're not fucking black and that's not your dad who owned that restaurant. One fucking lie after another!" He took her head into his hands and whispered into her ear, "And I don't know where you got this coke or how you plan on selling it without a scale and without knowing how to fold a simple envelope, but you know what? You sold me about six grams of coke. Not three! Dumb fucking not-black chick!" Mike released Allie's head, patted his breast pocket, and walked away through the dining room.

Allie stood for a moment, unsure of what her next move was. Then a flutter in her gut told her to get back to the car, back to the coke. She followed Mike out of the restaurant and down the sidewalk.

When each of them was at their own car, Mike turned around

and looked at Allie. "Give me the rest of your coke," he said, and he took two steps to the Prelude and put his hand on the passenger-side door.

"That was all I had," Allie said. "The whole scale thing was made up so I could hang out with you. I think you're really, super cute." A complete lie now that Mike seemed angry and ugly. (Allie couldn't help but think how Wai Po would be disappointed in the number of lies that had been slipping out of Allie's mouth as easily as the air she breathed.)

"Lemme see. Open the car." Mike's eyes were prickly. He barely blinked.

"Yeah, okay. Just a second." Allie was shaking as she fit the key in the door. When she got in, she hit the button on the automatic lock, then stabbed the key into the ignition. Mike pounded on the glass as Allie jerked the car into reverse, trying to get the clutch and gas synchronized. Mike leaped at the car, and even though Allie saw him do it, the thunderclap his body made as it landed on the low roof of the Prelude startled her and she let out a raspy scream.

Allie burst out of the parking lot and onto Fairfax Avenue. Mike's legs hung cartoonishly down the side window. Just as she started to speed up, the legs disappeared. Allie watched through her rearview mirror as Mike landed solidly on both feet in the breakdown lane. He ran after the car for only a moment before stopping, throwing up his right fist, and cursing her with words she couldn't hear. Allie pulled up close to the VW Bug in front of her, tailgating, and then quickly lost sight of Mike.

4

Allie drove down Fairfax with her eyes continually flashing in the rearview mirror. She didn't see any red trucks and she didn't see police cars. Her hands had a palsied tremble and her heartbeat was so strong she thought she could hear it over Prince, whose voice was making the whole car feel like it was vibrating.

When she hit Wilshire, Allie turned left. Wilshire ran into Beverly Hills, this much she knew. And Beverly Hills bumped against Westwood, she was almost certain. And Westwood was where Allie's only and best friend in L.A., Kathy Kruger, lived.

As a kid, Allie had gone to nine different schools in nine different parts of the city. She always made friends, but would lose touch with them within weeks of moving. No parent would brave the Los Angeles traffic to get a kid to another side of town, so once Allie was gone so were her friends. The most lasting friendship Allie had was with Kathy—they were in the same high school for half of junior year and all of senior year.

Allie came up with a new plan. She would hang out with Kathy for a while, sell enough coke to Kathy's friends to pay her tuition bill, and then track down her mother and let her help negotiate with Jonas so Allie could get back to the Bay Area. Meantime, if her mother didn't know where her father was, she would use Kathy's phone to call every Frank Dodgson in the Los Angeles phone book until she had found him. Allie's gut sucked in at the thought of the dead restaurant. *Another time*, she whispered. That was what she told herself when she needed to put off thinking about things. She had done it often as a kid and had found it a wonderfully effective way to glide through forgotten school pickups, no-show parents at parent-teacher conferences, or an after-school friend commenting on the lack of snack foods in Allie's house.

Allie pulled into a gas station and parked the car. She checked under the front seat and pulled out the Wonder Bread bag, just to make sure it was still there. There was a phone booth outside the mini-mart. Allie took a dime from her wallet, then got out of the car, leaving the purse and the coke behind. She clicked the automatic lock with a satisfied smile.

Kathy answered on the first ring.

"Oh my god!" Allie said into the phone, "I can't believe I'll actually get to see you!"

"I'm in L.A. How could you possibly see me?" Kathy was always so logical. She had seemed thirty years old when she was sixteen. And she almost looked thirty, too. Tall, rigid, blond hair clipped sensibly short. Men loved her: she was like Katharine Hepburn, or Candice Bergen. A no-nonsense woman with an almost magical sex appeal.

"I'm in L.A., too!" Allie screamed. Sometimes Kathy's steadiness made Allie whirl out of control.

"Are you at your dad's? What are you doing here?" When Kathy was happy, her voice was as even and flat as when she was mad, or irritated, or sad. Allie assumed Kathy was glad to hear from her.

"I don't even know where my dad is. I went to his restaurant and it was closed!"

"You mean closed for the night? Or closed down?"

"It was closed down. I mean there is no restaurant—I'm freaking out here!" It didn't seem right to tell Kathy the accumulation of things that were freaking her out just then.

"Odd," Kathy said. "And he didn't call you and tell you anything about it?"

"I don't have a phone, remember? Listen, I'm at Wilshire and Hills. Where's your new place?"

"Oh, I'm just around the corner. But I have a date in like five minutes with this guy. He's a lawyer."

"A lawyer?! How old is he?"

"Forty."

"Forty?! He's older than my mother!" *Gross!* Allie thought. But then she remembered that only hours ago, she had her shirt off in a fitting room with a thirty-three-year-old guy. *That* was even more gross.

"I know. But he's totally cool. Smart, handsome, the whole shebang. I swear I think I'm in love."

Although Kathy had (unlike Allie) seemed interested in boys in high school, she never dated. She and Allie hung out in the library, quizzed each other for upcoming tests, and went to the beach and read, their bellies never getting tanned as they lay facedown in front of their books in the sand. And even now that the switch had flipped in Allie and she was suddenly boy-crazy, she had never imagined that it would happen to Kathy, too. Kathy seemed too smart for love. Like she could see how fleeting it was, how irrational these crushes were, how they came on with the force of a tidal wave that, as had happened with Marc, could leave you as damaged as a seaside shantytown.

"Oh my god, I can't believe you're in love." Allie wished she were in love. With someone new. Someone who loved her back.

"Wait, let me call him and see if you can come to dinner with us. I know he wanted to bring one of his clients along, so maybe a fourth would be good."

"I don't know. I've had a pretty crazy day and I just drove

all the way down here—I probably smell." Allie raised her arm above her head, leaned in, and sniffed.

"You've never smelled a day in your life," Kathy said. "Come on, it'll be fun. Our first double date together. Give me the number where you're at and I'll call you right back."

It seemed like she was waiting for hours. Allie watched people come in and out of the gas station. She picked up the phone and listened for the dial tone to make sure it was working. She watched more people.

When Kathy finally did call back, Allie picked up the receiver before the first ring had finished. "Hey!"

"Okay, so Bud has this new client and the guy is single and Bud said you should definitely join us for dinner. This guy's really cool. Plus he's someone of quality."

"Quality," Allie said. Wai Po talked about people of quality. In third grade, when Allie was hanging out with Alice Woo, Wai Po approved, saying Alice was *VERY HIGH QUALITY. NO BARGAIN MEAT THERE.* "Okay. Sure. How old is this guy? Is he Bud's age?" Allie was starting to feel hopeful. Maybe true love would follow what Allie now saw as one of the most regretful days of her life.

"I don't know. I didn't ask. He's a movie producer. I think."

"Cool! How great would it be to go out with a Hollywood producer!" Allie could feel nerves jiggling on the ends of her limbs. A date! With a real, live, grown-up movie producer! She hadn't been on an actual date since Marc.

"Listen, we're supposed to be there now, so swing by and pick me up and we'll go together."

Kathy's apartment was less than two blocks from the gas station. Allie wanted to run in and see it, poke through Kathy's drawers, see what kind of food she had in the fridge, but they were in a rush, according to Kathy. They had to be on time.

Allie pulled away from the curb and followed Kathy's directions.

"Whose car is this?" Kathy said, and she looked around as if there was something more to see than just seats in the back.

"My friend Beth's."

"Why does it say CALL GIRL on the license plate? Beth's kinda giving people the wrong message, don't you think?"

"It says CAL GIRL. CAL. As in Berkeley."

"Are you sure there aren't two Ls on there?" Kathy seemed so confident that Allie wanted to pull the car over and look at the plate herself.

"It says CAL," Allie said.

Kathy pulled on her seat belt. She was the only person Allie knew who regularly wore a seat belt. "I'm really happy to see you," Kathy said, and she put an arm around Allie and hugged her in a half-touching way. Kathy had never been that affectionate in high school. Not like Beth, who liked to crawl into Allie's bed and wrap her legs around Allie to warm up.

"You're my only friend in L.A.," Allie said. "There's no one else to write letters to."

Kathy smiled. She was the only person who knew about the fifteen-page letters Allie used to send Penny only to get back almost-formal postcards from places like Budapest or Zagreb, where people were still passionate about Mighty Zamboni.

"So why are you here? I thought you had to work in Berkeley all summer." Kathy opened her window and adjusted the rear-view mirror.

"My job was in Oakland, not Berkeley."

"Turn right here. What's with the Wonder Bread?" Kathy kicked the bag with the point of her black leather pump. She was wearing a short cotton skirt and a blouse. Allie thought she looked more like a secretary than a college student.

"Well, that's sort of the reason I'm here now—"

"Left there! Quick!" Kathy pointed across Allie's chest. "Turn into the parking lot there. Park next to the BMW. That's Bud's car."

"Okay," Allie said, turning the wheel.

"Not so close!" Kathy said. "Pull out and in again so you won't nick his door when you get out."

"Don't worry." Allie cut the engine. "I won't nick your boyfriend's *BMW*."

"Sorry," Kathy said. "I'm just not used to you driving. I was always the one with a license and a car." Kathy unbuckled her seat belt and got out of the car.

Allie got out, held the automatic lock up at eye level, and gave it a click. It was true, Kathy had been the one in charge when they were in high school. Kathy decided what movie they'd go to, which girls they'd hang out with, what they'd eat, whose house they'd sleep at. Allie always felt like a tourist and Kathy was the confident and able insider who helped her navigate it all. But now, after going away to college and feeding herself and falling in love and losing all her money and getting her heart broken, Allie didn't quite feel like Kathy's tagalong. She felt almost as grown-up as Kathy had always seemed. And after having stolen a bag of pure cocaine (as well as having watched a man masturbate!), Allie felt like there were ways in which she'd even passed Kathy in the life-experience lane.

"Come on." Kathy turned toward the door of Manuel's Taqueria. She waited for Allie to catch up.

"Do I look okay?" Allie asked.

"Of course," Kathy said, and Allie knew it must be true. Kathy had never been one for false flattery. "By the way," Kathy said, her hand poised on the giant bar-like door pull, "don't tell Bud that you've smoked pot."

"I did it twice," Allie protested. If only Kathy knew that that was the least of Allie's transgressions!

"I know," Kathy said, "but he's *totally* against drugs. It's one of his things."

"Well it's not like I'm FOR drugs. I've just tried them. And believe me, my experience with them hasn't really turned out well."

Kathy paused, her hand still on the door pull. "Did you try anything other than pot?"

"I tried coke," Allie confessed. "It was awful. That's sort of why I'm here."

"Cocaine?" Kathy shook her head in a way that made Allie regret telling her. "That's hard-core." And then she finally pulled open the door and stepped into the restaurant ahead of Allie.

It was dark inside. There were strings of glowing chili peppers draped across the ceiling like clotheslines, and the walls were covered with straw hats, Mexican flags, and what Allie guessed where burro blankets. Tinny-sounding Mexican music came out of randomly placed speakers. Kathy seemed to know where she was going; she picked up speed as she approached a far corner table. A slender man in a suit stood and kissed her on the cheek. As Allie got closer she saw that yes, indeed, this was a full-grown, forty-year-old man with creases radiating around his eyes and tufts of gray popping up behind each ear. But he also appeared fit and didn't have a lecherous look to him. Maybe, like everything else in life, Kathy knew how to pick guys, too.

Across the table from Bud was an overweight, middle-aged, glossy-faced man in a wheelchair. He had a thick, almost-wet, blondish mustache, which gave him a walrus-like look. His hair was long and straight, with a yarmulke of baldness on the crown of his head. There was a pointer with a rubber tip attached to his forehead and a board somewhat like an Ouija board across the arms of his chair. He was grinning, his head rocking back with what appeared to be excitement. Allie tried to catch Kathy's eye, but Kathy wouldn't look at her.

"Allie!" Bud said, and he stuck out his hand. Allie shook it without taking her eyes off the man in the wheelchair. "This is my friend and client, Roger." He pronounced it Roe-Jay. "He's from Paris."

"You're a French major, this should be easy for you," Kathy said. She toward Roger. "I'm Kathy, by the way." Then she leaned forward to shake Roger's hand. Before she could get there, his arm spasmed. Kathy chased the hand across the board, trapped it, held it for the amount of time a shake would have taken, and released it. She was wearing her polite, nervous smile. Allie had seen it thousands of times over the years; it popped up frequently in front of teachers and parents. It reminded Allie of a pencil drawing: a single horizontal line to indicate a mouth.

"Have a seat," Bud said, and he pulled out the chair beside him for Kathy, then pointed at the chair in the corner for Allie. The wheelchair was blocking access, so Allie grabbed the two handles and tried to pull Roger back. Roger made a long, low squeal.

"Brakes," Bud said, "you need to release the brakes."

"Oh." Allie tried not to laugh. When she looked toward Kathy, Kathy jolted her head away as if to indicate she would have no part in making fun of this incident. Beth would want to talk about this, Allie thought wistfully. Beth loved to laugh about everything she and Allie encountered in Berkeley: the bearded guy who wore dresses, lived in a tree on Telegraph Avenue, and shouted down to pedestrians, "Jesus hates you!"; the Gertrude Stein–looking woman in the black judicial robe, who wandered around campus blowing bubbles from a pink plastic bubble-maker; or Polka Dot Man, who silently held yoga poses for hours in Dwinelle Plaza, wearing his white polka-dot jumpsuit. And then Allie remembered Beth's car, Jonas, Vice Versa, and the fact that she was supposed to have been back at Beth's apartment with the coke hours ago. *Another time*, Allie said in her head, and she longed for some unimaginable future where there were no terrifying or uncomfortable thoughts she needed to banish.

Allie looked down to the back wheels of the chair, saw a little red lever, and kicked it up with her foot. She rolled the chair back, got into her seat, and pulled the chair forward by the armrests. "I guess I can't lock it from where I'm sitting." She tilted her head to make her eyes even with Roger's falling head. A loose lank of tin-blond hair jerked across his face. "Do you think you'll be okay?"

Roger banged the felt-tipped pointer on the word YES that was prominent in the upper right corner of the board. NO was on the other corner, MAYBE in the middle, the alphabet in the center, and then a few simple word combinations on the bottom: *I need, I would like, Please, Thank you, Help.*

Bud ordered two pitchers of beer for the table. When the waiter brought out the bumpy orangey glasses, Bud poured a beer for each of them and raised his glass for a toast.

"To old friends and new," he said. "And to this foxy little lady!" He leaned over and kissed Kathy on the mouth, his fat lips completely concealing her face below her nose. Kathy had her hands on his shoulders, as if to push him away, yet she stayed with the kiss. Allie was impressed. Kathy had never been demonstrative. She would have sighed or rolled her eyes had Allie kissed someone like that in public.

"Okay," Kathy said, when she pulled away from the kiss. She straightened her already straight hair.

"You need to help him drink," Bud said abruptly, pointing at Allie with his cup.

"Oh!" Allie laughed, picked up Roger's beer, and put it to his mouth. Roger chugged, his mustache dipping into the cup, then rocked his head back in what seemed like glee. Allie wondered if she should wipe the beer foam off his mustache. She lifted her napkin once, hovered it for a moment, then put it back down without touching it to Roger's face.

Bud and Kathy turned to each other and talked with their faces only inches apart. At first, Kathy was wearing her stern mother face, as if she was scolding Bud. Then she seemed to relax. Allie wondered if love was one of those things, like drugs, that made you behave in ways you wouldn't normally. She decided to make the best of the situation and turned to Roger.

"So," Allie said. "How do you know Bud?"

Roger spent a good twenty minutes tapping out that he'd just met Bud. Bud was defending him in a case that was a matter of mixed information and not any wrongdoing on his, Roger's, part.

"What do the cops think you did?" Allie asked. She fed Roger another sip of beer before he could answer. The waiter returned for their order.

"I'm going to order for you, Roger," Bud said. "Enchilada platter all right?"

Allie jerked the beer back so Roger could slam down on the YES or NO. He chose YES.

"Me, too," Allie said, and she turned back to Roger, whom she was finding far more interesting than lovey-dovey Bud and spoony Kathy. "I'm dying to know," Allie said, as she fed Roger more beer, "what were you accused of doing that you needed a lawyer?"

Allie pulled the beer back and Roger tapped down on the letter *I*. Then the letter *M*.

"I'm—" Allie started. Roger emitted a howly yowl and dropped his head from side to side. Then he tapped down on NO.

"Not you." Allie sipped some beer. She liked beer but it made her so full she always felt the need to unbutton her pants when she drank it, which before tonight had been only a few times with Marc.

Roger plopped down on the NO again.

"Okay," Allie said. "Let's start over."

Roger tapped on the letter *I*, then pulled himself up and swayed from side to side.

"*I*," Allie said. "Just *I*, right?" Roger squalled like a kazoo and Allie laughed. She liked this. It was like doing the word jumble in the paper, or the crossword puzzle.

By the time the enchiladas had arrived, Roger had tapped out that he made movies for a living.

"Right! You're a producer!" Allie said, and Roger tapped YES, YES, YES.

Allie fed Roger a bite of his enchilada before each of her own bites. She forked it up just the way she liked it, with a bit of rice and lots of the sauce smeared in. Every now and then Roger's head would jerk just as she was reaching his mouth, and enchilada sauce would smear across his mustache or on his chin. Allie wiped him up, the red enchilada sauce staining his face and facial hair, and carried on.

Eventually, Kathy and Bud made an effort to include Allie and Roger in their conversation. Allie was sorry about this, as whenever Bud spoke he made sure not to ask any questions or leave any open-ended ideas that might inspire Roger to try to tap out an answer. The one time he did put forth a question, he caught himself immediately and said, "Well of course you think *The Godfather* is the best movie made in the past ten years—or I guess I should say eleven years since it came out in '72, right, Roger? Yes, that's definitely right, it was '72."

"So, Roger was telling me about his case," Allie said, as the waiter was clearing their plates. Two more pitchers of beer had arrived moments earlier. Allie had that swimmy feeling in her head that came when she drank too much. Her eyes felt like they'd been weighted with tiny silver beads. She imagined using toothpicks to prop her eyelids open, like Bugs Bunny or the Road Runner.

"It's open and shut!" Bud said. He was shouting slightly. Allie wondered if he were drunk, too.

"What's the case?" Allie asked. She felt her tongue slipping up on the letter *S*. Normally she'd stop drinking at this point, or even far before this point, but this day had wound her nerves so tightly she needed the unraveling brought on by alcohol.

Roger squealed and rocked back against his chair. The wheels slipped a little and Allie reached out, grabbed the board, and pulled Roger forward.

"Open and shut! Open and shut!" Bud slammed a lazy fist on the table. His beer splashed onto his wrist. He lifted his arm and licked the beer off. *Okay,* Allie thought, *definitely drunk.* Kathy looked as sober as she had when Allie had picked her up.

"Yeah, Bud said it was all a mix-up." Kathy spoke as if she were intimate with the case. "And that Roger is no more a criminal than you or me. Or maybe just me." Kathy looked at Allie and gave a little laugh.

"What?" Allie said. She could feel beer in her ears. It was making the noise in the room wobbly.

"I think you've done a little more criminal activity than I have." Kathy squeaked out a tense laugh.

Allie wasn't sure if she were hearing correctly. Did Kathy think Allie was a criminal because she had smoked pot twice?

Or was it because she had done the cocaine? Allie hadn't even told her about the bag of stolen coke in the car, but certainly she couldn't confess to that now.

"I have?" Allie asked.

"Let's just say you've changed a lot since high school," Kathy said, and she pushed her mouth into the closed-lip smile.

"You're committing a crime tonight!" Allie wished her words weren't so mushed together. "You're not twenty-one and you're drinking!"

"We didn't get carded," Kathy said.

"You're still committing a crime," Allie said.

"I'm just saying I've never deviated as far as you have," Kathy said, and Allie knew then that the drift she was feeling from Kathy might be permanent.

"What about Roger? Are you okay with what he did?" Allie turned to him. Roger's head had dropped to one side and his eyes were shut. Was he actually sleeping?

"Roger is not a criminal in the slightest!" Bud said with a spray of enthusiasm. "The girl looks thirty. I saw for myself." He laughed. "She's got stretch marks and everything hanging down." Bud held his palms below his ribcage and lifted them up and down as if he were weighing something.

"Who?" Allie asked. "What are you talking about?"

"Roger's case! The girl! It was all low and hanging!" Bud shut his eyes as he laughed.

"Hanging boobs?" Allie felt as though popcorn was exploding in her head. She wanted to clear out her brain, eliminate this frustrating confusion.

"Of course he's not talking about boobs!" Kathy glared at Allie. Allie tried to roll her eyes.

"Yeah, I am," Bud said to Kathy, and he refilled everyone's

beer, even sleeping Roger's. How many was that now? Allie had lost count long ago.

"Wait, so what about the girl's boobs?" Allie picked up her glass and sipped. She really wanted to stop but it felt like she was defying Kathy if she drank more.

"She had these sad, droopy-eyed boobs," Bud said. "I mean, there is no one who would ever think that she was only seventeen. Especially since she had an Alaska driver's license that said she was twenty-four. And it's not like Roger had ever gotten a girl from Alaska in one of his movies before! How the hell was he supposed to know what a real Alaska license looks like?"

"Oh, did she need parental permission to be in his movie?" Kathy asked. "Or, like a mother on set, right? I would love to put my kids in movies! I mean, it would be so interesting to be on the set and see how everything works, but not to have to be in front of the camera and worry about having movie-star looks, you know what I mean?" She stared at Bud, then Allie. Allie figured Kathy wanted them to shout out that she *did* have movie-star looks, but she kept her mouth closed. She didn't think Kathy deserved her support after insinuating that Allie was a criminal.

"I don't think you want your kids in one of Roger's movies!" Bud laughed again and pulled Kathy into his shoulder as if he were going to give her a head noogie. He didn't give the noogie but he did kiss her on the forehead. Roger woke up. He lifted his pointer in the air like a walrus lifting his nose, and trumpeted. Allie lifted her chin and trumpet-squealed with him.

Kathy and Bud stared at Allie as if she'd just insulted Roger. "Will you *please* stop that," Kathy said. Roger trumpeted more and more, panting with a smile between his efforts.

"Fine," Allie said, and then she turned to Bud. "Why wouldn't you want your kid in Roger's movies? I love Roger's movies! Roger makes the best movies in the whole wide American world!" After trumpeting with Roger, feeding him his dinner and beer, and wiping up his mustache numerous times, Allie was feeling a protective affection for him.

"You've seen Roger's movies?" Bud was grinning so big Allie could see his fillings.

"Maybe!" Allie said. "Name one."

"The Summer of Naked Sin Parties! The Year of Licking Dangerously! Star Whores!" Bud laughed, lifting his mug as if he were toasting each title.

"You're kidding, right?" Kathy asked. She was wearing her nervous line-grin again.

"No, I'm not kidding!" Bud almost looked offended. "Roger makes porno movies."

Allie burst out laughing. "Seriously?!"

Roger banged the pointer multiple times on YES, YES, YES, YES. Then he and Allie threw their heads back and trumpeted once together.

"That's disgusting," Kathy said. She was leaning away from Bud, her eyes darting around but never landing on Allie. Allie felt a drunken, shameful joy in seeing Kathy's straight and narrow ideals challenged by the upstanding lawyer boyfriend who they all now knew was defending a porno movie producer in a child porn case. Surely this was worse than smoking pot twice!

"It's not disgusting!" Bud said. "Those girls make a lot of money! And Roger treats them well!" They all looked at Roger. He tapped on the YES again. Kathy turned her head toward the wall. The waiter approached with the dessert menu.

"I'll order for all of us," Bud said.

"I don't want dessert." Kathy's mouth appeared to be made from cardboard.

"Well then three of those fried ice cream thing-a-ma-jigs," Bud said to the waiter.

"I'll share mine with you," Allie said to Kathy, and she reached her hand out across the table as if to tell her that even if she was a bitch, Allie was forever grateful for the friendship they'd had and was still on her side. Kathy leaned away from the extended hand.

"And another pitcher of beer!" Bud said, and Roger squealed again.

Allie was finding it difficult to wipe the fried tortilla with ice cream off Roger's face. She wasn't sure if he was shifting out of reach, or her hand was missing the target. It was like playing darts with a moving board.

"How do you drive?" Allie asked.

Roger tapped out D-R-I-V-.

"You have a driver?" Allie asked.

"Oh, Roger's driver!" Bud said. He and Kathy had been tensely whispering to each other. "He said he'd be here with the van at eleven."

"It's eleven ten." Kathy scowled at her gold watch.

"I love your watch," Allie said.

"You've seen it before," Kathy said. "I got it for graduation."

"I know," Allie said. She was just trying to warm things up between them. And she really did love that watch, although it forced her to recall how painful it had been to have dinner at the Sims Surf and Turf with Kathy's parents after graduation while Allie's father worked at the restaurant and her mother was out of the country. Since there had been no one to watch her get the diploma, Allie had skipped the ceremony, but Kathy had begged her to go to the dinner. After Kathy had opened the box with the watch, her mother handed Allie a wrapped present. It was a book about how to survive your first year of college. That weekend, Allie read the book straight through and then, later, found that college was nothing like the book anticipated it would be and none of the advice seemed pertinent. Certainly there were no chapters on what to do when you accidentally stole a bread bag full of cocaine.

"You want to roll Roger out while I get this lovely little lady home?" Bud stood and tried to pull out Kathy's chair for her, but Kathy didn't budge. Bud pulled and pulled, as though he was attempting to move a stone sculpture.

"I'll drive your car," Kathy said, and she finally stood. "You're drunk." She looked at Allie. "And you're too drunk to drive, too."

"I don't even know if I can walk!" Allie said. "I'll get a ride with Roger." Allie wasn't sure where she'd go, but going with Roger seemed like a good place to start.

Bud and Kathy walked ahead as Allie tried to push the wheelchair through the restaurant. There was greasy-looking carpet on the floor, which somehow made it hard for the wheels to move. Allie started and stopped several times. Then, just as she got some momentum going, she missed the door being held open by Bud and pushed Roger into the door frame. Roger squeal-laughed.

"Smooth move." Bud laughed.

Allie pulled back and aimed for the doorway again. It felt as though she was trying to thread a needle, but she and Roger made it outside.

Bud said a brief, sloppy good-bye and slipped into the BMW that Kathy had pulled up beside him. Kathy waved quickly out the window and Allie waved back. She wondered if that would be the last time they'd see each other. Then she wondered if she'd be sad about it tomorrow. Right now, she felt relieved.

Allie looked around. "Where's your van?" she asked Roger.

Roger tapped out C-O-K-E.

"Coke?" Allie asked. "You want a Coke?"

Roger's head flopped down hard on the NO.

"Oh!" Allie said. "You want cocaine?" She figured anyone who made movies in Hollywood, no matter what the genre, did cocaine.

Roger hit the YES, then spelled: I H-A-V-. Allie wondered if Bud wasn't really as against drugs as Kathy thought. If Roger did coke so openly, he surely had offered it to Bud before. Although that didn't necessarily mean Bud did it. Beth *loved* coke, and Allie had been best friends with her for almost two years before she tried it herself.

"Don't waste what you have," Allie said. It seemed harmless to give just a little of the Wonder Bread coke away, and cruel to deny a guy in a wheelchair with a head pointer and an enchilada-stained mustache what was probably one of his few physical joys. She let go of the wheelchair and staggered to the Prelude. When she looked back at the wheelchair, it was rolling toward a parked car, but slowly enough that Allie didn't worry. She retrieved the bread bag, locked the car, and returned to Roger, who had gently bounced into the parked car. Allie held the Wonder Bread bag against one of the wheelchair handles and her purse against the other handle as she pulled the wheelchair off the car it had hit and directed it to the sidewalk beside the driveway. The air was the perfect temperature, neither hot nor cold. If she weren't so drunk, Allie thought she'd probably enjoy a ride in the Prelude with the moon roof fully open, the blur of smudgy gray night sky above her head.

"You think your driver's coming?" she asked Roger.

Roger tapped YES.

"Want coke while we wait?"

Roger tapped YES, YES, YES.

"Okay." Allie rummaged into her purse and pulled out a Bic pen. She snapped off the cap and dug the pointed concave tip into the bag and pulled out a tiny pile. When she placed the cap under Roger's nose, his head tilted and jerked and the contents spread into his mustache like powdered sugar.

Roger knocked the pointer on the letter *A*.

"Try again?" Allie asked, and Roger lifted his head and squealed. "How about this?" Allie shoveled her cupped palm into the bag then held the heap under Roger's nose with the thought that maybe a twentieth of it would make it up his nostrils. Roger snuffled and rubbed into her like a dog rubbing into dead animals it finds in the woods. Allie remembered Mike licking her palm. It was a shame he turned out to be such an enormous jerk.

The van pulled up while Roger was still nuzzling his whiskered walrus face into Allie's hand. "Okay, finish up, our ride's here." Allie pushed Roger's head up with her free hand. Roger had his tongue out, so she wiped her palm clean on it. She didn't get the same erotic jolt as when Mike had done it.

A Hispanic man in a gray cotton zip-front coat stepped out of the van. "Roger! How you doin' tonight, sweetie?" He came over and collected Roger, rolling the chair toward the open sliding door of the van that had a silver ramp sticking out like a tongue.

Allie held her wet palm out, looking at the driver, looking at Roger, trying to decide what to do. "Can I have a ride, too?" she finally asked.

"Jump in!" The Hispanic man smiled at her and nodded his head toward the van. Allie blundered into the front seat and waited while the guy fastened Roger's wheelchair into the back with seat belt–looking straps. "You in Roger's movies?" he asked.

"No, just a friend," Allie said. The Wonder Bread bag was twisted shut and sitting on her lap like a small baby.

"I'm Jorge," the guy said, and winked. "Where you going?" He stepped through the van into the driver's seat. Then slowly, as if he were driving a truck carrying glass panels, Jorge pulled out of the driveway and they cruised away.

"Where are we going . . ." Allie's brain felt impossibly heavy. She closed her eyes to give herself a minute to think and her head lolled forward. Allie jerked up, looked at Jorge, and smiled as if that would erase the embarrassment of almost passing out mid-conversation.

"Well, Roger's house isn't far, so I'll just drop him off first." Jorge had a gentle face: soft and kind, with no sharp edges. His eyes were perfect circles. Allie wanted to touch his cheek, but even as drunk as she was, she knew she shouldn't.

Allie looked at the blur outside the window. They were in Beverly Hills now, driving past well-lit mansions, gates, driveways that had separate entrances and exits. Her gaze was fixed on a pink stucco house that looked like a Moroccan palace when a gasping, barking sort of sound erupted from the backseat. Before Allie could turn and look, Jorge had put the car in park and was pulling Roger out of his chair. The van was spinning, but Allie knew they were parked. She watched as Jorge straddled Roger's chest and performed CPR on the floor of the van in front of the chair.

"Pick up that radio, hold the side button, and tell them we're at Alpine near Lomitas Ave. They need to call 911." Jorge wasn't yelling, although his voice was urgent and stiff.

Allie picked up the small square speaker. She pushed the button on the side. "Uh, call 911," she said, almost whispering. "We're at Alpine and Lomitas and I think Roger's having a heart attack." There was a smokey wooziness in Allie's head. She tried to remember how much coke had been in her palm when Roger had snuffled it up. How much did people usually do in one sitting? Jonas had taken about eight pinches of the bread-bag stuff. Was a palm-full more than eight pinches? Could a *full palm* of coke really have gone up Roger's nose? Wasn't most of it in his mustache? Allie's heart thumped. Her eyes burned. She wanted to scream and cry in frustration. Everything she had done today had been wrong. Completely wrong! No wonder Kathy hated her.

The ambulance was there. Allie hadn't heard it, or maybe she had somewhere in the back of her panicked, drunken head. Two men in white jumpsuits were hovering over Roger with paddles on his chest.

"Is he dead?" Allie's voice quavered. Roger was flat on his back, his mouth open like a bird's beak, his eyes staring straight up. He didn't look like a quadriplegic. If it hadn't been for the pointer jutting up from his forehead like a unicorn's horn, Allie would have thought he was a normal middle-aged paunchy man. A snorer, for sure.

"Not totally," one of the paramedics said, and he jolted back as the paddles electrocuted Roger's giant, bloated body.

Allie righted herself in the front seat. Wai Po's voice was in her head. *DO NOT USE HATCHET TO REMOVE FLY FROM FRIEND'S FOREHEAD.* Allie shut her eyes and fervently prayed that she hadn't just killed Roger, hatcheted him with cocaine. She could barely finish the prayer words in her head when she dropped into a dead-drunk sleep.

5

Allie opened her eyes and looked at the ceiling. It was white, or more gray, really, with a spiderweb-looking crack that radiated out from where a chip of plaster was missing. Once her mind caught up with her eyes, Allie sat up, alert, wary. Nothing was familiar.

One side of the room had a Spider-Man and His Amazing Friends poster. The other side had a poster of Snoopy dancing with Woodstock. There were tiny stickers scattered on most of the walls: smiley faces, rainbows, dragons, more Spider-Man, and Strawberry Shortcake. Allie was in a stumpy bed with a red blanket and Fox and the Hound sheets. Next to her was a peeling plywood dresser covered with more stickers. On the other side of the dresser was another bed, with Strawberry Shortcake sheets. The room smelled like an elementary-school cafeteria: stale, crowded, sweaty, sour.

There was a weight in Allie's lap. She lifted the sheet, expecting to find a cat or maybe a rabbit. Instead she found the Wonder Bread bag, molded into a lumpy tube. Allie shook it so the coke fell to the bottom, untied the twisty, looked in, then shut the bag. All seemed normal.

The dirty pink purse was also in bed beside her. Allie spread it open and found the keys with her lucky rabbit foot. She stroked the gummy fur and instantly felt calmer.

Allie got out of bed, carrying the bread bag and her purse. She was in her Flashdance shirts and her acid-wash jeans but she was barefoot. The door to the room (more stickers) was ajar. There were fingerprints and peanut butter and other shiny viscous smears on it, so Allie toed it open. "Hello?" she called into the hallway that faced her. Framed photos hung from both walls. Jorge? Allie stepped closer. Yes, there was Jorge and two children, a boy and a girl. And a wife: black hair, overweight but curvy, a smile like a giant glittering diamond in the middle of her face.

The hallway smelled of coffee and burned cheese. Shag carpet wormed through Allie's toes. "Hello?" Allie crossed the length of the hallway and stepped out into a living room. There was a radio on somewhere. It sounded like it was playing the news in Spanish. Allie followed the sounds of the radio into a kitchen where the woman from the photos was talking on the phone. She jumped as if she were excited to see Allie, waved enthusiastically, then did a few *uh-huh*s into the phone.

"*Mami*, I have to go now, the girl is up." She switched to Spanish then, which to Allie sounded like *acata acata acata acata ack*. And then she hung up the phone and walked toward Allie.

"Hey," Allie said, and she waved with the hand that wasn't holding the bread bag.

"Are you okay?!" The woman put her arm around Allie's shoulder and led her to a red wooden chair at a linoleum-topped table. There were pots steaming on the stove. The radio had an antenna and sat like a giant insect on the chipped plastic countertop.

"Yeah, I guess." Allie slumped into the chair and stared at this woman as if she might be the better judge of Allie's state of mind. Currently, Allie only felt a strange disorientation, and fear that something even worse than her having stolen a bag of cocaine had gone down.

"Jorge said you were a friend of Roger's and you passed out

from shock after he—" The woman smiled and lifted her shoulders as if she didn't want to say the word *died*. Allie felt like she had to vomit. What sort of karmic revenge would come at her for smearing a palm-full of cocaine into the face of a drunk quadriplegic?

"He didn't know where to take you," the woman said. She seemed not to notice the guilt that was pushing Allie into the chair with such force that she expected at any minute to be spiraling through the linoleum floor into the chalky earth below.

"Yeah, of course," Allie said.

"And he thought maybe the best thing for you was to just sleep through it, so he brought you here."

"Yes," Allie said, although she had no idea where *here* was. For all she knew Jorge had driven her across the border into Mexico. Allie hoped it wasn't going to be too hard to get back to the Prelude. Although, she thought, she certainly deserved whatever difficulties came upon her now.

"I'm Consuela. I'm Jorge's wife." Consuela sat in the chair opposite Allie and stared at her with a questioning smile, as if she expected Allie to burst out in tears.

"I'm Allie," Allie said, though just then she wished that she weren't. She'd love to be any normal non-drug-thieving person who hadn't possibly killed a man in a wheelchair and didn't have some thug named Vice Versa after her.

"What's in the bread bag? It sure isn't bread, but I didn't want to open it. You were clinging to it like it was your blankie."

"Oh, yeah." Allie's heart pounded. "It's my parents' ashes."

Consuela gasped and put her hand to her heart. "Oh you poor thing. I bet after what happened with Roger—" She stopped, as if she couldn't bear to continue.

"Did the police come?" Allie could feel her head swirling.

"Yeah, Jorge said the police came, Roger's assistants came, there were people all around and you were just sitting in that front seat sleeping it off."

"They're not going to arrest me or anything are they?" Allie's voice cracked and she felt a cry creeping into her throat.

"Arrest you? What for!" Consuela took Allie's hand from across the table, and Allie started crying. Really crying. Head on the table. Snot dripping into her mouth. Strange choking animal sounds. Sobbing.

Consuela rushed around to the chair and pulled Allie's head into her soft, deep, warm belly. She rocked Allie back and forth. "Roger will be fine," Consuela said. "My father had a heart attack and now he's like Charles Atlas or something, running in marathons and everything." Consuela separated Allie from her middle and held her wet face in her hand.

"You mean he's alive?" Allie was so relieved she wanted to laugh.

"Yes, he's alive! He's in the hospital. He'll probably be out in a week." Consuela stared at Allie as if she were trying to make sure Allie understood what was being said.

"Oh god, I thought I killed him!" Allie's voice broke on the last two words, *kill-ed hi-im.* "I gave him the coke that gave him the heart attack!"

"Someone always gives it to him. He has a problem!" Consuela scooted into the chair beside Allie. "He's addicted. Jorge tells him every night to stop doing it, but he does it anyway. If it hadn't happened last night with you, it would have happened tonight."

"But he probably never does as much as he did with me." Allie sniffed.

"Listen," Consuela said. "You probably saved Roger's life. Maybe now he'll stop doing coke. He was either going to die or have a heart attack from it. It's his good luck that he had the heart attack!"

"Maybe." Allie sniffed and tried to smile.

"Don't think about it now." Consuela stood and went to the stove. "Now you eat tamales. I've got cheese and I've got beef." Consuela put two on a plastic plate that had a picture of a teapot in the center. She set the plate in front of Allie, then handed her a fork and a knife, each with a fake wooden handle. Then she sat across from Allie with her own plate of tamales. "Is there anyone you need to call? I hope no one was looking for you last night."

"No, no one's looking for me." The only person who wanted to find her, Allie thought, was Vice Versa. She had no idea what he looked like but she pictured him as a blood orange–colored gryphon: half-lion, half-eagle, with claws that would slice through her flesh like a box cutter into butter.

"You can call anyone from our phone. Roger gives Jorge the codes for calling long-distance so that we don't have to pay for it. I think Roger's company pays for it. And, you know, I hate that dirty movies are paying for my phone calls to my mama in Mexico, but Roger is a good guy, and he treats our children well. They don't know he makes dirty movies." Consuela laughed.

"He seemed like a good guy." Allie unwrapped the corn husk off each tamale and took a bite. They were so good she didn't want to talk. She tried forking a little of each together to get just the right salty-savory balance.

"Yeah, he gives pornos to Jorge and Jorge brings them home and gives them to the garbage men. They think it's better than the six-pack of beer our neighbors leave them at Christmas." Consuela was watching Allie as she ate. "You like that, don't you?"

"They're amazing," Allie said, taking another bite. She couldn't say anything else. She was too focused on eating.

"Have some more." Consuela got up and went to the pot on the stove.

"You know," Allie said, "if you really don't have to pay for long distance, there are a couple people I should call."

"Honestly!" Consuela plopped down two more tamales on Allie's plate. "It doesn't cost us anything." She rubbed Allie's shoulder and looked down at the Wonder Bread bag. "It's nice that you always have your parents with you."

"Yeah," Allie said. "It's like free long-distance day and night."

Consuela let Allie use the phone in her and Jorge's bedroom. The bed was made with a poinsettia-red quilted bedspread that reminded Allie of a roadside motel. There was a thick wooden cross over the bed, with a dried brown palm frond stuck behind it at an angle. On the dark, wide dresser were framed photos and a small colorful statue of the Virgin Mary with a crown on her head and a cross at her heart. Allie imagined it would be nice to have Catholicism, to believe in the power of a Hail Mary. Wai Po's words had always been Allie's prayers—incantations she repeated over and over again, the rabbit foot clutched in her hand like a rosary.

Allie sat on the edge of the bed, dropped the bread bag down next to herself, and picked up the receiver. She looked at the telephone number printed in the center of the dial. Area code 213. Wherever she was, she was still in Los Angeles. Allie dialed the long-distance code Consuela had written on the back of a business card that had NOBGOBBLERS, INC. printed in cherry-red. Roger's name and a telephone number were also on the card. When the dial tone returned, she punched in Beth's number. The digital clock on the nightstand said it was eleven thirty-eight.

Beth answered with a quiet, trembling voice.

"What's wrong?" Allie asked.

"What do you mean *what's wrong?*!" Beth was whisper-yelling. "There's, like, a fucking seven-foot black man taking a dump in my bathroom *right now*. And the guy isn't fucking leaving my apartment until you come back with my car and the, like, seven tons of coke you stole from Jonas!" Her words came out like the swish of a washing machine.

"Is it Vice Versa?" Allie whispered, too, although there really was no reason.

"No. His name's Rosie."

"Seriously?"

"Yes, seriously!" Beth's whisper was sounding hoarse. "And where the fuck are you? You were supposed to be back in *two hours*! Are you on, like, the fucking Gilligan's Island cruise with my car?!"

"Are you tied up?" Allie pictured Beth bound at the feet, with her arms tied behind some chair and duct tape over her mouth. Then, since Beth was talking on the phone, she erased the duct tape.

"No, I'm not tied up! I just can't leave. This guy is fucking living with me until you come back. And he eats, like, nonstop? I swear he had, like, two large pizzas for lunch. TWO. By himself. And it's not even noon yet!"

"You didn't have any pizza? Not even a slice?" Allie tried to stop whispering, but her voice kept slipping there in reply.

"Allie, where the fuck are you?! I swear I'm going to call the police the next time this guy takes a bathroom break and the only reason I haven't called yet is because you're carrying, like, a suitcase of coke and, like, I totally don't want you to get arrested. They told me that if you called I'm supposed to, like, tell you to just come back, return the coke and they won't hurt you?"

"Do you believe them?" It seemed impossible to Allie that Jonas would employ a guy named Vice Versa and a seven-feet-tall-double-pizza-eating man if he didn't intend to use them in violent ways.

"Not really. This guy has a gun *down the back of his pants*. Like you know when people have, like, plumber's butt? He's got gun butt. Every time he bends over I see a pistol sitting there above his crack just wedged into his pants. And he's huge. I swear. Totally enormous."

"So what should I do?" Allie felt her face going hot. Her hands started to shake.

"I don't know." Beth's hushed voice sounded so sad, Allie wanted to cry again.

"I'm trying real hard to figure this all out," Allie said, although she had yet to formulate a plan that seemed good enough to share with Beth.

"I know," Beth said. "Oh! I forgot to tell you. Your dad called? He said he moved and he wanted to give you his new phone number."

"Did he say anything about his restaurant? I'm in L.A. now. I went to his place and it's closed."

"He barely said anything about anything."

"I know," Allie said. "He doesn't like talking on the phone. He doesn't even like talking in person. But at least I know he's alive now."

"You ready for the number?" Beth said.

"Yeah." Allie grabbed a black Magic Marker off the night-stand and wrote it on the bread bag as Beth recited it to her. "Why do I have to have a father who never lives in the same place long enough for me to memorize his phone number?"

"Why do I have to have, like, a seven-foot man who just ate two large pizzas taking a ten-hour dump in my bathroom?" Beth asked.

"Okay, okay. Sorry. Listen. I'm going to start by calling my dad to see if he can help somehow. I'll try to get the pizza-eating-dumper out of your apartment as soon as possible. I promise." Allie picked up the bread bag and looked at her father's number. It was smeared from her hand. "Shit. Give me my dad's number again, I can't read what I wrote."

"Oh my god!" Beth said. "I just heard the toilet flush! He's coming out!"

"Didn't he hear the phone ring?"

"I don't know! He probably has the fan on in there—it's like a jet engine. And I, like, picked up in the middle of the first—" Beth hung up.

Allie held the phone against her ear as if Beth would reappear on the line. The phone started beeping and then an electronic voice asked her to hang up and dial again. Allie hung up but she didn't dial again. Instead she went to find more tamales.

Back at the kitchen table, Allie ate and stared at the smeared number on the bread bag. Even if she did get a hold of her father, what would she tell him? *By the way, Dad, I just stole a few kilos of coke and I'm trying to figure out how to give it back—minus the salary Jonas owes me, of course—without getting murdered, killing anyone else, or going to jail.*

Consuela was at the kitchen sink, wearing pink plastic gloves and a half-apron with oysters printed on it. She was doing the dishes and singing along with Spanish-language radio. When the song ended, she removed the gloves, wiped her hands on the apron, and looked at Allie. "You look so worried," she said. "I promise you, Roger will be fine. Do you want me to take you to see him?"

"Um . . ." Allie barely knew Roger. But she did feel she should go see him. She needed to apologize.

"It won't be scary. Jorge stopped by and said he's sitting up and pointing and everything." Consuela smiled.

"Okay, I guess." Allie looked down at the newspaper that was folded open on the table. There was a boxed-in square with the dates and times for bands at the Hollywood Bowl. Mighty Zamboni was listed. Allie snatched up the paper and looked at the date. It was three days old. Her mother had played here only two days ago.

"It takes me forever to read the paper," Consuela said as she started to put away the clean dishes that were drying on a dishtowel on the counter. "I just got to that today!"

Allie stood up, holding the paper. "Can I use the phone again?"

"*Sí, sí!*" Consuela said. "I promise you, it's free long-distance!" She waved both hands at Allie as if to shoo her back into the bedroom.

Allie dialed the number for the Hollywood Bowl. A man answered. He sounded whiny.

"Hey, do you know where Mighty Zamboni went after they played there?" Allie asked.

"I'm not Mighty Zamboni's manager," the guy snorted.

"I know but they were just there, so they're probably doing the whole state, right?"

"I have no idea what they're doing. They're not a band that interests me."

"I really need to find them," Allie said. She switched to a whisper so Consuela wouldn't hear, and added, "My mother's the tambourine girl for Mighty Zamboni and I need to find her."

"Why on earth are you whispering?" the guy said. He talked to Allie as if they'd known each other for years and he was allowed, entitled even, to be irritated with her.

"Because the woman whose phone I'm on thinks my parents are dead," Allie whispered.

"What is wrong with you that you tell people your parents are dead if they're not?"

"Please just tell me where Mighty Zamboni is now," Allie said in her normal speaking voice.

"Fine. Hold on." There was a clanking sound as the guy let the phone fall.

Allie opened the drawer of Consuela's bedside table and poked through it while she waited. There was a red leather Bible with a pink feather bookmark. There were also condoms and a tube of K-Y Jelly. Most of the Catholics Allie knew used birth control in spite of the pope's insistence against it. But she didn't know anyone who kept their birth control and their Bible in the same place. Allie loved imagining that Consuela and Jorge had a vigorous, hearty sex life. Eat some tamales, put the kids to bed, say a little prayer, and then BOOM. Roll around and make each other happy.

"Miss?" The guy was back on the phone.

"I'm here," Allie said.

"Leonard, the gaffer, said he talked to some of the Zamboni roadies and they mentioned they were playing the Santa Barbara County Bowl next. He thinks they're opening for either Blondie or Billy Idol."

"Blondie or Billy Idol?" Allie said. "How do you confuse Blondie with Billy Idol?"

"Both blonds, I guess," the guy said.

"All right, well, thanks," Allie said, and she hung up the phone and stared at it. She had the slightly jittery feeling under her skin that she always had when she knew she was going to see her mother. Allie had spent hours, days, years fantasizing about being with her mother in a traditional way. Fantasy Penny would cook for her, feed her, push Allie's face into her belly as Consuela had, and let her cry. In reality, she'd never experienced her mother like that. But there was a difference between their past encounters and now, Allie thought. In the past, Allie had never been in a tough situation in which she honestly needed Penny to help her out. But now, with the bag of coke, Rosie holding Beth hostage, and no clear plan, maybe Allie's mother would rise up and *be* a mother. A mother, Allie assumed, would never let her daughter be murdered by a man named Vice Versa.

Allie picked up the phone, called 411, and asked for the Biltmore Hotel. When she was ten years old, she and her father had driven to Santa Barbara to see Mighty Zamboni play. Allie and Frank had stayed in a tiny, tar-and-gravel-roofed motel just off the freeway. But her mother had stayed at the Biltmore Hotel, on the ocean. Allie had loved visiting her mother at the Biltmore. That night, when she lay awake on the cardboard-feeling mattress in the motel, Allie entered an hours-long fantasy in which she was staying at the Biltmore alone with her mother—breakfast in bed, afternoons at the beach, evenings sitting outside on the patio, eating what was then Allie's favorite food, mac 'n' cheese with bacon bits and bread crumbs baked on top.

Allie wrote the number to the Biltmore on her hand. She wasn't going to mess with a Magic Marker on a bread bag again. And then she punched in the long-distance code and dialed the hotel. It seemed impossible that her mother would stay anywhere else—Penny seemed to identify herself by the things to which she was loyal: she always drove a convertible (only Cadillacs since she'd been with Jet); she always smelled like Giorgio Beverly Hills perfume; and she always wore her black hair as long as, or longer than, Cher's.

When the front-desk clerk picked up, Allie asked for Penny Klein's room. As a young girl, she had been embarrassed that she was the only kid in the class (no matter which class or school it was) whose parents didn't have the same last name. Even Rachel LeBlanc's parents, who were divorced, had the same last name.

"There's no one here registered by that name."

Of course. Penny always shared a room with Jet Blaster. "Can I have Jet Blaster's room."

"I'm sorry, there's no one here with that name either."

Jet always thought he was so famous that he had to register under fake names. The guy was about sixty years old now, showing up in *People* magazine's "What Ever Happened To . . ." issue. Allie's mother had been in love with him since she was a young girl. And when she got pulled out of the audience by bodyguards and asked to meet Jet backstage after a Hollywood Bowl concert twelve years ago, six weeks after Penny's mother, Wai Po, died, she decided to leave Allie and Frank and go on the road with Jet as his tambourine girl. The night before she left, Penny sat on the edge of Allie's bed, leaned over Allie, and tucked her in so tightly that the blanket felt like a belt.

"I got a better job," she had said.

"I didn't know you had a job." Allie was wearing a fake Lanz nightgown with lace around the bib and hem. She had found a real Lanz nightgown in the JC Penney catalog and shown it to Wai Po, who bought the exact pink floral flannel and sewed the nightgown for Allie within a week. It was Allie's favorite possession, and, while wearing it, she always imagined herself as a character in her favorite movies: *Chitty Chitty Bang Bang* (she'd be Jemima), *The Sound of Music* (Louisa), *Bedknobs and Broomsticks* (Carrie).

"I'm a housewife, a mother, and a wife. Those are jobs." Penny's voice was like a prong. "But they're not the job I've always dreamed of having. My dream job is to be the tambourine girl in a band. And now someone's offering me that job, so—" Penny smiled with her lips pursed, then pushed a coil of red hair behind Allie's ear and kissed her on the forehead. Penny was twenty-six years old and still looked like a teenager with her straight, shiny hair and her smooth, velvety skin. On the rare times she took Allie shopping, the clerks often asked Penny if she were Allie's babysitter. These were the moments when Allie felt proud of Penny. But when her teenage-looking mother told her she was leaving to be a tambourine girl, Allie felt a wave of embarrassment. Maybe her mother was too pretty to be a mother. Or too sexy. Penny wore tiny shorts that showed the spot where her thighs met her butt, she had tank tops that exposed the outline of her small breasts. She was rounded like a woman, but the size of a girl, not even an inch over five feet. Allie's third-grade friend Donna's father always called Penny "Sexy Pretty Penny," as in, "How's that Sexy Pretty Penny? Does she pack you a good lunch every day?" This made Allie and Donna fall into each other with laughter—Allie's giggles always infused with the discomforting tanginess of shame.

"It's no big deal. I'll be home between gigs," Penny had said. Allie had never heard the word *gigs* before and she said it over and over again in her head as if it were a bell she was ringing.

"Okay," Allie said.

"Okay?" Penny asked.

"Okay," Allie said. It didn't occur to her that she might have some influence in this decision, that she could actually ask her mother to stay home.

When Penny had left the room, Allie retreated to *Chitty Chitty Bang Bang*, imagining the scene with beautiful Truly as she came in and tended to the children with a lacey long dress and a delicious British accent.

After that conversation, Penny was continually on the road with reunion tours, fund-raisers, and opening for bands that Penny claimed wouldn't exist today if it hadn't been for Mighty Zamboni (according to the occasional postcards that arrived). Allie and her father played along with the idea that Penny would be home any day now, any minute. But other than three drop-in appearances on three different Christmas days, the gigs went on through elementary school, junior high, and then high school.

At least once a year, Allie and her father would learn that Penny was coming to town, thanks to the pair of laminated passes that appeared in their mailbox a week before the show. The only concert Allie's father ever attended was the one in Santa Barbara. The two of them ate catered food with the band in a dining room near the dressing rooms. Allie's mother dragged Allie around by the elbow, introduced her to everyone, and asked if they looked like sisters. Her father was treated like an old friend with whom Penny had lost touch. When her parents sat on either side of her, eating pasta and talking about the California drought, Allie felt as though they were three strangers seated together on an airplane.

After that, Allie only went to the shows in Los Angeles, always bringing along a friend. Frank would drop them off and pick them up, never asking how the concert, or Penny, was.

"Can I have Gomer Pyle's room?" Allie asked the Biltmore operator. That was a name Penny once told her Jet used.

"Miss, who are you looking for?" The operator sounded impatient.

"My mother is the tambourine girl in Mighty Zamboni," Allie said, "and I assume the band is staying there, but I don't know the name they're using."

"I'm sorry. I can't connect you unless you know the registered name of the guest you're trying to reach."

"Okay. What about Alvin Bridgewater?" That was Jet's given name. It sounded as ridiculous to Allie as Jet Blaster.

"There's no one under that name either," the woman said.

Allie heaved in a big breath, then pulled the phone from her ear and hung up. She looked down at the coke and thought about what big trouble one little bread bag had brought. Allie picked up the phone again and called Kathy, who answered on the first ring.

The enthusiasm in Kathy's voice faded when she heard Allie on the line. Allie felt the rejection stinging in her eyes. "It was great seeing you last night," she said.

"That was a crazy night," Kathy said. "I'm not sure things are going to work out for me and Bud."

"I'm sorry," Allie said.

"Thanks," Kathy said, and then there was nothing but silence.

Allie let the silence stretch as long as she could before bursting out with, "So, I just wanted to let you know that Roger had a heart attack in the van last night."

"What do you mean he had a heart attack? Are you still drunk?" Kathy sounded angry, as if she already knew that Allie was responsible for the heart attack.

"What? What do you mean am I still drunk?" Allie felt confused. What did her being drunk have to do with the fact that Roger was in the hospital?

"You were trashed. It was embarrassing." Kathy sounded twenty years older than she was, making Allie feel thicker and more ashamed than ever.

"Okay, well, I didn't drive. I got in the van with Roger, who proceeded to have what seemed like a pretty violent heart attack. It was one of the scariest things I've ever seen." Allie looked up at the cross looming over her head. She knew that in not telling Kathy about the coke she had given Roger, she was presenting an alternate story to the truth of what had happened, another lie in the long series of lies that had been accumulating ever since she stepped into the fitting room with Jonas. But right now she couldn't take any more criticism.

"Am I supposed to tell Bud? 'Cause I really don't want to talk to him again."

"No," Allie said. "I'm sure someone will tell him eventually."

"I gotta go," Kathy said. "My friends are waiting."

A rush of tears moved forward in Allie's eyes. Was that really it? Last night Allie had felt relieved to let Kathy go, but now when she couldn't even find her mother in the hotel she *knew* she was staying in, Kathy's rejection felt like sandpaper against her cheeks.

"I'm sorry I disappointed you," Allie said, and she sniffed up the snot that seemed to be plummeting from her nose.

"Something like this would have happened with you eventually," Kathy said. "I mean, look at your rock-'n'-roll-druggie mom."

Allie hung up. The jaggedness in Kathy's words stunned her. *Another time*, she said in her head. She would think about Kathy some other day. For now, she'd follow the advice Kathy had given her weeks ago for getting over Marc: *Imagine putting teeny, tiny Marc on a leaf, setting him in a stream, and letting him float away.* In her head Allie saw miniature business-skirt-bound Kathy, clinging to a spiky oak leaf like a drowning pinhead beetle, rushing down a white-water stream over craggy, giant rocks.

After several seconds with this fantasy, Allie felt better. She picked up the phone and called Kathy back.

"What?" Kathy said.

"Can you just tell me the name of the place where we ate so I can go get my car?"

"Manuel's Taqueria," Kathy said.

"Okay. Well, thank you for being my friend in high school. I needed you then."

"Everyone's got to move on, Allie," Kathy said impatiently.

"The moving on's already happened," Allie said, and she hung up.

Consuela was drinking a cup of coffee and reading the paper at the kitchen table. She said something in Spanish to the paper as Allie entered, then looked up at Allie. "You okay? You want to go to the hospital now?"

"Do you mind if we go later?" Allie asked. "I've got to drive up to Santa Barbara to see someone."

"Sure. But if you drive all the way to Santa Barbara, we can't go to the hospital today. At three I have to pick up my kids from their fancy camp that Roger pays for, and I don't want to take them to the hospital."

"Roger pays for the camp?"

"Oh yeah," Consuela said. "He pays for all the kids in the neighborhood to go to a fancy camp in Beverly Hills. He's a good man. Even if he does that nasty porno."

"What are your kids' names?" Allie asked. She had a feeling that Consuela was probably the best mother in the world.

"Jesus and Maria." Consuela pronounced them Hay-soos and Ma-ree-ah.

"Jesus and Maria," Allie said, mimicking her.

"Yeah. Or Jesus and Mary!" Consuela laughed.

"I want to have kids and name them Jesus and Maria," Allie said, using the Spanish pronunciation again. She was serious. She wanted to *be* Consuela and be married to Jorge and make tamales and talk to the radio and talk to the newspaper and take in stray, smashed girls, and let them sleep in the kids' beds, and laugh at nothing or everything.

"You could! No qualifications needed, you just have the kids and name them!" Consuela laughed again.

"Hey, do you think you could drive me to my car?" Allie hated to ask another favor of Consuela, but calling a cab seemed like one more place where trouble could occur.

"Where is it?" Consuela asked.

"Manuel's Taqueria."

"That's at the end of this street!" Consuela said. "But I'll drive you if you don't want to walk."

Allie had her purse on her shoulder, the bread bag in one hand and a grocery bag with tamales, a warm can of Tab, and a baggie of homemade tortilla chips in the other. Consuela had wanted to pack homemade salsa for Allie, too, but she couldn't find a container that wouldn't leak.

There were many cars in the parking lot of Manuel's. The lunch crowd, Allie supposed. She opened the door of the Prelude, dropped the bread bag and grocery bag on the floor, put her purse on the seat beside her, and started the engine. As she was backing out, three women in jewel-colored suits walked across the parking lot into the restaurant. Allie wished that if she weren't Consuela, she were one of them. They clearly had jobs. Apartments for which they'd paid the rent. No best friends who dumped them. No boyfriends who stole student loans. No coke in a bread bag. No fathers with changing phone numbers and closed-down restaurants. No missing mothers. When those three women entered Manuel's Taqueria, they knew exactly how long they'd stay and where they'd go next—everything in perfect order. Allie, on the other hand, felt her life made as much sense as a raven at a writing desk.

6

After having rolled down her window three times at traffic lights to get directions from neighboring cars, Allie finally made it onto 101 North, headed toward Santa Barbara. About sixty miles away from Santa Barbara, she picked up KTYD, a radio station that seemed to be playing only songs she knew by heart. So the last hour flew by: Allie ate tamales, drank Tab, and belted out Eagles, Police, Jackson Browne, Eurythmics, Stevie Nicks, Rolling Stones, and Little Feat.

Allie turned down the radio as she pulled into town and followed signs to State Street. It was perfectly clear and sunny, as if everything she saw before her had been sliced out with a razor blade. Allie opened the moon roof and pushed the buttons to bring down all four windows.

At the first stoplight, Allie asked a brown-haired surfer in the crosswalk how to get to the Biltmore Hotel.

"Huh?" he asked, and leaned his long, dark body into her window.

"Do you know where the Biltmore Hotel is?" Allie asked. She pulled her head back so their faces weren't so close. There was something about his lanky limbs and thin neck that reminded her of Mowgli from *The Jungle Book*. He didn't resemble Mike in Los Angeles, but the fact that he looked like a surfer, like Mike, made Allie feel slightly edgy and suspicious.

"Turn around, drive until you hit the beach, take a left and keep following the shoreline past the cemetery, up the hill." The surfer jogged away from the window as the light changed.

It wasn't hard to find the Biltmore. The hotel looked like a massive estate—a home for Thurston Howell III. It sat on a rolling green lawn that led straight to the ocean across the street. Like most of the buildings and homes in Santa Barbara, it was Spanish-style: stucco, red tile roof, arches, no sharp angles. Allie parked the car along the beach road. She pulled up the emergency brake and looked alternately at the hotel on her left and the beach on her right. A group of surfers in wetsuits were in the water, bobbing on their boards, resembling a flock of idling black ducks. Each time a wave came in, they all leaned forward and paddled toward it, trying to place themselves for the best ride. There was almost a politeness about the way they entered the waves, never running into each other, rarely cutting each other off. Mike was probably one of the few bad-spirited surfers in the world, Allie thought. But, still, she couldn't look at this crowd without thinking of him.

Allie opened her purse and clawed through the rubbish for lipstick. She found the one Beth had given her. The lid was off and there were tobacco bits stuck to the tip from when she had carried a friend's cigarettes in her purse. Allie dug around some more, found an old receipt, wiped off the tobacco, smoothed out the tip of the lipstick and put it on. Penny always seemed to take note of how Allie looked.

There were tobacco bits in her comb, too, but Allie ignored them as she picked through her red curls. She turned the rearview toward herself and examined her face. Maybe mascara would help, but the one she had was like rubbery, black bread crumbs. She licked her first finger and smoothed each of her brows into a gentle arc. Allie's eyebrows were light brown, as was her body hair. The first time Marc saw her naked he asked if she was a natural redhead. She was. It was the only thing she had, besides her almond eyes, that she thought made her look interesting. Maybe the freckles helped, too.

"Go in," Allie told herself, aloud. She looked at the hotel again, then picked up her purse and the grocery bag that now held trash. The bread bag she left behind on the floor of the car under the seat.

The Biltmore lobby had a thick, glossy, red-tile floor and tapestry couches. Allie walked past the front desk, stuffed her plastic trash bag into the open hole of a copper ashtray stand, then dropped down onto the end of a couch. She sunk in deep, as if she were made of heavy stone, and slouched against the big, padded armrest. She would sit there and wait until her mother walked in or out.

Allie flopped her head onto the armrest—she was woozy with tiredness. She dropped her Candie's mules on the floor and tucked her bare feet under her bottom like a nesting flamingo. And then she was asleep.

There was murmuring near her. Allie opened her eyes. A couple was on the couch beside her, whispering. Allie was nearly certain that they had said something about Jet Blaster. She sat up and looked at them.

The woman had gray hair down to her waist and was wearing a dress that looked like a Navajo blanket. The man had hair like a fur cap. Their faces were pointed toward the center of the lobby as they talked to each other. The woman said it again, this time more clearly: *Jet Blaster.*

Allie looked to where their eyes were directed and saw a small circle of people, but no Jet. And then someone shifted to the right and Allie could see Jet signing autographs for a group of middle-aged women who were mostly taller than he. Allie always wondered if one of the reasons he chose Penny that night at the concert was because she was small, three inches shorter than Jet (and fifteen inches shorter than Allie's dad).

Allie sat up and slipped on her shoes. Her eyes stayed on Jet as she approached him. The women made room for her but stayed close themselves. It was obvious they were hoping for something more to happen.

"Hey," Allie said. She tried not to smile, but she couldn't help it. Smiling was a reflex trained into her mouth by Wai Po *(A SMILE WORTH A THOUSAND OUNCES OF GOLD; A PERSON WITHOUT SMILING FACE MUST NEVER OPEN A SHOP; A SMILE GAIN YOU TEN MORE YEARS OF LIFE; IF YOU HAVE NOTHING ELSE TO OFFER, OFFER YOUR SMILE).*

"Hey!" Jet had the same wolfish grin for her as he did for the women standing by.

"How's it going?" Allie stepped back so she could take in his outfit: a black snakeskin coat that only went as far as his waist, a fishnet shirt, black leather pants with laces in place of a zipper.

"Jet Blaster," he said, and stuck out his dainty, manicured hand.

"It's me. Allie." Allie hadn't seen him in over two years, but she didn't think she looked that different.

"Allie! Great! Come back to the room with me, we'll chat." Jet linked his arm into Allie's and waved good-bye to the women. He didn't speak until they were in the elevator.

"Whole place is only two flights, but it's easier not to run into my fans on the stairs." Jet winked. He still hadn't unhooked his arm from Allie's. She felt heat where their elbows touched. Jet had never been affectionate with her; in fact, he'd barely looked her way each time Allie had visited Penny. Allie had always imagined that he hated the fact that Penny had a kid, was still married, even, and didn't belong to him alone.

"You look gorgeous," Jet said. Allie stared at his hair, which was unnaturally black and as glossy as a beetle's carapace. She wondered how her mother could ever touch that hair. "You were at the Grambier concert, right?"

"What? No. I haven't seen you since the Hollywood Bowl concert two years ago." Allie pulled her arm away and stepped ahead as the doors opened.

"No, I'm positive you were at Grambier." Jet caught up and put his palm on Allie's lower back. His boots had what looked like a three-inch heel, but he was still only eye-level with her.

Jet unlocked the door to the suite, opened it, and motioned with his arm for Allie to enter. She saw her mother's yellow satin nightgown draped over the bed. Penny had always worn nightgowns, hemming them by hand in front of the TV at night.

"Well, maybe it wasn't Grambier, but wherever it was it was a helluva fucking fun time," Jet said, and he unlaced his pants and laid a delicate, pointed penis in his palm. Allie was so surprised by the sight of this, his pale fingerling of a dick surrounded by chaparral-like pubic hair, that she didn't quite register what was happening until Jet put his hand on the back of Allie's head and tried to direct her down.

"HEY!" Allie bucked up. "Jet, it's me. ALLIE."

"Allie?" Jet said her name half-smiling, eyes nervously darting around the room as if he expected a whole party of past lovers and girlfriends to pop out and yell *Surprise!*

"Allie! Penny's daughter Allie!" Allie glanced down at the dick. He still hadn't tucked it away. She found it obscene, slimy-looking. An overgrown slug.

"OH, Jesus Christ! Allie!" Jet laughed, flicked his penis in, and tightened his laces. "Sorry about that! I thought you were this girl I met in Ohio at a concert there."

"No." Allie sat in the oversize chair and crossed her legs. Her brain was spinning: her mother had left their family for a small-penised man who took blow jobs from girls at concerts; this same man had just tried to get Allie to give him a blow job; additionally, he was dressed like a middle-schooler on Halloween.

"Wow, sorry. But—" Jet put his palms up and shrugged.

"You're some boyfriend," Allie mumbled. She still felt like a kid around Jet and couldn't summon the nerve to directly confront him.

"Oh please." Jet waved his hand, then sat on the edge of the bed. "You don't even know what you're talking about. Your mother and I have an open relationship. She's probably off fucking some surfer right now while I'm sitting here babysitting her daughter."

"You're hardly babysitting me," Allie said.

"Well you're hardly handling this like a grown-up. It was a reasonable mistake." Jet fell back on the bed and ran his hands through his hair. Allie wanted to leave but she knew the only way to her mother was Jet.

"Listen," Jet said, staring at the ceiling. He had beady little insect eyes. "Since you are grown-up, and your mother is who-knows-where—" He sat up and slapped his dainty hand against his crotch. "There wouldn't be anything wrong with us having a little fun together." He smiled, revealing pointy eyeteeth that were longer than his front teeth.

Allie jerked her head away like a kid who wouldn't eat what was being handed her. She refused to look at him. Was her mother truly foolish enough to be in love with such a puny-minded egomaniac? Then again, she herself had fallen in love with a guy who absconded with her student loan and scholarship money. Allie hoped that by the time she was Penny's age, she would outgrow such idiocies.

"Okay, okay, sorry." Jet exhaled and flopped back onto the bed. "But I seriously have no idea where your mom is."

"She's still with the band, isn't she?" Allie felt a stone rising in her throat like an elevator. She needed her mother now. She needed someone who cared whether Allie lived or died. Someone who wouldn't dismiss Allie as a complete dumbass for having tried coke and then stolen it.

"Yeah, yeah, she's still with the band. I just mean, there's no point in your hanging out here because who knows if she'll even show up."

Allie didn't trust Jet. She figured that now that he knew there was no way he was getting a blow job, he wanted her out of the room. "Well, she'll have to be here in time to leave for the show. When's the sound check?" As a young girl, Allie had loved mentioning the sound check to her friends. It made her feel important, an insider: *"Well first I went to my mom's sound check and then I went to Fleetwood Mac's sound check, but their sound check didn't go off too well because Stevie's mic was feeding back."*

"Four thirty." Jet flipped onto his belly so he could read the clock on the nightstand. "Fuck!" He rolled onto his back and sat up.

"It's four thirty now," Allie said, and she stood. "Do you think I can have a ride to wherever the concert is so I can find my mom?"

"Oh, she wouldn't go there without me. She'll be here any second." And then, like a cue in a stage show, the door opened and Penny popped her head in.

"Jet!" she said. "We're supposed to be there *now*!"

"Hey Mom!" Allie was surprised by the choking happiness that beat in her throat. She rushed to her mother.

"Allie! What are you doing here?!" Penny stepped in, let the door shut behind her, and hugged Allie, enveloping her in that familiar smell: Giorgio perfume and old blankets. Penny looked smaller than ever. She was dressed like Pocahontas in suede fringe pants and a suede fringe vest. Her hair was lighter than Allie remembered, more dark brown than black, and with a slight wave, as if she had gone to bed with it damp.

"Can I come to the concert with you?" Allie asked.

"We don't have any backstage passes," Jet said. He was off the bed now and was finger-combing his hair in the wall mirror.

"They're really strict about the passes." Penny gave an exaggerated pout.

"Mom! I'm your daughter! And we haven't seen each other in two years!" The happiness was curdling in Allie's throat. She was strangely amnesiac when it came to her mother: always anticipating some great, joyful love, only to be disappointed, every single time.

"I know." Penny's pout turned into a clowny fake-frown. "But I didn't know you were coming. And I gave the two passes we had to the salesgirl at this little clothing store where I got this outfit—"

"Where are the fucking clothes you left the hotel with?" Jet asked.

"She's sending them over here. I didn't feel like hauling them around with me all day and I wanted to wear this." Penny's pouty voice vanished when she talked to Jet.

"How much is that going to cost me?!"

"You can afford it!" Penny spoke sharply, revealing a hint of a Chinese accent. Wai Po had spoken like Chinese characters in Jerry Lewis movies. But Penny, who didn't seem to have inherited any features from her white father, sounded as American as she was. Or, as one saleswoman at the I. Magnin department store said when Allie and her mother were shopping years ago, "You sound so normal!"

"Just because I can afford it doesn't mean you should waste my money on it! Let's go!" Jet walked toward the door, opened it, and pulled Penny out by the arm.

"I'll go with you." Allie tamped down her disappointment and rushed alongside her mother to the elevator.

"But really, sweetie, we don't have a pass for you!" Penny pushed the L button, then stuck her fingers into Allie's curls. "Doesn't she have the prettiest hair?" she asked Jet.

"Yes. But don't start paying for any haircuts. We're on a budget now." Allie thought it was interesting how different Jet's tone was when he was trying to get a blow job from when he was trying to protect his money.

"Mom," Allie said. "I really need to talk to you. I need to spend some time with you."

"Honey, that lipstick is too orange for you," Penny said, and Allie reflexively reached up and smeared it off onto the back of her hand.

The elevator landed on the first floor. "We have to be there now," Jet said. He walked out of the elevator and inched Penny along by the elbow.

"Well, can I drive you there, Mom? We can talk in the car." Allie was almost jogging to keep apace—there was a foggy panic in her head, as if this were the only chance she'd ever have again to spend time with her mother.

Allie and her mother were in the Prelude, following a black limousine that held Jet. The other members of Mighty Zamboni had left earlier; Penny complained that they had all grown impatient in their middle age and never waited for her and Jet, even though Jet was the only star and she was the only girl and therefore they were the only ones worth looking at. Allie wondered if anyone was looking at any of them. She hadn't seen Jet's face in the *National Enquirer* for more than two years. And even that had been a picture of him looking dimpled and egg-shaped, wearing a Speedo on the beach in France, with the caption, "Guess who?" Allie had studied the picture while in line at the grocery store. A blurry image of a woman in a pink bikini stood behind Jet. It was impossible to tell if it was Penny.

"Did your father get you this car?" Penny stroked the seat. "Where did he get the money to buy you this car?"

"This is a friend's car, Mom. I can't even find Dad right now."

"Did you drive here from Berkeley just to see me?"

"Yeah, well, sort of. Mom, what happened to Dad's restaurant?"

"He closed it and is opening another one somewhere, I can't remember where." Penny played with the power-window button. "Who paid for the vanity plate? You're not really a California girl, you know. You're much too ethnic for that."

"It's not my car, Mom," Allie said.

"Well, that's good because the license plate is totally wrong for you." Penny spoke as if Allie had escaped a near-tragedy.

"Why did Dad close the restaurant?" Allie asked, hoping to keep her mother on track.

"Everyone eats gourmet now. Also, the rent was getting too high."

"Where's he living? Do you have his phone number?"

"I don't know where he is, Allie, but he did give me his number." Penny took a pen from the glove box, then searched the floor for a piece of paper. "Why do you have a loaf of bread?" She jabbed the pen at the loose flap above where the twisty held the bag shut. From her leather-fringed purse, Penny plucked out an old receipt and a palm-size address book. She opened the book and copied a number from it onto the receipt, then put the pen and the phone number into the glove box.

"Do you frequently talk to Dad?" Allie asked.

"He calls maybe once or twice a year." Penny pulled down the sun visor and looked at herself in the mirror. "He phoned me at the Hollywood Bowl a few days ago to wish me luck with the show. Sweetheart, tell me the truth, do I look older to you?"

"You look young as ever, Mom. You always look beautiful." She did. Allie often had the urge to show new friends pictures of her mom so they could see how pretty she was.

"Oh, aren't you the sweetest thing!" Penny smiled and ran her thin hand down Allie's cheek. That small gesture felt way better than it should have. Allie wondered if it was instinct that made her long for her mother's touch, or if she were particularly needy right now.

"I need to talk to you about that bread bag, Mom. It's kinda connected to my tuition at school." Allie sped up. The limo seemed to have forgotten she was following. There were now two cars separating them.

"Do you need money? I'm really sorry, but I don't have any money. Jet handles the finances and the man is as tight as—" Penny stopped talking and shook her head.

"As tight as what?"

"I don't know. There's some saying, *tight as*, but I don't know what the *as* is. But he's that tight. He's as tight as that thing that everyone says as tight as about."

"In fact I do need money but you've never really given me

money before so I didn't even think to ask you for it." Allie wasn't bitter about this, or angry, it was simply how things had always been.

"Well sweetheart, what exactly do you need?" Penny squeezed Allie's hand, which was resting on the stick shift.

"Will you pick up that bread bag and look inside?" Allie asked. "It's full of pure cocaine that I stole from a dealer in Oakland."

"This *whole bag* is full of coke?!" Penny asked, and she grabbed it from the floor.

"Yes, Mom. The whole bag. That's why—"

Penny appeared to have stopped listening. She opened the bag, stuck in her curved, red pinky nail, pulled out a tiny pile, and shoved it up her nose. "Christ, that's good!" Although Allie had been fairly certain her mother had done drugs, it was still somewhat shocking to see this person she called *Mom* snort a long fingernail full of cocaine.

"I didn't mean to steal it. I was sort of whacked out of my mind on some coke that must have been—"

"This shit is great!" Penny said, and she dipped her nail into the bag again and poked around as if she was breaking up lumps.

"Well now this guy named Vice Versa is out looking for me, another guy named Rosie is holding my friend Beth hostage, and I have to figure out how to return the coke without being killed by Vice Versa, Rosie, or Jonas."

"Who's Jonah?" Penny took a hit up the other nostril. Allie cringed as if she'd just watched her mother slice open a vein.

"Jonas. The dealer I stole it from." Allie put her hand on the bag and clasped it shut. "Mom, these are people with guns. You've gotta leave most of it in the bag, okay?"

"Why would you return it?"

"I'm not interested in stealing! I just took it to pay myself back the money Jonas owed me for working in his store!" Allie hit the brakes hard, stopping at a red light. The limousine cruised on ahead.

"Okay, okay, relax," Penny said, and she watched a young family crossing the road in front of them. "Lotta Mexicans around here."

"Yeah, well, they're probably looking at you and saying *lotta Chinese around here.*"

Penny laughed and Allie smiled. She had forgotten how bubbly her mother's laugh was, how fun it sounded.

The light changed and Allie caught up to the limo. Almost immediately, they turned into the windy, tree-lined road of the Santa Barbara County Bowl. Giant eucalyptus bows hung like heavy, weighted arms over the car. The air smelled like it had been wiped down with Mr. Clean.

"I still don't see why you have to return it."

"God, Mom! Wai Po must have had some saying about not stealing other people's stuff." Allie flipped through the words in her brain like songs in a jukebox. She wanted to find just the right Wai Poism for this moment.

"Well, Wai Po's dead, so it doesn't matter what she'd say." Penny took another fingernail hit from the bag. Then she lifted the bag, dangled it in front of her face, and watched it swing back and forth. The bottom was starting to sag more, as if a baseball were sitting there. Allie pushed the bag down into her mother's lap.

"I want to go back to school next semester," she said. "I want to stay in Berkeley and graduate with honors. I want to return this car to my friend, Beth. I don't want to be a coke-snorting thief. I want to be someone Wai Po would be proud of."

"Wai Po didn't go to school and you certainly don't have to go to school," Penny said. "I never went and I'm doing exactly what I always wanted."

"Yeah, yeah, I know. You're a tambourine girl. Dream come true."

The limousine pulled into a hidden, roll-gated tunnel behind the stadium. Two guards, white guys who looked like weight lifters, approached Allie's side of the car. They both wore combat boots. One had a shaved head and the other had hair that looked like a shar-pei puppy.

"Miss," the shaved guy said into the window. "Do you have a pass?"

"This girl's with me." Penny held up a performer pass that was encased in a plastic shield. There was a shoelace-like string dangling from it. "She's the medic." Penny opened the Wonder Bread bag, dipped her pinky in, then leaned over Allie and out her window so she could put her finger under the guard's nose. He sniffed, wiped his nose, then lifted a walkie-talkie and stepped away.

The dog-haired guard leaned his head in the window. "Some of that there for me, too?" He grinned, exposing missing molars. Penny obliged him, then sat back in her seat.

"Go on in." Shaved Head waved his arms toward the dark opening of the tunnel.

"So you can get me a backstage pass now?" Allie tried to modulate her voice so it wasn't as raw as she felt.

"Oh sweetie, you know I would have given you a pass if I had one! But since I don't have one, why not use the coke to get you in?"

Allie parked behind the limousine in the tunnel. Penny pulled her purse up onto her shoulder, picked up the bread bag, and got out of the car.

"Mom." Allie was whispering even though no one was nearby. "You can't take the coke."

"Why not?"

"It's not mine!"

"Well, just let me have a little bit. Jet won't spend money on drugs anymore. I told you. He's as tight as . . . as whatever."

"Yeah, I know. But you can't take the coke. I need to return it. Or most of it. Or something."

Penny huffed, "Oh, come on! There must be a couple kilos in here!" She marched off with the bread bag through the door that had the word TALENT in gray spray-painted block letters on it. Allie rushed after her.

Several people, mostly roadies, were milling around the talent area, which was a hallway with what Allie guessed were dressing rooms off of it. Penny seemed to know where she was going, so Allie followed behind, keeping an eye on the Wonder Bread bag. Penny was swinging it back and forth as if she were about to hurl it.

"Don't drop the coke," Allie whispered.

They turned into a large communal dressing room that appeared to have been decorated with cast-off seventies furniture. There were black leather belts with giant gold buckles holding the cushions to the orange plaid couch. And the club chair was made of orangy-red rubber—it looked inflated and cartoonish. No one was there but Penny and Allie.

"Wait here while I go to the sound check," Penny said, and she walked out with the bag of coke.

"Don't do any more of that!" Allie called after her mother, but Penny didn't answer.

Allie sat on the couch and looked around the room. She had spent a lot of her life waiting for her mother. What difference did another twenty or thirty minutes make?

After an hour spent reading the three magazines from the three-legged coffee table (*Sassy*, *Rolling Stone*, and *Interview*), Allie got up and used the bathroom. The bathroom fan was so loud it sounded like there was a helicopter hovering in the room. When Allie emerged, she was startled to see everyone from Mighty Zamboni around her, mid-action, as if they'd been there all along.

Johnny and John-John, Mighty Zamboni's guitarists, who were lovers and looked like twins, were sorting through a rolling rack of clothes debating what to wear. When the band was at its peak, Johnny and John-John had each had a wild spray of white hair. Now they both were bald.

The drummer, Tigger, was sitting in the oversize chair, reading *Hollywood Wives*. He still had the same mop of brown hair he'd had when Allie was a little girl. Tigger had always been Allie's favorite. He was smiley. And fat enough that there was no point in trying to pretend he was one of the cool people of the world.

Jet was sitting on the end of the couch, a glass of what looked like scotch in one hand, one leg swung over the arm so his leather-bound crotch was neatly displayed. Penny sat beside him.

"Hey," Allie said, to the room in general. Johnny and John-John looked at her and nodded their chins. Tigger lowered his book into his lap.

"We haven't seen you in a while," he said.

"Yeah, I'm in college now," Allie said, and she went to the couch and sat beside her mother.

"Jet, remember Allie?" Penny said.

"Mom, I was just with him at the hotel."

"Oh, yeah, I forgot!" Penny laughed and bounced against the back of the couch.

Jet ignored them both, then lifted his glass and emptied it.

When she was younger, Penny used to tell Allie that she was the Yoko Ono of Mighty Zamboni and that's why the band didn't treat her or Allie very well. But Allie never took it personally. None of these guys had families, although Johnny had three kids with a Swedish woman who sometimes sent the kids on tour with him. Each of them, including Allie's mother, seemed so far off from the world of families that it was impossible to imagine any of them having to think about others.

"I need the bathroom." Penny stood up and left with the bag of coke. Allie took a deep breath. She hoped she could somehow reconcile the amount missing with the amount she was to return to Jonas when her mother was done with the bag.

"You know, you look totally different now than you did two years ago," Jet said. "That's why I was confused about who you were."

"I look exactly the same," Allie said, and turned her head away.

"No you don't. You didn't have boobs two years ago. You didn't have hips. You were a skinny little kid. And now you're a woman. Or womany-ish. You can't blame me for not recognizing you. When Penny told me you were coming I was expecting this little girl."

"Penny didn't know I was coming. I was a surprise."

"I mean *if* she had told me you were coming. If she had said, *Jet, Allie's coming*, I would have been looking out for some skinny little kid with frizzy red hair."

"My hair's not frizzy."

"It was. Two years ago."

Tigger looked over the top of his book as if he were appraising Allie's hair. "Your hair does look a lot better," he said.

"Fine. Whatever." Allie's hair *had* been frizzy. She had never known what to do with her curls, so she had washed them and brushed them, and the end result was a vibrating head full of wiry red hair. Eventually she figured out that she shouldn't shampoo her hair—just rinse it, condition it, and run her fingers or a comb through it every couple days.

Penny came out of the bathroom and sat down on the couch between Allie and Jet. "Fucking great bathroom!" she said. "Amazing. Totally amazing bathroom. Huge. Huge fucking bathroom. And there's a bathtub in there!" She wiped her finger along the bottom of her nose. Allie put her hand on the bread bag and tried to pull it out of her mother's grip, but Penny wouldn't let go.

"Let's go to catering. I'm hungry," Jet said, and he hoisted himself off the couch and walked out of the room, the empty glass still in his hand. Tigger put down the book and followed. Johnny and John-John went, too. Once they'd left the room, Penny opened the bag, stuck her long red pinky nail in, and did a few little heaps of coke. Allie forced herself to stop keeping track of how much her mother took. This was beyond her control.

"Mom," Allie said, "do you and Jet really have an open relationship?" The thought repulsed her, but her curiosity was greater than her distaste.

"No! Where did you get that idea? Do I look like someone who would have an open relationship! Please!" Penny unwound the bag and took another hit.

"Uh, well . . ." Allie wasn't sure if she should give her mother the truth or not. Then she remembered Wai Po saying *A SPARK CAN START A FIRE THAT BURNS THE ENTIRE PRAIRIE*, and decided she didn't want her words, her story with Jet, to be the spark that caused any fires in her mother's life.

"Well what?" Penny said. She jiggled her feet and wiped her nose.

"The guy I was working for, Jonas? He pulled out his dick at work yesterday." Allie hadn't intended to share this story with her mother, but it felt right at the time, like she were indirectly telling her about Jet exposing his penis.

"Oh honey!" Penny wrapped an arm around Allie and pulled her in for a hug. "Men can be such dorks! Was that the first penis you'd ever seen?"

"No, not really. I had a boyfriend but we broke up."

"You had a boyfriend?! That's so exciting!" Penny squeezed Allie again. "So, are you a virgin or not?"

"Not," Allie said, and she felt herself blushing.

"Sweetie, believe me—" Penny picked up Allie's hand and held it—"that's not going to be the first time some man whips out his dick. Now that you're more womanly you have to get used to ignoring them. Just look away and walk away."

Allie was stunned to hear that this was a part of the experience of growing into a woman. But she couldn't say her mother was wrong. In only two days, two entire penises had been displayed for her. It did seem doubly sad, however, that one of them had belonged to her mother's boyfriend.

"Now." Penny let go of Allie's hand and stood. She was still holding the bread bag. "Let's forget about this Judah's penis business and go eat!"

"His name's Jonas," Allie said, and she followed her mother to the door.

7

Billy Idol and his band were also in the County Bowl dining room that served the performers and their roadies. They were sitting at a round table, like a family, laughing and shouting over each other to be heard.

Mighty Zamboni sat at another round table. They were silent, grunting.

Billy Idol was even more beautiful in person. This, Allie thought, was one of the few advantages to her mother: real live access to her celebrity fantasy. Billy Idol's eyes were enormous, like giant hooded buckeyes. His nostrils flared on either side of a perfectly centered slice of nose. Of course there was the hair—white as cocaine, spiked up like a sea anemone. And then the mouth, that wonderfully snarling, pulpy mouth. Allie had spent many hours imagining Billy Idol's curled lips biting into her own lips. And now that he was only a few feet away, Allie was convinced that an encounter with Billy Idol might be like painting Liquid Paper over her memory of Marc. She would only remember Marc had been there when she scratched away the surface.

Billy Idol was holding a fork with something red and runny falling off it while he laughed so hard that he had to push his chair back from the table. He was one of the most joyful people Allie had ever seen. She wanted his joy to rub off on her.

"Are you opening for him?" Allie kept her eyes on Billy as she talked to her mother.

"We're not *opening* for him," Jet said. "We're the first act and he's the second act."

"Isn't the first act the opener?" Allie looked at Jet and smiled. She knew she was being cruel, but she couldn't help it.

"Not necessarily," Jet said. "You don't know anything about this business." Everyone was silent for a moment. Allie poked at her tamale. It wasn't half as good as the ones Consuela had made for her earlier. The dining room had a buffet with both Italian and Mexican food. Allie took the Mexican food, just like her mother. A love for Mexican food was one of the few things she and Penny had always had in common.

"Do you know them?" Allie asked. "Can you introduce me?"

"To Billy Idol?" Penny said. "Oh honey, you don't want to meet him."

"Yes, I do."

"We're not allowed to talk to them," Tigger said. "Billy said some unflattering things about us in a radio interview." Tigger had both Mexican and Italian food on his plate. It was heaped high, like a serving platter.

"Don't even fucking look at them!" Jet said. Allie kept staring.

"Allie, please listen to your stepfather!" Penny said.

Allie laughed. "My stepfather? He didn't even recognize me! And you two aren't married!"

"Ah, but Jet and the Queen of Hearts got married in Las Vegas," Tigger said.

Penny turned to Allie. "The Queen of Hearts is what they call me now that Jet and I are legal. You know all these other women have wanted to marry him over the years—"

"But the Queen of Hearts decapitated the competition!" Jet said, and he did a karate chop in the air.

"Wait, I'm confused. What do you mean you got married?"

Allie felt like she wasn't getting the joke. Her mother, as far as she knew, was married to her father, Frank.

"We were doing a show in Vegas last July," Tigger said, "and Jet had a little too much to drink and—"

"He thought your mom was this Chinese stripper we met after the show!" John-John said. Jet and the rest of the band, save Penny, laughed loudly. Allie got the feeling they were trying to out-laugh Billy Idol's group.

"He did not think I was the stripper!" Penny said. "That was a joke." Penny looked at Allie with frowny concern. "Wipe that worry off your face, honey! It really was a joke. There was this Chinese stripper who was hanging around backstage and everyone kept teasing that Jet thought he was marrying her. But he didn't. He never even talked to her."

"Yeah, I only had eyes for the Queen of Hearts!" Jet said. The band burst out laughing again.

"They just love to tease me about this," Penny said to Allie. "It's their on-running gag."

"So you two really did get married? Like a serious, legal commitment?" Allie felt nauseous. Could she and her mother be so distant that Allie didn't even know she'd married—*again*—a year ago?!

"Of course. It's totally legitimate and the hooker wasn't even in the chapel." It appeared that Penny had forgotten she had ever been married to Frank, even though the evidence of that relationship was sitting right beside her.

Jet shrugged his shoulders, still laughing, then hunched over his plate to eat. There was a shine on his chin from fettuccini sauce.

A thunderclap of laughter erupted from Billy Idol's table. Everyone looked over except Jet, who stayed focused on his food.

"Mom," Allie whispered into Penny's ear. "Aren't you still legally married to Dad?" Penny kicked Allie's foot under the table and shook her head nervously.

"Yes, you are. You're married to Dad!" Allie whispered again.

"Don't worry about it," Penny said.

"What are you two whispering about?" Jet asked. He sounded like an angry old man.

"Billy Idol," Allie said.

"You're not allowed to talk about him," Jet said. "No singer from England is worth talking about! Pretend he isn't there."

Allie turned in her seat so she was directly facing Billy Idol's table. She caught the star's eye. His lip curled up as his eye clicked shut in a wink. Allie felt a flush of electricity run across her skin. The current was so strong it momentarily wiped out any anguish she had over discovering her mother's additional marriage.

Penny took the Wonder Bread bag on stage. Allie could barely believe it. She hadn't seen a move like that since fourth grade, when Dorothy Lancaster took Allie's Malibu Barbie, insisted it was her own Malibu Barbie (once upon a time, they each had one), and carried it around everywhere at school, tucking Barbie into her armpit as she leaned over the desk to write.

Allie stood in the dusty dark of the wings, watching the show. The salesgirls to whom her mother had given the passes were singing along to every song, standing as close to the edge of the stage as possible. Allie thought she saw tears in one girl's eyes when the band started playing "Miracle Oracle Lovers," a song that Allie had always thought was so stupid as to be embarrassing (. . . *the oracle of love has declared the miracle of love within the debacle of* . . .).

Allie turned and left the backstage area.

Billy Idol was alone on the grubby plaid couch in the lounge where Allie had hung out earlier with Mighty Zamboni. He was reading *Sassy* magazine.

"Hey!" Allie stood in the doorway, leaning in. Her head felt cloudy and wet with nerves and excitement.

"C'mon in!" Billy Idol said, in his wonderfully choppy British accent. "I'm catchin' up on my literature!" When he said *literature*, it sounded like *lit-tra-chure*.

"Anything good I should know?" Allie asked. She sat on the red puffy chair and tried to arrange her body so that she looked leaner, sleeker—one leg crossed over the other, her head held up as if by a string.

"Ya! If you use a bleedin' eyelash-curler before puttin' on mascara it will make your eyes look bigger." Billy Idol sneered.

"Good one!" Allie couldn't believe she was actually having a conversation with Billy Idol. She was so in love with him that the chaos, danger, and disasters that had preceded this moment almost seemed worth it, because all that stuff—including the bread bag that she'd love to forget—had led her here.

"You with Mighty Zamboni?"

"No," Allie said, too quickly. She realized she was embarrassed by Mighty Zamboni.

"But I eyed you over there eatin' with them."

"My mother's the tambourine girl. But she moved away when I was eight. I don't really know her."

"The Chinese bird?"

"Yeah, she's half."

"So you're a quarter."

"Yeah. What are you?"

"White boy," Billy Idol said, and laughed.

"You dye your hair, right?"

"Oh yeah. I think it's really a mucky brown or something like that. Makes me look all rock 'n' roll, don't it?"

"I like the white," Allie said. She hoped Billy Idol would talk to her about his hair color for hours. Or talk to her about anything, as the sound of his voice was as beautiful to Allie as the sound of his music.

"I like your red. Funny. A Chinese with red hair. Bloody hilarious."

"I guess." Allie smiled.

"I'm goin' to write a song about you. 'China Girl with Red Hair.'" Billy started thumping out a beat on his black leather thighs.

"My dad's black," Allie said.

"You're fuckin' kiddin' me!" Billy Idol laughed.

"No, I'm serious. And I have one Jewish grandfather. He's dead."

"You're a fuckin' bloody 'malgamation of the whole fuckin' world, aren't you?" Billy Idol grinned.

"I guess." After so many years of following Wai Po's wishes that she pretend to be white, Allie had never realized how cool her black-Jewish-Asianness was. Now that she saw it through Billy Idol's eyes, it actually seemed like something to be proud of.

"You're like the bleedin' United Nations in one bloody girl-package, are you not?" His grin spread wider.

"Maybe." Allie smiled. There was silence for a moment. And because she had no idea what to say next, how to keep this conversation running, Allie offered the only thing she thought might capture Billy Idol's interest longer than her Chinese-black-Jewishness. "Do you want some coke?"

"You got some fuckin' coke? What's a China-blackie-Jew like you doin' with coke?"

"Someone gave it to me. Hold on, I'll go get it and meet you back here in a sec."

Billy waved *Sassy* in the air as if he planned to continue his reading while Allie was gone. "I'll be right here, doll!"

Mighty Zamboni was in the middle of "Thunder Falls Arcade," a song with a rolling tambourine shimmer throughout the chorus. Allie positioned herself by the side of the stage, almost in a crouch. The minute the chorus started, Allie ran onto the stage, grabbed the Wonder Bread bag that sat at her mother's feet, and ran off again, as efficient and swift as a ball boy at Wimbledon. Penny barely noticed the distraction as she was also harmonizing, eyes shut, hair swishing behind her head while she whacked the tambourine in a series of quick little spanks.

Allie's heart thumped happily as she returned to the room and found Billy Idol still on the couch reading *Sassy*.

"Don't tell me you're carryin' the blow in that bread bag!" He tossed the magazine to the ground and patted the seat of the couch beside himself.

"Crazy, huh?" Allie scooted in next to him. She was so close she could feel the heat off his thigh.

"Give us a peek, will you?" Billy took the bread bag, removed the twisty, let the neck unwind, and looked inside. "You gotta be bloody kiddin' me? This is real?" He stuck his long, angled index finger in, pulled out a bit, and rubbed it on his gums.

"What do you think?"

"You a bleedin' dealer? A China-Jewish-blackie bird dealer?" Billy Idol was grinning so big that Allie had the urge to lean over and lick his teeth.

"No. My boss is. Or former boss. I have to return it to him soon. And, really, I shouldn't give any more away but if you want just a little—" Allie shrugged. How could she let her mother do some and then withhold it from Billy Idol?

"I'll take as much as you'll bleedin' give up!" Billy Idol laughed and the gold cross earring in his left ear shimmied and shook.

Allie's head was jumbly and her heart was wobbling around like a top that was about to fall. She hadn't done any of the coke with Billy, but the longer she sat with him, the more she felt as if she had. Desire was like an oil fire burning in her veins. Other than when she knew she was in love with Marc, Allie had never felt such a strong pull toward another human being.

Billy spun the bag shut and handed it to Allie. It seemed even rock stars had their limits.

"D'you wanna have sex?" He opened his leather pants and pulled out his dick. It was as white as flour, the size of two Babe Ruth candy bars, side by side. Allie wondered if this was how things would be until she hit middle age. After nineteen years on the planet, she had seen a total of *zero* live dicks in her life. Then she turned twenty and was introduced to Marc's. And now, in less than forty-eight hours, she had seen three more.

The difference between this display and the previous two was that Allie was happy to see this penis. "Yeah. If you do. You don't have VD, do you?" She dropped the bread bag on the floor and waited. Because Allie had only been with Marc, she wasn't sure how these encounters usually operated.

"I don't have any venereal diseases that I know of. But the worst anyone can get is gonorrhea and my blokes tell me you just take some antibiotics for that and, bam, it's gone!" He pushed his leather jeans down like a snake shedding a skin.

"I don't have my diaphragm," Allie said, with a little panic in her voice. She hoped they could still make this work.

"No worries, doll! I got me willie snipped so I'm only shootin' spit!" Billy kneeled on the gritty couch beside Allie and unfurled her curls with his finger. Within seconds, she was naked, too, and they rolled, bounced, and flipped around like dolphins in a tiny, shallow tank. It certainly wasn't the greatest sex Allie had ever had, but it was the most exciting and, strangely, the most joyful. It was as if Billy Idol were the happiest man on earth, and she, Allie, was able to feed off it if only for those few minutes.

Afterward, Billy Idol lay on his back and patted his belly for Allie to lie on top of him. "That's nice," he said, and swirled his hands along her back and down to her ass.

"I can hear your heart beating." Allie wished she could record it and carry it around with her. It was a beautiful heartbeat, deep and powerful. Sexy.

"I must apologize to you, darling. We had beautiful bleedin' intercourse and I never even got your name." Billy ran his palm along Allie's face. He stuck his finger in her mouth, swirled it around, and then pulled it out.

"Allie."

"Allie."

"Yeah. Allie."

"Beautiful China-black-Jewish-American curly-haired United Nations amalgamated Allie doll."

"*C'est moi.*" Allie laughed and wondered, how do you make time stop? How do you pause life so that nothing changes?

"*C'est* bleedin' *toi!*" Billy slapped Allie's ass and laughed again.

All too soon Billy's band was knocking on the door. It was almost time to go on stage. Allie unstuck herself from Billy's perfectly ridged body. They dressed side by side. Then he pushed his snarling mouth against hers one more time.

"Allie. It was bloody wonderful spendin' time with you. You are one beautiful bird." Billy winked, went to the door, and left.

Allie's flesh was still vibrating. She didn't want to leave the room where she could smell Billy's almost rose-scented skin, and his woodsy sweat, and the perfumed gel that held up his hair. But Mighty Zamboni would be back in seconds, and if Allie had any hope of returning to the Bay Area, she had to abandon the idea that her mother would help her, and leave quickly, before Penny snatched away her only negotiating chip.

8

Once Allie was on the road, away from the County Bowl, the pain of Penny's betrayal motored in with the force of a speedboat.

Allie had to pull the Prelude over to cry. It was a flooding, thrusting cry—pouring out of her like a rush of opened dam water. She had found her mother, she had seen her mother, and, as usual, her mother had failed her. Periodically, as she was crying, Allie lifted her arm and tried to smell Billy Idol in the crook of her elbow. Anything to help pull her out of this moment and return her to the state of bliss she had been in only thirty minutes ago. Eventually she calmed and was able to sit up.

When she was younger, Allie had cried every birthday or holiday when her mother was missing. But by the time she was twelve, she had stopped crying. She still yearned for Penny at certain times, such as when she took the bus down to JC Penney with her father's credit card tucked deep into her pocket to buy a minimal wardrobe for school. Or when she got her first period in eighth grade and was too embarrassed to ask her dad to buy pads. Instead, Allie had stuck folded paper towels in her underpants and, whenever she could, borrowed pads from girls at school. This went on for a year until Frank must have figured she'd had her period and began stocking the bathroom vanity.

And Allie had missed the energetic fun her mother had brought to the household—putting on records and dancing, a glass of wine in one hand and a wooden spoon for a microphone in the other.

Alone with her father, it was a placid life: two people in the same room, Allie doing homework, her father, who always smelled like burned beef, watching TV. A white Styrofoam container of something would be sitting on the coffee table in front of Allie—the dinner her father had brought home for her from the restaurant. Theirs was a silent existence, spaces of hollow time punctuated with hellos and good-byes, like they were riding a city bus together, only acknowledging each other when one of them got off or stepped on.

Allie thumped her head into the center of the steering wheel. Just once, she would like to leave her mother and feel happy and filled up rather than depleted. She cried her last bits—as if she were wringing out a sponge—then calmed, her shoulders rising and falling as she breathed.

"Okay," Allie said. "Time to move on." She popped open the glove box and slipped out the scrap of paper with her father's phone number. The red ink Penny had used made the number look urgent, important.

There was a steakhouse across the street, with a wooden tiki mask taller than Allie guarding the front door. With the paper in one hand and her purse in the other, Allie marched in. At the hostess stand stood a brown-haired girl who was skinnier, taller, more angled, and yet also sultrier than any human Allie had ever seen in person.

"Number?" the hostess mumbled. She didn't smile.

"Huh?" Allie held up her father's phone number.

"You eating tonight?" The hostess dropped her head toward her shoulder as if it were suddenly too heavy to hold up.

"Oh. No. I just wanted to use the phone if that's okay."

There were wooden benches in the entranceway. People were lined up on them, waiting for their table. Everyone seemed to be watching the hostess stand, or maybe they were watching the hostess.

"You know how it works," the hostess said. "Dial nine to get an outside number."

"Is it okay if I call long-distance?" Allie asked.

"Are you kidding? I make all my long-distance calls from this phone. There's no way I'm going to call from home and pay for it!" The hostess picked up three menus, called "NINTZEL," and then walked off with a trio of men.

Allie went behind the hostess stand and glanced down at the list. There were two pages of names, only a quarter of them crossed out.

A woman approached, put her hands on the edge of the stand, and clacked her nails. "How long for a table for four?"

"Ummm . . ." Allie ran her pointer finger along the list as if she knew what she was doing. And, actually, she did know. Allie had sat people at her father's restaurant since she was old enough to reach the hostess stand. She could look at a list of names and say exactly how long each person would wait. "A little over an hour."

"Fine. Sloane. With an E on the end." The woman stood and watched as Allie wrote down the name.

"I'll call you at the bar if you want," Allie said. That's what she had always said at Frank's restaurant, and she assumed it was the same here. As she was speaking, the hostess returned. She was about five inches taller than Allie.

"We'll call you at the bar," the hostess repeated, and Sloane walked away.

"I told her it'd be over an hour," Allie said.

"Thanks," the hostess said. "Did you make your call?" She indicated with a cigarette-slim finger the phone tucked into a nook below the podium.

"Ah! Thanks!" Allie picked up the receiver, looked at the scrap of paper that had FRANK written in all capital letters, punched nine, then the number. The hostess called another name and walked off with an older couple, both wearing red: she in a red dress and shoes, and he in a red dinner jacket. Allie wondered if they had deliberately matched up like that.

A thin, square-shouldered man approached the podium just as Frank answered the phone.

"It'll be more than an hour," Allie said to the man.

"What'll be more than an hour," Allie's father said. His voice, when he used it, boomed.

"Hold on a second, Dad, I'm hostessing."

"Allie, don't call me if you can't talk." Frank hung up. Allie felt an immediate panic. She was worried that that was the only moment she'd ever have to talk to her dad. Things had been so out-of-the-ordinary lately that a death—hers or her father's—didn't seem like an unreasonable thing to anticipate.

"Five," the man said. Allie took his name, then called her father back. When the phone started ringing, she dropped down into a squat behind the podium. The hostess's legs approached.

The phone rang fifteen times. Allie was now sure she had blown her one chance. And then, finally, Frank answered.

"Dad," Allie said. "We were just on the phone. Why did it take you so long to pick up again?"

"I wanted to make sure you really wanted to talk to me. I figured you'd wait if you did." Allie could hear echoed laughter from a sitcom in the background. She imagined her father in the dark living room lit only by flickering blue TV light. He looked good in that light, with his peanut-butter-colored skin and his massive body. Frank was six-four, with hands the size of baseball gloves. As a kid, Allie liked to stare at his ears, which looked like tiny butterscotch snails curled up on either side of his giant rectangular head.

"I do want to talk to you," Allie said.

"What do you need?"

"Did you close the restaurant?"

"Moved it. We're reopening in a week."

"Why didn't you tell me?"

"Why do you need to know?"

"I don't know. That restaurant's been there my whole life. You're my dad."

"That I am," Frank said.

Allie paused, then said, in a rush, "I'm sort of in trouble."

"Pregnant?"

"No." The hostess's legs walked off with another group.

"If you're not pregnant, you're not in trouble."

Allie paused. She didn't know how she could possibly tell her father she had stolen a Wonder Bread bag full of coke and fled to Los Angeles, where she had almost killed a quadriplegic, had a disappointing reunion with her mother, and had sex with Billy Idol.

Frank spoke again into the silence. "So I suppose you didn't get the money back from that thieving boyfriend of yours?"

"No." Allie's chest heaved at the thought of Marc. She had rarely told her father about her failures, humiliations, and disappointments. Not even in third grade, when Oliver Jones got all the kids to call her Little Orphan Allie because her mother didn't show up for the Mothers' Day luncheon. Not in fourth grade, when she felt ugly and invisible when she and all the girls in school (many of them blondes) were collecting Barbie dolls and not one person had a doll that looked anything like Allie. And not in the past year, when she discovered a whole new range of emotions in falling in love and then having her heart destroyed. If Allie had known ahead of time that Frank wouldn't help her out of her financial jam, she never would have told him about Marc decamping with the cash.

Allie slumped her head against the phone, letting it drop into the nook of her shoulder.

"Be a good girl," Frank said. "Work hard at that job and listen to our great first lady and *just say no to drugs*." Frank had always loved Ronald Reagan, and Nancy by association.

"Got it," Allie said, and her father hung up before she could say good-bye.

"You okay?" The hostess tilted her body and looked down at Allie.

"Yeah." Allie stood. The hostess's thick brown hair was cut in a perfect line across her shoulders.

"I'm going to seat this party of four. If anyone else comes in, tell them the kitchen closes in an hour and they probably won't be able to get served by then." She walked off with four menus and four people trailing behind her.

Sloane approached the podium again. "How much longer?" she asked. "Sloane."

"Yes, Sloane, with an E on the end." Allie ran her finger down the list of names. "You still have about fifty minutes."

"You're shaking," Sloane said.

"Too much coffee," Allie said. Of course she hadn't had coffee all day; Allie's anxiety was simply radiating out her fingertips.

"Caffeine's a stimulant. You shouldn't do stimulants." Sloane had tiny red veins snaking across her cheeks and nose. They reminded Allie of maps, and roads or rivers as seen from an airplane.

"I try to stay away from them," Allie said. "I swear."

The hostess returned. "Name?" she said to Sloane.

"Sloane with an E on the end," Allie said. "They're here." She pointed to the name on the page.

"About fifty minutes," the hostess said. Sloane returned to the bar.

"Do you mind if I make another phone call?" Allie asked.

The hostess pointed her long, fin-like hand to the floor. Allie dropped down into a crouch, picked up the receiver, dialed nine, and then called Beth.

Beth picked up on the first ring.

"Hey, it's me," Allie whispered.

"Hey!" Beth wasn't whispering. Allie heard a grumbling beside her. Then Beth's voice, barely muffled by her hand over the receiver. Allie could make out: *Be quiet, it's Allie!*

"Who are you talking to?"

"Oh, no one."

"Well, it's got to be someone."

Beth sighed. "Okay, it's Rosie? But he's really cool now. We're like, I don't know, totally hanging out—" Beth got cut off. It sounded like the phone had fallen onto something soft, like a bed. Allie could hear stifled giggling and the grumbling voice again.

"Are you *with* Rosie?" Allie wasn't sure she could envision it. Beth in her chic little Spanish-style apartment with a drug-gangster hit man named Rosie.

"Listen, he's totally not who I thought he was last time you called. We're having, seriously, like, the best time together? I mean, I don't even want to leave the apartment!" More giggling, more grumble voice, and then what sounded like the smacking sound from kisses.

"So he's not a guy with gun-butt who's taking ten-hour dumps in your bathroom?"

"Come on, Allie! That was before I knew him. I swear, this guy is just like you but with a penis! Like, after you sneeze you wrinkle your nose up like a rabbit a few times. Rosie does the exact same thing!"

"I had sex with Billy Idol," Allie said, to get away from the subject of how similar she was to Rosie the gun-toting thug.

"No way!" Beth laughed as if it wasn't true.

"I swear. Way."

"You swear? Like, where did you meet him?"

"I stopped in to see my mom, and her band was opening for him." Allie had told Beth about her mother leaving to be the tambourine girl for Mighty Zamboni. They even went to the library together and sorted through old magazines so Beth could see Penny in photos of the band. The only picture Allie owned of her mother was taken the day Allie was born. She was wrapped in a pink blanket, nestled in Wai Po's arms with Penny sitting beside her.

"Where did you have sex? Like, what does he look like naked?!" Beth asked.

"He had a really big dick," Allie whispered, with her hand cupped over the mouthpiece of the phone. The grumbling voice grumbled enthusiastically. "Is Rosie listening to me?"

"He's pushing his ear in so he can hear," Beth said.

"*Where* are you guys?"

"Under the covers." Beth started laughing and Rosie joined in. Then Beth must have muffled the phone again—better this time—because Allie only heard hushed talking until Beth came back on. "OH, you know what else?! Rosie has the exact same birthmark as you. That patch of blue skin on the small of your back?"

"Mongolian spots?" Allie wasn't really interested.

"Yeah! Only his skin is way darker than yours, 'cause he's black, you know, so the spots don't look as blue as yours? They're sort of dark purple."

"Got it. Listen, we need to figure out how to un-mess my messed-up life now," Allie said.

"How's your life messed up? You just had sex with Billy Idol!" Beth said.

"Uh, Beth? Do you remember that you were being held hostage the last time we talked?" Allie put her mouth closer to the phone and lowered her voice. "And I stole a bread bag full of cocaine after Jonas showed me his dick?!"

"Jonas showed you his dick? Is that why you took the coke? I thought it was because he didn't pay you," Beth said.

"Well, yeah, both. I guess. He pulled out his dick—" Allie looked up at the hostess to see if she were listening. The hostess was staring at the list of names as if it were a crossword puzzle. "—And I was hallucinating on that baby-jar stuff and I just freaked out."

Allie heard more grumbling, then Beth said, "Rosie said it's okay to freak out about the dick, and it's okay to be mad about not getting paid, but you shouldn't have taken the coke."

"I know," Allie said. "I wasn't in my right mind."

"Rosie said," Beth was laughing as she spoke, "he's seen Jonas's dick, and he understands why someone would look at it and run—" She interrupted herself with more laughter. Allie didn't join in.

"Okay, enough about the dicks," Allie whispered impatiently.

"Wait, Rosie has one last thing to say—" Beth muffled the receiver for a moment, then came back on. "He says don't you think it's interesting how the same act, like a guy showing you his dick, is either pervy or great depending on the guy?"

"Is he pointing this out because I didn't do anything crazy when I saw Billy Idol's dick?" Allie asked.

"Yeah," Beth said, then she translated the grumbling that continued in the background. "Rosie said people are never responding to the act, they're only responding to their perception of the person committing the act."

"All right, well, thank Rosie-Paul Sartre for his insight and please ask him if Vice Versa is going to murder me when I come back to the Bay Area." Impatience was starting to pulse in Allie's veins.

"Vice Versa's in L.A. now looking for you," Beth said.

"Looking for me where?" Allie's throat clicked and spasmed.

"Like, he probably went to your father's restaurant?"

"My father's restaurant is no longer there. Did he find the new

restaurant?" Allie could feel her face inflaming. The trembling in
her hands increased. She wanted to wiggle her nose, bewitch herself through space, land in Beth's apartment, take the phone out
of her hand, and repeatedly whack her in the head with it. Did
she actually *tell* Vice Versa the name of her father's restaurant?

"Rosie says if you run into Vice Versa and he shows you his
dick, pretend he's Billy Idol!" Beth started laughing, and then she
got the hiccups and laughed even harder. Allie realized Beth was
completely smashed. She often got the hiccups when she'd had
more than three drinks.

"You're too drunk to help me out now." Allie looked up and
saw the hostess watching her with giant, glowing eyes. "I'm sorry
I have your car." Allie tried to reshuffle her brain, calm herself so
she could stand up and exist in the world, in this moment, like a
normal person. "And I think you have Stockholm syndrome." She
hung up and stood beside the tall hostess.

"I need to use the bathroom," the hostess said. "Could you seat
this deuce at that far table in the corner?" She pointed to a table
Allie couldn't see.

"Sure." Allie looked down at the list. Focusing on the deuce was
the perfect way to re-center herself. "James!" she called out, and she
picked up two menus from the stack under the podium, stepped
out, and held them against her chest. "James, party of two!"

The James couple approached Allie side-by-side, hand-in-
hand, like a pair of proud, chest-puffed doves.

"Right this way." Allie turned and walked through the restaurant, deliberately placing one foot in front of the other. *I am alive, I
am in a steakhouse, I am seating the James party of two. No one in this
restaurant is trying to kill me. I'll think of Vice Versa another time.*

By the time she had seated the couple, Allie felt reoriented.
The hostess was still gone when she got back to the podium, but
Sloane was there, waiting.

"Is the table for Sloane available yet?!" She rapped her nails against the podium again.

"I'll call you when it's ready," Allie said sternly. Sometimes you had to get tough with the really hungry ones. Sloane walked away quickly, stiffly. Allie knew this type—Sloane was used to getting everything she wanted exactly when she wanted it.

Allie picked up the phone to call her father again. "Dad," she said, when he answered. "If someone wanted to find you in L.A. how would they do it? I mean, is the address to the new restaurant listed somewhere?"

"What are you getting at, Allie?" Frank never sounded happy to hear Allie's voice on the phone and he appeared to be even more inconvenienced by this call than most others.

Sloane approached once more. Allie held up her index finger, making the one-minute signal, but Sloane would not accept it. "My husband said that that couple you just seated came in after us!" Sloane said. She was wrong.

"Dad." Allie looked down at the ground, refusing to make eye contact with Sloane. "If a man named Vice Versa shows up at the restaurant or your house, don't open the door."

"Who is Vice Versa and why would he show up?" Frank was using the gruff tone that used to make Allie run to her room and hide in the closet. He had never even spanked her, his voice was always punishment enough.

"He's just some mean-nasty black guy that's been giving me trouble."

"What kind of trouble has he given you?" Frank's voice went up in a way that Allie had never heard before. There was a sudden silence of the TV in the background. Had Frank actually turned off the set?

"I haven't quite met him yet—"

"Then how do you know he's a *black guy*?"

"Come on, Dad! The guy's name is Vice Versa! Can you imagine a white guy named Vice Versa?"

"Allie, I have raised you better than that! Do not assume that just because his name is original he is a black man."

"Sorry, Dad." Allie glanced at Sloane, who refused to leave the podium. She turned away, the phone cord wrapping around her shoulder, her back to Sloane.

"Excuse me! I'm a customer here and you are being paid to help ME!" Sloane said.

Allie whipped her head toward Sloane and spat, "I don't work here!" She turned back to the phone. "Listen, Dad. He's some guy that my employer in Oakland hired to kill me."

"Why would your employer want to kill you?" Frank spoke softly. As if maybe he were worried about Allie, or even scared for her.

"I don't know," Allie lied, "but just stay away from this guy."

"Allie!" Frank's voice was coming out like a bark. "Tell me exactly what kind of trouble you're in. When you say *kill* do you really mean kill? As in commit an act of *homicide*?"

Sloane was leaning across the podium, trying to get her face in front of Allie.

"You've only been waiting twenty minutes!" Allie said.

"Allie!" Frank's voice shook the phone against Allie's ear. "Is there honestly a person roaming Los Angeles who is looking for me so he can get to you and extinguish your life?!"

"That couple you just seated came in after us. My husband is sure of it," Sloane said.

"They were here twenty minutes before you." Allie pointed to the recently crossed-out name on the list.

"Allie!" Frank shouted, and then the phone went dead. Allie looked at the receiver. Of course her father would hang up again. When she was a kid, if she asked a question twice on the phone (*are you sure I can't go to the movies with Kathy?*), he simply hung up. Allie put the phone back into the receiver and looked at Sloane.

"My husband is certain they came in before us. He recognizes the woman from the bank," Sloane said. "He took note when she walked in."

"I am not kidding you." Allie surprised herself with her stern voice. It felt as though she were channeling her father. "I will call you when your table is ready and until then do *not* approach me at this podium."

Sloane's mouth was half-open. "Get me your manager," she said. Her voice was shaky.

"Find the manager yourself," Allie said, and she picked up the phone again and dialed Frank's number while glaring at Sloane. The phone rang and rang.

A waiter approached and tapped Allie on the shoulder.

"Yes?" Allie asked. She kept the phone at her ear, still ringing.

"I got an empty four-top that's waiting to be filled. Do you mind getting off the phone?" He stared at Allie with his head tilted away, as if from exasperation. It was a scolding look.

"Yeah, okay," Allie said. Her father had probably had enough of her drama. She hung up the phone and picked up four menus.

Sloane was the next party of four on the list, but there was no way Allie was going to give them the table now. "Tavis!" Allie called out. She bit the inside of her mouth to alleviate some of the sudden guilt she felt for bypassing Sloane. Wai Po would have castigated her with one of her sayings. Maybe *LAW CONTROL THE LESSER MAN, RIGHT CONDUCT CONTROL THE GREATER ONE.*

At eleven, when the final customer, including the Sloane party, had been seated, Allie straightened the menus, ripped the used pages out of the ledger, and tidied the hostess stand. The hostess had never returned, so Allie had taken over. She had dialed her father's apartment eleven times in between seating tables, but Frank had never answered. It was likely he was dead asleep, his hands placed neatly atop the covers as if he were being laid out in a casket. That was how he always slept. Allie imagined that her father was so solid that he became immoveable at night. A slab of marble carved into the shape of a man.

The scolding waiter approached Allie just as she was about to leave and handed her a wad of soft, folded bills. "Your tips," he said.

"Is this from everyone?" Allie asked. At her father's restaurant, all the servers gave the hostess ten percent of their tips.

"Everyone who's clocked in tonight," he said, and walked away just as the hostess returned. Her hair looked stringy and wind-blown, her straight-edge cut now misaligned. There was a rim of white powder around her nostril.

"Where were you?" Allie asked.

"Doing you-know-what-with-you-know-who." The hostess checked the menus and book, saw that it was all properly arranged, and smiled.

"I don't even know you," Allie said, "so I really have no idea what you-know-what-with-you-know-who is."

"Doing *it* with Bill." The hostess pointed to the back of the restaurant with her thumb. "The manager?"

"I don't work here," Allie said. "Do you know that? Do you understand that I just walked in off the street to use the phone?" Frank's powerful voice was seeping out of her again.

"Oh my god!" The hostess laughed. "I thought you were someone who worked here who was showing up but not on her regular shift! Oh my god! That is so funny! But, you know, I'm kinda glad you don't work here, 'cause, like, some woman was complaining about you to Bill and he, like, wanted me to fire you!"

"You can't fire me," Allie said. "I quit." She tucked the wad of bills into her pocket and walked out.

9

Allie stopped at four different hotels on Cabrillo Boulevard along the beach. They were all sold out. She gave up, gave in, and went back to the Biltmore. With their elevated prices, they wouldn't be sold out. The bread bag was dangling from her fist as Allie stood at the reception counter. There was almost four hundred dollars in her purse from the money Mike had given her, less what she paid for gas, plus what she earned in tips from hostessing.

"Can I help you?" The woman on the other side of the counter looked as tidy and fresh as a 1970s Pan Am stewardess. She didn't hide the fact that she was examining Allie, her eyes clicking up and down as if she were checking for lice or disease.

"I'd like a room for tonight," Allie said.

"We're sold out for tonight."

"No way," Allie said. "How could you be sold out?"

"We're often sold out weeks in advance. Can I find you a room for another night?" The woman tilted her head and forced a smile that had the same effect as if she'd given Allie the finger.

"Forget about it," Allie mumbled. She turned and walked toward the elevators. Penny would let her sleep on the couch, especially if Allie gave her more coke.

Allie gave a rhythmic knock on Penny and Jet's door. After a suspiciously long pause, Jet came out wearing an open silk-kimono robe. Allie didn't look down.

"Can I talk to my mother?" Allie kept her voice matter-of-fact.

"She's sleeping," Jet said.

"Can I crash on the couch in your room? I'm homeless. For now."

"Aren't you a coed somewhere?" Jet gave a sinister smile, revealing his little, carved, dagger teeth.

"A coed?" If Allie hadn't felt so much anger toward Jet, she would have laughed at his ancient phrasing.

"A college girl. Aren't you in college somewhere? Don't you have a dorm room or a sorority or something like that?"

"It's summer. Can I talk to my mom?"

"She's sleeping, I told you."

"She did a whole pile of coke before the show. There's absolutely no way she's sleeping."

"Where'd she get the coke?"

"Billy Idol," Allie said, and smiled.

"She did not!" Jet waved his hand.

"Can I talk to her?" Allie leaned to either side of Jet, trying to see into the room. The lights were out. Maybe her mother was in the bathroom.

"She's sleeping."

"Jet! Where is she?!" Allie was growing impatient. Over the course of the day, the child-to-adult status of her relationship with Jet had irrevocably changed. She now saw him as a small-minded, small-world, perverted little pedophile.

"She's at the bar," Jet said.

"Why aren't you at the bar?" Allie asked.

"I don't like the clientele," Jet said, and he pushed the door shut.

The stairs were faster than the elevator, so Allie trotted down. Billy Idol and his band mates were at the bar, along with all of Mighty Zamboni minus Jet. Everyone was roaring with laughter, including Penny, who sat on the lap of the black-haired drummer from Billy Idol's band.

"OH MY GOD, LOOK WHO'S HERE!" Penny screamed. She rushed to Allie as if they were sorority sisters meeting up at a mixer.

Allie untangled her mother's arms from around her neck. Penny grabbed at the bread bag and tried to tug it out of her daughter's hand.

Allie immediately regretted her decision to stay at the Biltmore. "Leave it alone," she snapped, and she pulled back so quickly that Penny stumbled.

"It's my China Blackie bird!" Billy Idol got up from his stool, came over to Allie, and led her away from Penny.

"That's my SISTER!" Penny caught up to them, then flopped her belly onto a barstool, bottom out. She wobbled around the stool like a nine-year-old. Allie was only slightly embarrassed. These were rock stars, they were used to idiotic behavior.

"It's your daughter, you bleedin' sot!" Billy Idol said, and everyone, including Allie, laughed.

"Hey," Allie said, and she sort of leaned into Billy's chest the way a cat might if it wanted to be scratched.

"How you doing, China?" Billy pulled up a stool and patted it so Allie would sit.

"She's got coke!" Penny yelled. She popped off the stool and stumbled into Billy Idol and Allie, throwing one arm across each of their shoulders.

"Mom, you need coffee or something," Allie said.

"I need more of that COKE!"

"Shh!" Allie said. "It's too much for you, Mom."

Billie Idol leaned in close to Penny and quietly said, "Last I heard it's illegal in America, so you best keep quiet about it. Now why don't you be a good bird and go sit on my mate's lap and let him order you a café or something?"

Allie wondered if she'd ever stop swooning over his accent, which made her feel like a melting popsicle: sticky, watery, going down.

Penny snatched at the bread bag with two hands. Billy Idol detached Penny's hands, then threw her over his shoulder like a bag of grain. "Nigel, you got this one, mate?"

"Hear hear," Nigel said, and he patted his skinny, snakeskin-bound thighs.

It was as miraculous as if Marc had fallen in love with Allie again. She was in Billy Idol's suite. In his bed. Naked. And they were *talking*. Billy didn't want any more coke and he was too tired for sex, so they were snuggling. Face-to-face. Flesh against flesh.

Allie told Billy the story of her childhood, her mother leaving to be the tambourine girl, her father devoted to his restaurant. She told him about Wai Po, how she was the only person who kept track of Allie: saving her report cards, framing her drawings and paintings, showing up to school plays and sitting in the front row. She didn't tell him about Jonas, Vice Versa, or Rosie—that story seemed too sordid for this moment, too dark.

Billy told Allie a long and interesting story of being born in Middlesex, moving to the States at age three, then returning to Britain when he was seven. His words hit Allie in damp little pats as he spoke. Eventually his voice rocked Allie into the most peaceful sleep she'd had since Marc broke up with her.

When she woke in the morning, Billy Idol was gone. Beside Allie's head, on Biltmore stationery, was a note written in all capital letters:

DEAR CHINA-BLACKIE,

THANKS FOR THE FUN, THANKS FOR THE COKE,
THANKS FOR THE GAB. YOU ARE A DOLL EVEN
THOUGH YOUR MUM IS A BIT OF A WANKER.
HERE'S THE BEEPER NUMBER FOR IAN, MY MAN-
AGER. CALL HIM IF YOU'RE EVER IN TROUBLE
AND YOU NEED MY HELP.

LOVE, BILLY

Allie's heart fluttered. Here it was, written proof that *someone*,
Billy Idol even, was ready to help her. She would save this number
for a real emergency. For now she was okay moving on by herself.
She was off to Los Angeles to find her father. Hopefully, she'd get
to him before Vice Versa did.

10

There was a moment, as she was driving into Los Angeles, when Allie felt a pang of loneliness slice up through her core. Now that she and Kathy had "broken up," Allie didn't have a single friend in L.A. All her friends at Berkeley had strong hometown ties: framed pictures of Senior Cut Day in high school, loads of people who would come visiting, long-distance phone bills that were higher than their rent. Allie loved looking through their photo albums, seeing pictures of groups that were so big everyone's head appeared to be the size of a ladybug, hearing about Thanksgiving holiday when friends would travel in packs, visiting house after house late into the night until they had eaten dessert maybe fifteen times. Allie had never had a pack. The only people in L.A. that she might be able to call friends now were Jorge, Consuela, and Roger. And she had only known them for hours.

Still, since Allie had no idea where to find her father, and Roger was stuck in the hospital, that was probably as good a place to start as any. She could sit in Roger's hospital room, make amends for almost having killed him, and use the phone until her father finally picked up.

Once she got on the 405, traffic came to a dead stop. Allie could have played Chinese Fire Drill by herself. When she first heard about Chinese Fire Drills, she had tried to convince Wai Po to do one. They were in Wai Po's car, a spotless four-door red thing that smelled like vinyl. (Wai Po told Allie she kept the car in good shape so Allie could have it when she turned sixteen.

When Wai Po died, Penny sold the car and kept the money, using a portion of it to buy a one-way ticket to Wisconsin to join Mighty Zamboni, which was based there.)

"You just put the car in park," Allie had told her grandmother, "and then we get out, run a full circle around the car, and get back in again."

"WHY?" Wai Po had said, in her usual shout.

"For fun," Allie had said. "You do it at a stop sign."

"BUT WHY IS THIS FUN? I AM OLD WOMAN. IT IS NO FUN TO GET IN AND OUT OF CAR AND IT IS NO FUN TO RUN AROUND CAR."

Wai Po was fifty-five at the time, and to seven-year-old Allie that did seem old. She agreed that ancient, hobbled Wai Po, who had the posture of a troll, should not gallop around the car. But now that Allie was twenty, her mother was thirty-eight, and her father was forty-eight, fifty-five didn't seem that far gone.

Allie put the car in neutral in the middle of a river of automobiles that filled her rearview mirror and stretched out in front of her as far as she could see. Heat waves undulated off the cars. The man on her right was picking his nose. Did he think that *no one* was looking through his glass windows? On her left was a bald man in a red convertible. Allie rolled down her window and leaned out.

"Hey there!" she shouted.

The man turned and smiled at Allie as if he'd like to get off at the next exit and get to know her. "Hey!" he said.

"Do you know how I get to Cedars-Sinai hospital?"

The man's face changed, his hopes dashed. "Just get off at Santa Monica Boulevard," he said. "It'll be easy from there."

"Thanks!" Allie waved and turned her head. She could feel the man staring at her, his desire was like an invisible net trying to entangle her. Allie rolled up the window as if that could protect her from his gaze.

Allie pulled up the emergency brake and sat in the silence thinking about her night with Billy Idol. If anything could erase the stain of Marc, it was being naked with Billy Idol *a second time.* And yet why was Marc slinking back into her thoughts?

The traffic inched ahead. Allie released the emergency brake and let the car roll. She played a little game, trying to see how long she could inch forward in traffic without shifting into gear or hitting the brake. The bald man beside her kept apace even though he could have moved up in his lane, ahead of Allie.

Allie was about to declare herself a winner in the no-gear/no-brake game when her windshield exploded with a thunderous crash and Allie felt something large, warm, and heavy, like a bag of laundry, slam into her head. It happened too quickly for her to scream. Carefully, she lifted her hand and felt her head for blood or bullet holes. And then she opened her eyes to what was possibly the ugliest creature she had ever seen sitting on the passenger seat: an enormous black bird with a featherless neck and head that were pink like a fresh-picked scab. Its beak was arced like an old man's nose and it was screeching like an old woman, shaking puzzle piece–shaped bits of glass off its wings.

Allie was still too surprised to know what to do. Her head felt lumpy and warm, as though giant bruises were bubbling up. A small group of people rushed to the car before she had sense enough to get out, and now they stood gathered around her: a blondish family, two black men, and the bald man, of course, who was taking pictures with a camera the size of a brick, which hung from a thick black strap around his neck.

Allie turned off the engine, opened the door, and got out of the car. The Wonder Bread bag was on the floor below the bird.

Her purse was next to the bird on the seat. Allie hoped the bird wouldn't leave droppings on her purse.

"Thing looks like a condor," one of the black guys said.

"I bet you're right!" the blond father said, and he patted the man on the back as if he'd just discovered gold.

"You okay?" The bald man put one hand on Allie's upper arm, then let go as he clicked off more photos of the bird.

"I think so." Allie touched her head again.

The bird hopped onto the driver's seat and banged its beak against the driver's-side window. The tapping had an urgency to it, like the clicking before a bomb goes off. The crowd laughed.

"Go out the front! There's no window!" Allie yelled at the bird. Everyone laughed again.

The bird hopped onto the console between the seats and spread its wings. They were probably longer than Allie's legs— feathered tips touched each side of the car. The bird started to squall and flap, creating a chaos and tension that reminded Allie of stirred-up dirty lake water.

A siren sounded in the distance. Allie's heart beat so powerfully she thought it might be visible through her two shirts. She ran to the other side of the car, opened the door, and grabbed her purse and the bread bag off the floor. The bird leaped forward onto the hood of the car just as Allie was closing the door. Allie could hear the clicking of the bald man's camera. She looked down into the mass of jewel-colored cars to see if the siren was coming closer. There it was, a cop car, in the breakdown lane. And traffic was starting to roll.

The bird looked back at Allie, still and upright, like it was posing for a picture. Then it dropped dead, beak-first. The crowd gasped. Allie knew that if she had been anywhere but Los Angeles, people would have stuck around and tried to revive the bird, or maybe they would have checked to make sure it was truly dead. But traffic ruled here, and traffic that was moving forward could never be ignored.

Allie grabbed the giant bird in both hands, the bread bag dangling from her right fist, her purse sliding off her left shoulder into the crook of her arm. The bird was much heavier than she imagined, more like an eight-year-old than a baby. She went to the trunk, opened it, and dropped the bird on top of Beth's school books, which had been there since the end of the semester, and two empty Tanqueray bottles from when Beth had hosted a T and T party outside the football stadium sometime last fall.

Cars were moving around Allie, like river water around a giant boulder. She slammed the trunk shut, rushed to the driver's seat, brushed the round-edged glass out onto the freeway, then got in the car. Her Candie's crunched the glass underfoot as she shifted herself into place. She started the car, put it in drive, and moved forward. Even at twenty miles an hour, the wind made her eyes tear up and snarled her hair. Allie wished she had a scarf, like Grace Kelly in that movie when she cruised down the curvy, cliff-side roads in Monaco. And she wished she had sunglasses, too. With the Los Angeles haze coming right at her, Allie's eyes felt as though she was in a smoke-filled bar. She put her hand on her forehead and felt the hot olive that had suddenly grown there. She would have cried, maybe. But her eyes were too dry and at that moment she needed to just get to the hospital. Along with the phone, there'd be food there. A bathroom. After she found her father, she could call Beth again to make sure things were still cool with Rosie. She might even call Marc and find out if he'd made any progress on getting money out of the bar so he could pay her back. Of course, all this was dependent on Roger being glad to see her. And after what Allie had done, almost killing him by smashing an open palm of cocaine in his face, she couldn't blame him if he didn't want to talk to her.

11

Roger squealed and tapped his head pointer against the board that was placed on a tray across his lap. He didn't appear to be wearing a hospital gown: his chest, arms, and shoulders were bare above the sheet tucked under his armpits. He was hairier than Allie would have imagined—somehow the growth of body hair seemed incongruent with life in a wheelchair. In his useless, flaccid arms were wires and tubes, taped against the openings where they entered his veins, and his wrists were bound with soft, white binds to the arms on the bed. Machinery lit up and beeped all around him, giving the impression that Roger was in dire circumstances, but Roger's vigorous banging against the word YES gave Allie confidence that he would be all right.

"Remember me?" Allie said, and she dropped into the molded plastic chair beside the bed. Roger slammed more rapidly on the YES.

"I'm really sorry," Allie said. "I'm really sorry this happened." She looked down at the bag of coke, then tucked it under the chair with her purse.

NO NO NO NO, Roger tapped.

"I feel like it was my fault. I gave you way too much."

NO NO NO NO, Roger tapped.

"Yes, yes, yes, yes, yes," Allie said. "I was an idiot. Irresponsible. I almost killed you." Allie dropped her head in shame. She was embarrassed by everything: the fact that she had lost $7,000 to a man who apparently didn't love her, lifted her shirt for Jonas so he could see her breasts, and stolen the coke. Now Allie understood why her mother didn't leave until Wai Po had died. It was hard to mess up with that cranky, choppy voice yelling at you about what you should and shouldn't do. But when it felt like no one was watching over you, the bad stuff became easy.

"I'm *such* an idiot," Allie said.

Roger stared at her silently, his pointer resting on the NO.

A nurse walked in. Allie stood to give her more room. "Is he going to be okay?" Allie asked.

The nurse was reading Roger's chart. She went to the tubes, checked everything as if they were wires in a car engine. "Yup." Her hips flared out like a bell. When she moved, they swung from side to side. Her oatmeal-colored hair was pulled back into a tight bun. Her face looked older than her figure.

"No surgery?" Allie asked.

"Oh, he's had surgery," the nurse said. "They put a stent in his artery." She was writing in the chart now.

"So now he's fine?" Allie asked.

"Like new," the nurse said, and she looked up and smiled.

"You're like new!" Allie said to Roger, and she couldn't stop herself from thinking: *If not a little heavier, balder, more waxy-looking, and pinniped with limbs that don't quite function like new.*

Roger tapped on the YES. The bell-shaped nurse swung her way out of the room, and Allie scooted the chair closer toward Roger's head and sat.

"Roger, can I talk to you about something?" Allie guessed that a guy who did a palm-full of coke, produced porno, and funded camps for underprivileged children would somehow be able to understand the dilemma she was in without passing judgment.

The pointer clunked down heavily on the YES. Roger gave a panting smile.

Allie started with Marc and the loss of her money, lingered over the cocaine, touched down on the penises (Jonas, Jet, Billy Idol), and then ended with the lump on her forehead, or, more specifically, the condor crashing through the windshield of the Prelude and currently resting in peace, she hoped, in the trunk. There was something liberating about talking to someone who couldn't interrupt with questions, ideas, instructions, or a coherent reaction. Roger's response to each point on her list was the same walrus-like honk as he raised his pointer in the air.

"So what do you think I should do?" Allie asked.

H-O-W, Roger tapped.

"How," Allie said.

"B-I-G," Roger tapped.

"How big?" Allie said. "How big what? Penises? Coke?" She held up the bread bag. Roger didn't respond. "Santa Barbara County Bowl? Jet? Jet's short, like this." Allie held her hand an inch over her head. She could feel that her hair was fluffed up into a wild, wiry puff from the ride with no windshield. Still no response from Roger.

"The bird?" Allie asked, and Roger trumpeted.

"Big," Allie said. "Enormous. Like something out of a dream. Or a nightmare. You know?"

YES, YES, YES, Roger tapped. O-K, Roger tapped.

"Okay?" Allie asked. And then Roger tapped out the word *think*. "Can I use your phone while you're thinking?" Allie asked, and Roger trumpeted.

Allie used the bedside phone to call her father. After dialing his home so many times last night, she had memorized the number.

"Hello?" Her father's voice wasn't booming.

"Dad?" Allie said uncertainly. The calm voice was unsettling. "Yeah?"

"Why are you home? I thought you were reopening the restaurant."

"I got people down there working. They don't need me hanging around telling them how to do their jobs."

"But that's what you do," Allie said. "You hang around and boss people."

There was silence for a moment and then her father said, "Sweetheart, when are you coming home?"

"You mean to your home?"

Silence, and then, "Yes, your father would love to see you."

"You want to see me?" It felt like a wire cable was running through Allie's spine—straightening her, alerting her.

"Yes. Of course."

"Well, where do you live now, Dad? I don't even know where you live."

"You got a pen?"

Allie dug through her purse and pulled out a pen and a magazine subscription card. "Okay, go ahead."

"Thirty-nine twenty-six Las Trachas Avenue."

"Where is that?"

"In the Hollywood Hills. Just off Sunset." Allie heard a rumbling in the background and then her father said, "Wait. It's 5926. I was confused."

"You were confused about your own address?"

"Old age," Frank said, and his voice sounded soft and worn.

"Dad, are you okay?" The wire in Allie's spine tightened, yanked upward.

"When are you coming to see me, sweetheart?"

Allie stopped talking and waited for something to be revealed through the air on the phone. Her father had never called her *sweetheart* before. She couldn't help but be touched even though her heart, her stomach, and her vibrating spine were telling her that something was terribly wrong. Was Vice Versa sitting there with a gun to Frank's head?

"I'm going to stop off and see some friends," Allie said, "and then I'll get there as soon as I can." She was gathering time enough to come up with a plan.

"So I'll see you today?"

"Uh, yeah. Dad, where's the new restaurant?"

"Sonoma Boulevard in Venice."

"Same name?"

"Of course."

"So, maybe we should meet there, right?" Vice Versa couldn't kill them in the middle of an under-construction restaurant. There would be at least twenty people on the site working to get the place ready.

"I'm not going in today, sweetheart. Just come home."

Frank never called any of his residences *home*. It was always *the apartment*, or *the condo*, or *the house*.

"Okay, Dad," Allie said. "I'll see you at home."

Allie hung up the phone and looked at Roger.

"Either he has a gun to his head and someone is telling him to tell me to come home or he had a stroke."

Roger stared at Allie for a moment with his wet, droopy eyes. A small bubble of spit sat on his dangling lower lip. He let the pointer drop on the letter G.

"Gun," Allie said, and when Roger trumpeted in the air she felt a swirly shifting inside herself. Her father was large. She just hoped he was larger than Vice Versa and, somehow, bulletproof.

It took twenty-seven minutes for Roger to convince Allie, through frantic tap-spelling, that she should not call the police and send them over to her father's house. His final message: "No police. Ever." Jorge and a few "helpers" were on their way over, Allie learned. They would get the situation under control.

Finally, after room-temperature mac 'n' cheese in the cafeteria and two pass-throughs of the nursery where Allie stared at pink and beige puckered babies displayed like giant confections behind glass, Jorge arrived. He had two more of Roger's employees in tow, Hans and Luis. It was four p.m. They were supposed to have been there at two thirty, but a tractor-trailer jackknifed on the 405, turning the four-lane freeway into a single-lane road.

Jorge leaned over Allie, who sat in the orange plastic chair, patted her shoulder, and smiled. Luis and Hans slouched against the wall. Luis had feathered-back blond hair and wore a tight T-shirt that showed his pumped-up body. Hans was bulkier than Luis, but also with feathered blond hair. He wore an orange T-shirt under a black suit jacket. Allie thought they looked like they had walked off the set of a James Bond movie, although it was hard to tell if they'd play the good guys or the bad guys. They were almost too well-groomed to be good guys.

"Sweetheart, what happened to your head?" Jorge asked, and he pointed at his own forehead. Allie reached up and touched the bump. It throbbed like a loose tooth that was being pushed out by a tongue.

"Oh," Allie said. "I think this is the least of my problems."

Roger aimed his pointer at Allie and bounced his head. After having spent the past couple hours with him, Allie was starting to read his eye-and-pointer language. "You want me to tell them the whole story?" Allie asked, and Roger thumped down on YES.

"You won't tell Consuela, will you?" Allie asked Jorge. "I like her so much and I think she'll hate me if she knows how messed up I am."

"No, you don't look so messed up!" Jorge said. "But this is work, anyway, so I won't tell Consuela. It's between us here in this room." He sat on the edge of the bed with his right foot on the floor, his left knee flopped sideways.

Before Allie could begin her confession, a nurse walked in. Everyone watched her impatiently.

"You're not supposed to have more than two visitors at a time," she said to Roger. This nurse was small and elfish, with a scribble of brown hair on her head.

"We're all family," Allie said.

"Oh!" The nurse looked at Allie, surprised. "Are you his daughter?"

"Yes." Allie reached out and took Roger's bound hand. It felt thin, and soft, and boneless. "And these are my cousins."

The nurse looked around and assessed the faces: Jorge with his black hair and black eyes, blond Luis, and even blonder Hans. "Very interesting family," the nurse said.

"We're military brats," Hans said, and he ran his hand through his hair, pushing the feathered locks into a perfect array down the side of his head.

"Oh yeah?" The nurse crossed her arms and stared at Luis.

"A different mother in every station," Hans said, and the nurse laughed a little and finally walked out.

Allie told the story all over again, including working at Miss Shirley's, Jonas and his penis, the cocaine in the bread bag (and here she had to confess to her not-dead parents), Jet and his minimal gifts, Billy Idol (leaving out his expansive gifts), the dead bird, and the anxious feeling she had that Vice Versa was currently holding her father hostage while waiting for her.

"Roger's right," Jorge said. "When you call the police on drug dealers, they get even nastier. It's like starting a holy war. There's no way they'll hurt your dad, because they need him to get you, but since your friend Beth is also being held hostage by Rosie—"

"Sort of," Allie said. "I think she has Stockholm syndrome now."

"Either way, sweetheart, she'll be the first one dead if the police get involved."

"I feel sick," Allie said, and she slouched down into the chair, her chin dropping toward her chest.

"This is a no-death situation," Hans said, waving a hand.

"Jorge just said Beth would be *the first one dead*!" Allie said.

"We will find a peaceful solution." Jorge peered down at Allie to make sure she was listening. "Trust me on this."

"Okay," Allie said, and when she exhaled she tried to imagine her worries as her breath—a physical thing she could blow out of her body.

"Do you still have the beeper number for Billy Idol's manager?" Hans crossed the room and stood by Allie, who reached into her purse and pulled out the eviction notice and the piece of Biltmore stationery with Billy Idol's scrawl. She looked at them both, then handed the note to Hans. While Hans read the note aloud, Allie crumpled the eviction notice into a flowery ball and tossed it into the trashcan near the door. *Another time*, she thought.

"Can I keep this?" Hans asked.

"No," Allie said, nervously laughing. "I love that note."

"I can see why," Hans said, and he held it up to the light as if there were some secret code embedded in the paper.

"If you love Billy Idol so much, why don't you marry him?" Luis said. It was the first thing he had said since walking in the room. Allie was surprised by how soft and sugary his voice was, like Michael Jackson in the body of Michael Hutchence.

"I don't *love* him!" Hans said. "I admire him. There's a difference, you know." Luis rolled his eyes. Allie watched, transfixed. She wasn't sure if they were lovers or not.

"Sweethearts, we need to take care of Allie and her father now," Jorge said. "No more yakkity-yak about Billy Idol!"

"He gets grouchy when he's hungry," Luis said, nodding toward Hans with his chin.

"I don't get grouchy when I'm hungry, I get grouchy when I have to pay for bad food, and I had the worst lunch at Mama Mia's today," Hans said.

"I thought it was great," Luis said.

"I wonder if Spago will deliver food to the hospital?" Hans asked.

"We have other problems than what we should eat," Jorge said.

Luis scratched his calf and Allie could see there was a gun strapped there. "Do you all have guns?" she asked.

Hans turned his back to her and lifted up his T-shirt. There was a gun wedged down the back of his pants. Luis opened his jacket and showed her another gun strapped in a holster across his chest.

Jorge held up his empty palms. "I'm a driver," Jorge said, "and I have a family. My weapon is my heart. I bring love."

Hans and Luis laughed, but Allie liked what he said.

"Do you have a gun?" Allie asked Roger. Roger trumpeted with a loose-hanging smile.

"He has no way to discharge a weapon," Jorge said. "But he likes having one strapped to the back of his wheelchair so that whoever is pushing him has quick access to a gun."

"They took down Larry Flint," Hans said. "They could be after Roger, too."

"Who are *they*?" Allie asked, and Hans and Luis both shrugged.

"Allie," Jorge said. "We have much to do. We must replace the glass on the car, check on your father, return the cocaine to Jonas, free Beth from Rosie, and get you back in school unharmed."

"Okay." Allie smiled. No one had offered to do so much for her since Wai Po had sewn the patches on Allie's Blue Bird vest, then chaperoned the troupe's camping trip and set up the tent that Allie and three friends would sleep in (Wai Po had her own pup tent). She also taught the troupe a Chinese folk song so they each could earn a culture patch.

It was agreed that if someone were holding Frank hostage, they'd be expecting Allie to arrive immediately. So instead of going now, they would go tomorrow, after the (possible) gunman had stayed up all night guarding Allie's father and waiting for Allie. He'd be tired and edgy, paranoid even, and that would make him an easy target. In the meantime, Allie would be taken to Jorge's house to eat and sleep. Hans and Luis would take the Prelude to the shop where all of Roger's vans were serviced.

"I'm surprised you don't have a limo instead of a van," Allie said to Roger.

"Roger prefers vans," Jorge said.

Roger trumpeted and beat his pointer down on P, then O, then R.

"You like the vans because they remind you of porno?" Allie asked.

Roger thumped on the YES several times.

12

Jorge picked up limp, dewy, sleeping Jesus and put him in the bed he and Consuela shared. Then Consuela quickly changed the sheets from the Fox and the Hound to Snow White. The kids had only gone to bed thirty minutes ago, after homemade flan for dessert, but were conked out as if in a coma.

"These are girl sheets," Consuela whispered as Allie helped her tuck in the corners. Maria was sleeping in the other bed. A pink night-light lit up the room like the inside of a seashell.

"You could have left on the Fox and the Hound," Allie said. "I don't really care."

"A girl needs girl sheets," Consuela said, and she smiled in that big, warm way.

Allie and Consuela finished making the bed, then Consuela led Allie out of the room and into the single bathroom in the house. There was a Garfield coffee cup on the vanity, which held four toothbrushes and a tube of Crest.

"I can just use my finger to brush my teeth," Allie said.

"Towels are here," Consuela said, and she opened up the cupboard under the sink and pulled out a thin, grayish towel that had flowers embroidered on it. "Soap and shampoo are in the shower."

"Do I look like I haven't showered in a while?" Allie asked, and Consuela laughed.

"You look clean enough, but maybe hot water will bring down that knot on your head. And your hair's a little—" Consuela waved her hands around her own head to indicate the craziness of Allie's windblown curls.

Allie reflexively poked her fingers into the curls but couldn't push through the knots.

"Are your parents with you?" Consuela asked.

"My parents?"

"Your parents," Consuela said, and she lifted one fist and held the open palm of the other hand below it as if she were holding the bread bag with two hands.

"Oh, my parents! Yes. Jorge has them. He was going to hold on to them so I didn't, I don't know, roll onto them in the night and break the bag."

"*Sì, sì*, very good idea," Consuela said. "Jorge is very good about these things. When his mother, Maria Teresa Iglesias Paz, died, Jorge carried her around for forty days in a cigar box he had nailed shut."

"What did he do after forty days?" Allie looked at their reflection in the broad bathroom mirror. She was pale green under her halo of hair, next to Consuela, whose skin was the color of warm caramel and whose loose hair draped over her shoulder like a sleeping black cat.

"He drove her to Mexico and buried her in the family plot next to her own mother and father."

"Wow," Allie said, and she suddenly felt overwhelmingly tired, empty.

"You shower," Consuela said. "Then go to bed and when you wake up I will make you a chocolate *con leche y pan de yema*."

"Chocolate *con leche y pan de yema*," Allie repeated, as if in a dream. She had no idea what that was, but she was certain of two things: (1) her own mother would never make her chocolate *con leche y pan de yema* and (2) Allie would love it.

At four a.m. Allie woke up. She tiptoed out of the glowing pink bedroom, down the hall past the family photos of Consuela, Jorge, Jesus, and Maria, and into the kitchen where the red wall phone hung near the tin roll-top bread box.

The code for long distance was taped to the wall above the phone. Allie used the code, then dialed Beth.

"Hello?" Beth answered on the first ring. She didn't sound like she was sleeping.

"Are you up?" Allie whispered.

"We've been doing blow all night," Beth said. Allie could hear music in the background, Culture Club, maybe, and voices.

"Who's we?" Allie asked.

"Me, Rosie, Jonas, and some girl named La Star?"

"La Star? Is she black?"

"No! God! You're so racist!"

"But *La* Star?"

"She's, like, a total hippie chick from Santa Cruz. She's a naked model."

"Like a porn model?"

"No! She, like, models for art classes and shit like that. Right now she's walking around naked in between practicing poses for this class she's modeling for tomorrow?"

"Seriously? There's a naked hippie chick walking around your apartment doing blow and Jonas hasn't pulled out his dick yet?"

"Jonas says you made that up."

"I did NOT make that up," Allie said firmly, and she felt herself flush with rage. How could Beth not believe her?

There was silence for a moment. Finally, Beth asked, "Have you met Vice Versa yet?"

"No," Allie said. "Every time I think of him I start worrying that he's shot my father, or is torturing him, or something."

"Are you serious? Who do you think these people are? Vice Versa's, like, a mediator. He just wants to talk to you and get the coke back."

"Are you still being held hostage?"

"Not against my will," Beth said, and she laughed, then whispered into the phone so it sounded grainy and wet, "I think I'm in love."

"With Rosie?" Allie couldn't help but think this seemed improbable.

"Yeah. I've totally never felt this way about anyone before."

"But he ate two large pizzas all by himself then took a ten-hour dump in your bathroom! He carries a gun!"

"Have you ever hung out with a guy with a gun? It's really sexy."

Allie thought of Hans and Luis. They weren't sexy to her, but she could imagine how it might be sexy knowing that the person you were with could protect you like that. "Are you sure he's not going to use that gun to kill me?"

"Oh my god! I just told you these people aren't killers!"

"But the last thing Jonas said to me was something about Vice Versa being a mean motherfucker who would *kill* me," Allie said. "Jonas's words, not mine."

"Ah, Allie?" Beth spoke in a sarcastic monotone. "You were, like, tripping on mushroomy-acidy-coke then. Remember? Just find Vice Versa, like, return the coke and bring back my car."

Allie heard coughing from Consuela and Jorge's bedroom. "I've gotta go. But listen, a bird crashed through the windshield of your car and smashed it, but we dropped it off last night and it's getting fixed today, and this guy, this really nice guy in a wheelchair, or, well, in the hospital now, he's going to pay for it for me and the car will be like new before I get it back to you."

Allie could hear Beth talking to someone in the background. "I'm sorry, what'd you say?" Beth asked Allie, and then, before Allie could answer, she laughed. "Sorry, this naked girl, she's, like, doing these poses where her right foot is behind her head?"

"Really? Wow. Sounds kinda gross," Allie said.

"Oh my god! I, like, almost forgot to tell you Marc called!"

"How could you forget to tell me that Marc called? What'd he say?" Allie's heart flip-flopped at the mention of Marc. She hoped he would end up saving her rather than destroying her.

"He sold the bar—"

"That's great! My problems could be over!"

"No, wait, he's buying a fruit stand or something down in Emeryville and he wants you to invest with him."

"Seriously? Does he understand how badly I need the money?" It felt like a rush of wind blew through Allie's body. She needed to get the money before Marc invested it again. At the very least, she could save her college career. And if the missing coke was now more than what Jonas owed her (who knew how much Penny did when Allie wasn't looking and, of course, there was Billy Idol's share, too) Allie could throw a little money Jonas's way to make up the difference.

"Probably not. But listen, I've really gotta go! I don't want Jonas to know we're talking."

"I thought you said I was safe?"

"YOU ARE," Beth whisper-yelled, "but you know, he's still kinda pissed at you! I'll talk to you soon!" Beth hung up before Allie could say good-bye.

Allie quietly returned to bed. She lay awake thinking about Marc until the sun wiped out the pink glow from the room and made everything yellowish-white. How could she still have feelings for a guy who took all her money, left her penniless, and then

broke up with her? It was like her urge for Marc was biological—
her body wanted it even though her logical brain knew it was
dumb. About as dumb as stealing coke from a drug dealer. Although maybe not nearly as dangerous.

Nine-year-old Maria and seven-year-old Jesus sat across the
breakfast table, their chins hovering only inches above their plates,
and stared at Allie. Allie reached up and touched the olive on
her forehead—had it grown bigger during the night? Jesus said
something in Spanish to his mother while holding his gaze on Allie. Consuela replied in fast Spanish, then gave Jesus a little whack
on the shoulder before kissing him on top of the head.

"They go to rich kids' camp in Beverly Hills," Consuela said,
switching to English, "and all the white kids have nannies who
pick them up and bring them home, and you look like one of
those nannies, so Jesus is afraid that I am going to leave you in
charge while I—" Consuela laughed—"I don't know where those
women who have nannies go all day!" She turned to her son and,
smiling, rattled off a few quick sentences.

Jesus answered and Consuela laughed.

"He thinks I'm going to go shopping and to the gym!" Consuela said. "I don't know anyone who goes to a gym! The boys,
they go to the boxing club."

"Jesus boxes?" Allie looked down at him. He had thin,
noodley arms and shoulders that barely passed his jawline.

"No, Jorge, the big boys! The men!" Consuela laughed again
and went to the stove, where a cookie sheet was covered with
fresh, warm *pan de yema*. She put one on Allie's plate—it was Allie's second—and ripped another in half that she divided between
Jesus and Maria. The *pan de yema* tasted like sweet bread and was
so melty-soft in Allie's mouth that it didn't need butter.

Consuela had chocolate *con leche* simmering in a saucepan. She got up to stir it every few seconds, releasing the smell of cinnamon and chocolate into the air like a puff of smoke. Allie picked up her mug and tilted it so the last thick drips of chocolate would slide into her mouth. Allie wanted more chocolate *con leche*, too, but Jesus and Maria were still on their first cup and Jorge hadn't even come in for breakfast yet.

When Allie put down the cup, Jesus and Maria were staring again.

"Do they speak English?" Allie asked Consuela while looking at Maria. She had beetle-black eyes and thick hair in two braids that looked like horsetails.

"We're Americans," Jesus said. "Of course we speak English." He didn't even have a hint of an accent.

"Oh! It's just you were speaking in Spanish to your mom earlier—" Allie could feel her face filling up with a blush. She smiled and both kids smiled back.

Consuela pulled down another mug and poured chocolate *con leche* into it just as Jorge, freshly shaved and smelling of spice, walked into the kitchen. Jorge kissed his wife on the lips, then kissed each child on the head. He sat at the table and waited while Consuela gave him a plate with *pan de yema* and a mug of chocolate.

"You want more?" Consuela tilted the saucepan toward Allie.

"Only if there's enough," Allie said, but what she wanted to say was yes, yes, yes, yes.

Consuela took Allie's mug and filled it over the sink (even though not one drop spilled in the transfer), then returned the mug to her. Allie sipped the chocolate and smiled at the kids, who tried not to smile back. Finally Jesus cracked a grin and Maria started to laugh.

"Do you swear on your mother's life that you're not the nanny?" Maria asked.

Consuela brushed her hand across Maria's shoulder. "*Hija!* Do not talk about her mother, you don't know anything about her mother! She is not the nanny!"

Jorge looked from Allie to his kids and burst out laughing. "Sweetheart, do you think we have money for a nanny?!"

"Maybe Mr. Roger pays for it," Jesus says.

"I am your nanny!" Consuela said, and she leaned in and kissed Jesus all over his forehead until he brushed her away.

"You know," Allie said, "if you need a nanny, or want a nanny, I *would* be your nanny." Allie only thought of this as she said it. But now that the words were out, it seemed like a brilliant idea. She could live with Consuela and Jorge and Jesus and Maria in this little house. Vice Versa and Jonas would never find her here, and she'd learn from Consuela how to be a real mother. Jesus's bed was comfortable, and if he didn't mind sleeping with his parents she didn't mind sharing a room with Maria.

"No, no, sweetheart, you don't need to be a nanny," Jorge said. "Your car will be fixed this morning, we'll take care of all your business, and then you will go back to college."

"You're in college?" Maria asked.

"Yeah. I'm off for the summer." Allie hoped this wasn't a lie. She hoped she'd be able to pay off her late tuition and, once again, be an official Berkeley student who really was just on summer break.

Jorge stood and shoved the last bit of bread in his mouth. Allie stood, too. She cleared her dishes, held them over the sink, then leaned to the left and right, looking for a dishwasher.

"Don't worry about them!" Consuela laughed. "I do all the dishes once everyone has left the house."

Allie paused for a second. She tried to remember dishes growing up. There weren't any. Glasses in the sink, maybe. Her father would rinse them and stack them on a drainer without really scrubbing them. There had been a dishwasher in most of their apartments but Allie never really knew how to use it. Because neither Frank nor Allie ever cooked, there was only packaging to throw away, white foam boxes, to-go containers. Allie knew that when she had a family, there would be dishes. Lots and lots of dishes. And she would never complain about them.

"*Vamos*, Allie," Jorge said, and he gently took her arm.

Allie looked down and saw that Jorge had the bread bag in one hand and her purse dangling from the crook of his elbow. Like a perfect gentleman, it seemed, Jorge would carry everything, even Allie's purse. Even her fear.

Allie sensed the surfers in her peripheral vision; she knew they were walking behind her and Jorge as they entered the hospital. Normally, she'd turn and check them out, but her post-Mike repulsion to surfers remained. It seemed wrong that one bad guy could ruin a whole category of people for her, but that's how it was for now.

When she and Jorge got on the elevator with a crowd of eight or so people, the surfers squeezed on as well. There were too many bodies in the elevator for her to really see them, but she couldn't help but check out their broad backs and the fringe of blond hair that released below a baseball cap the taller one wore. After stopping at three different floors, the only people left were Allie, Jorge, and the surfers, whose faces she had yet to see. They wore baggy shorts, flip-flops, and T-shirts—everything sun-faded into a neutral stone color. They smelled of surfboard wax and sand, as if they had just come from the beach.

And then one of the surfers flipped a switch on the button panel and a buzzing erupted in the elevator. The cage bounced a moment before settling between floors. Allie put her hand on Jorge's forearm and the surfers turned and faced them. The taller of the two wore black Ray-Ban sunglasses that he pulled off and shoved into his pocket. It was Mike. Allie's flesh retracted and her stomach plummeted. It felt like the stalled elevator was actually dropping.

"You are so, *so* not black," Mike said to Allie. "And you've got, like, a tumor growing out of your forehead!" Mike and his pal both laughed.

Jorge took a step so that his body was blocking Allie from Mike. "Do you know these people?" he asked Allie.

"She sold me pure snow, bean-head, for, like, fifty cents a gram!" Mike said, and his friend lifted his hand so they could high-five.

"What do you want?" Allie asked. She recalled the thump of Mike's body when he hurled himself onto the roof of the car. That seemed like a different conflict, a different Allie—so long ago it might as well have been a story she had read in the newspaper.

"The coke, dumbass!" Mike said.

"The coke is gone," Jorge said.

"Give me the coke, you fucking beaner," Mike said, and he pulled a small pistol from his front shorts pocket. It looked like a black water gun and Allie wasn't sure it was real. Mike's friend pulled out a gun from his shorts pocket, too. It also looked like a water gun, although slightly bigger.

"Listen to me very carefully." Jorge's voice sounded stronger and more forceful than Allie had ever heard it. It was like he was playing a part in a movie. "We don't have any cocaine. The stuff she had earlier has been sold."

"I no understanda you, *señor!*" Mike said in an overblown fake accent that made him sound more Swedish than Mexican. He pushed the gun into Jorge's neck and grabbed the Wonder Bread bag with his free hand. "Here's the plan. Topher's going to stay behind with you two while I take this stuff to stately Wayne Manor. If you try to come after me, Topher will shoot. What room will you be in, in case I want to come back early for Topher?"

"Four-twelve," Allie said quickly.

"If you're lying—" Mike removed the gun from Jorge's neck and twisted it into the center of Allie's lump—"Topher will kill you both." The lump throbbed so powerfully it seemed to have replaced Allie's heart.

"I will," Topher grunted. His voice was phlegmy, a man with mashed potatoes stuck in his throat.

"It's room eight-twelve," Jorge said. That was the truth.

"Eight-twelve," Mike repeated. Then he lifted his free hand and flipped the switch. The elevator moved toward the next floor. Mike pulled his weapon from Allie's forehead and shoved it down the front pocket of his shorts. Topher tucked away his gun, too. Allie reached up and touched the half-moon indentation in her still-pulsing lump; she imagined it looked like a giant fingernail had poked her there. When the doors opened, Mike stepped out, leaving Topher with Allie and Jorge. They rode in silence to the eighth floor.

As they left the elevator, Jorge put his arm around Allie and leaned in toward her ear. "You okay?"

"Yeah, I'm totally fine." And Allie was. She was tired of being polite, tired of being scared, tired of being too obedient to insist that Jonas zip up his pants. Wai Po had been right when she said, *HAVE MOUTH AS SHARP AS DAGGER, BUT HEART AS SOFT AS TOFU.* The only way to get out of this mess now was to use her dagger-mouth and pray that her tofu heart stayed strong.

Allie and Jorge walked down the hallway with Topher on their heels. Jorge seemed to be ignoring Topher, so Allie did the same. Surely he wouldn't pull out the gun here. There were people everywhere.

When they got to Roger's room, Jorge turned to Topher. "We're not going to chase your friend," he said. "You can go, it's cool now." Jorge held up his hands as if he expected Topher to pat him down.

"Nah, I told Mike I'd stay with you for an hour," Topher said.

"He'll never know," Jorge said.

"Get in the room," Topher said, just as a group of white-coated doctors approached. They were fast in conversation, oblivious to Allie, Jorge, and Topher. Allie thought it must be nice to be one of those doctors. Their problems, if they had any, would be so different from hers.

"After you," Jorge said, and he held out his hand as if to let Topher pass.

"After you," Topher said.

"No, I insist," Jorge said.

"I fucking insist," Topher said, and he nudged the gun in his front pocket so it poked out into a little pyramid.

"I'll go," Allie said and she entered Roger's room. Jorge came behind her, then Topher brought up the rear, closing the door behind himself. Allie wasn't sure what he'd done, but Jorge must have given some sign to Hans and Luis, because they stood in one fluid motion, foot-long shiny silver guns cocked and pointed at Topher before Allie could even take in the scene.

The door started to open behind them and Jorge pushed it shut. "He's using the potty!" he called out. "Please come back in a few minutes."

"But I'm the nurse! I help him with the potty!" the voice returned. The door rattled alarmingly.

"He wants privacy," Jorge said. "Five minutes. Please."

Roger trumpeted loud enough for the nurse to hear. She must have taken it as the final word, because the door fell silent.

"His buddy took the coke," Jorge said.

Hans and Luis stepped toward Topher. Luis patted him down and removed the gun. He laughed, high and girly, as he shoved Topher's gun down the front pocket of his jeans.

"Is it a water pistol?" Allie asked.

"Almost," Luis said. His trilling voice startled Allie every time he spoke. "It's what you use to shoot a squirrel."

"Dude!" Topher said. "I bought that from a fucking Crip. It's hard-core."

"Dude," Hans said, in an imitation surfer drawl, "the Crips would have nothing to do with a guy like you." He and Luis took Topher by the shoulders and sat him down into the plastic orange chair. Luis stood so close to the chair that his hip pressed into Topher's ruddy cheek.

The bell-shaped nurse entered the room, unimpeded. She looked around from side to side as if she expected someone to jump out at her. "Is everything okay?" she asked as she approached Roger. "You went potty with all these people in the room but you didn't want me in here?"

Roger trumpeted.

"We're family," Allie said. She watched Roger point out the letters M-Y-D-A-U- and added, "I'm his daughter!"

"Where's the potty?" the nurse asked. "I'll clean it."

"I cleaned it," Jorge said.

The nurse stared at Jorge for a minute, then turned back to Roger. "You have a lot of family," she said, and she administered the errands she had come for, checking the IVs and looking at the openings where each wire entered his body, adding a new bag of something clear into Roger's left arm, checking his chart. No one spoke. Finally, the nurse patted Roger on his thin hand and left quickly and quietly.

Allie sat on the edge of the bed. She exhaled, long and slow, until she felt like an empty plastic bag. "How did you find me?" Allie asked Topher.

"How do you know him?" Luis squeaked.

"I met the other guy, the one who now has the coke, at a gas station." Allie turned back toward Topher. "But how did you find me?"

"Your picture was in the newspaper," Topher mumbled.

"I'm in the paper? No way." Allie had only been in the paper once before, when her Camp Fire Girls troupe was photographed walking in the Chinese New Year parade in Chinatown. Wai Po was in the picture, too, marching right alongside Allie, wearing a long silk dress she had brought from China to America when she was twenty years old.

"We saw it, too," Hans said. "The Metro section." He went to the counter where the sink was, sorted through the scattered *Los Angeles Times*, and pulled out the Metro section.

Jorge took the paper. Allie stood beside him and looked over his arm. There it was, a picture of the bird squawking in front of the broken windshield. Jorge read the headline: "Condor Crashes into Car on the 405." There was an interview with the guy in the convertible. He mentioned that the driver, "a young woman in a Flashdance-style T-shirt," had asked for directions to Cedars-Sinai hospital just before the bird hit her car.

"But how did you know it was me?" Allie asked. "There's gotta be thousands of Preludes on the road."

"Look," Jorge said, and put his slender brown finger on the photo. There in the corner of the frame, just behind the bird's left wing, was a slice of Allie's body, her hand grasping on to the Wonder Bread bag.

"We'd been waiting by the doors since six this morning," Topher said. "Mike figured if you went to the hospital yesterday, you'd go again today. No one shows up at a hospital once."

13

Jorge drove the van. Allie sat in the front seat and Hans and Luis sat on the bench in the way back. Topher—hands duct-taped behind his back and feet duct-taped together—was in between them. The first backseat could only hold one, as it was mostly open space for Roger's wheelchair. Allie turned on the radio and sang "Wild and Loose" along with Morris Day and the Time. She often sang when she was nervous. It helped shut down the obsessive thoughts swirling in her head.

"This is my wife's favorite song, sweetheart," Jorge said.

"Oh yeah?" Allie liked the idea that she and Consuela had something in common.

"Yeah. I'll tell her you like it, too," he said, smiling. "She thinks you're special."

"No way. Like how?" Allie couldn't recall anyone ever saying she was special. Unless you counted Jonas, who thought she was pretty special when she lifted up her shirt for him.

"Just special." Jorge shrugged. "You remind her of herself when she was younger."

"Really?" This made Allie feel like she'd better stay out of trouble, stay alive. If there was any chance she'd grow up to be a mother like Consuela with a husband like Jorge and two perfect little Jesus and Mary kids, then she sure as hell didn't want to die at the hands of Vice Versa (or anyone else!) this year.

"Yeah, really." Jorge pulled into the parking lot of the auto shop where the Prelude was being fixed. He put the van in park, cut the engine, and turned toward Allie. "She had a few wild years, but then she calmed down when she realized the wildness was no fun, you know?"

"Yeah, I know." Allie could feel herself passing rapidly through this current stage. Wildness was burning out of her like the end of a forest fire.

Jorge looked out the window and Allie followed his gaze. A Hispanic guy, who looked somewhat like Jorge but bigger, was waving his arms, pointing to a rolled-down garage door.

"Let's go get your car," Jorge said, and he started up the van again and drove toward the garage door that was slowly rising. Once they were inside, the door rolled shut behind them. The only light came from a single bulb hanging on a wire in the middle of the ceiling.

"The Prelude!" Allie said, and she got out of the van and ran to Beth's car, which, as far as she could tell in the dim light, was sparkling clean and had a beautiful glass windshield in one smooth piece. "It looks brand-new!"

"I told you it would." Jorge said, getting out of the van. He pulled from his pocket a bundle of bills so big it resembled a giant green rolled sock. "Roger's cash," he said, when he noticed Allie watching. Allie wondered how she would ever repay this debt.

Jorge handed several bills to his bigger twin. "My cousin!" he said to Allie, and he threw an arm up and around the man's shoulder.

"Oh!" Allie said. She was relieved to know that she had been right about their looking alike, that she hadn't just thought all Mexicans looked the same.

Hans and Luis came out of the van with Topher shuffling like a bowling pin between them.

"You ready to take us to your friend?" Jorge asked Topher.

"Dude, I told you, we were supposed to meet at his place and I lost the address," Topher said. "He probably picked me for this job because I don't know fuck about him—not even where he surfs."

"Of course you know where he surfs," Allie said. "Even *I* know that every surfer knows where all the other surfers surf." Beth had dated a surfer from San Luis Obispo for a while. He didn't even call his friends by their names but instead used the name of the beach where they surfed.

Allie turned, walked to the Prelude, and popped open the trunk. Even though she knew the condor was there, it startled her enough when she saw it that she let out a little yelp and jumped back. It smelled oceany and sour, like salted death.

Everyone, including Jorge's cousin and shuffling Topher on Hans's arm, rushed to the trunk and peered in. Jorge removed the empty Tanqueray bottles and tossed them underhand to an open trash can near the office door. The bottles exploded with a crackle as they landed.

"Fucking thing stinks," Hans said.

"That's the biggest fucking smelly thing I've ever seen," Luis squeaked.

"You're the biggest fucking smelly thing I've ever seen," Topher mumbled.

Everyone looked at Topher for a second. It appeared that no one could believe he was that dumb. Then Luis and Hans folded Topher into the trunk, on top of the bird. Jorge slammed the trunk and turned to Allie.

"We're going to find your father first, sweetheart, then we'll get the coke," he said. "People before things or money."

"Okay, Dad first." Allie wondered if Frank would save her or his restaurant first. Penny definitely wouldn't save Allie first. Allie had asked to be saved and her mother had responded by trying to steal the coke.

Before they left, Allie stepped into the garage office to use the phone. She wanted to check in on Beth, see if there was any new information on Vice Versa and let her know the Prelude was okay.

Allie had memorized Jorge and Consuela's long-distance code and she used it. Beth answered on the seventh ring.

"It's me." Allie looked around the garage office. There was a naked Asian girl calendar on the wall with Chinese writing printed on it. Someone must have bought it in Chinatown. The desk was metal, just like the filing cabinet. Everything was tidy, organized.

"I totally figured it was you. No one else has been calling me lately."

"Rosie still there?"

"Yeah. We're so in love it's sickening. The guy actually licks between my toes he loves me so much?"

Allie couldn't bear to hear anything else about Beth's and Rosie's deep and abiding love. "Listen, your car's all fixed up and I'm headed over to my dad's house now. Is there anyone there that you know of? I mean, is there like a gang there with machine guns or something?"

"What do you mean, my car's fixed up?"

Allie remembered that Beth hadn't been listening when she had told her about the bird, and she didn't feel like going into it now. "It's clean," she temporized.

"You're calling to tell me my car is clean?"

"Beth! I'm on the lam here with a hundred thousand dollars worth of coke and you're being held hostage, remember? I'm calling to find out if there's anyone at my dad's house with him!"

"If I ask Rosie, he'll know I'm talking to you. If I ask Jonas, he'll definitely know I'm talking to you." Beth sounded irritated, like she had better things to do than chat on the phone with Allie.

"Is Jonas still there?" Allie cringed at the thought. How could Beth spend so much time with Jonas in her apartment?

"Yeah, he's kind of on a bender. He locked up the dress shop and he and Rosie and a couple of other guys, I think one of them might even be Vice Versa, although I'm not really sure, have been hanging around the last two days? Jonas is sleeping on the couch right now. He's been so sweet, Allie. Are you sure he whipped out his dick? 'Cause he's been, like, a perfect gentleman?"

"What about when you did that crazy baby food–jar coke!" Allie was enraged. She wanted to dive through the phone lines, pop out of the mouthpiece holes like spaghetti, and strangle Beth. "Remember you were dancing and he was trying to get you to take off your clothes?! Remember, he was perving out on you?!"

"Oh my god!" Beth laughed. "I totally forgot about that!"

"How could you forget about that?! Are you high?!"

"Well, yeah, I have been high, like, ever since Rosie and I started falling in love. It's like, sex, coke, sex, pot, sex, alcohol, sex, coke, sex, pot, sex—"

"Yeah, I see the pattern." Allie had a flash of understanding drug use as the ultimate narcissism: feeding oneself something in order to feel a heightened and altered sense of only oneself. She forgave Beth for this, but wished she'd snap out of it so she could look beyond her mattress. "But listen, have you overheard anything about my dad?"

"No. They always seem to talk on the phone when I'm in the bedroom or something. I haven't heard anything about anything."

"So don't tell them I called, okay?"

"Rosie just walked in. Now he knows I'm on the phone with you."

"He's right there? Is he listening in?" How could Beth be so clumsy?! Though Allie knew she herself was the only one to blame for her troubles. As Wai Po had said, *EAT SALTY FISH, MUST ACCEPT BEING THIRSTY.*

"No, he's licking my toes." Beth laughed in a squealy sort of way. And then Allie heard shuffling and conversation through Beth's thin hand over the mouthpiece.

"Allie?" It was a big voice, thick as tar.

"Rosie?"

"The one and only. Listen, my dear, no one's out to extinguish your life. Why don't you bring back Beth's car, return the bread bag, and we're all good. Okay?"

"What about Vice Versa? I thought he was looking for me."

"Jonas called him off. I love Beth so much, I told Jonas I'd kill him if anything happened to her best friend."

"So Vice Versa's not in L.A. anymore?"

"No ma'am. He started partying here around oh-two-hundred hours."

"Is he still there?"

"Indeed. Hold on a moment." There was more shuffling and whispering in the background. Allie looked out the glass window into the garage. She hoped Rosie wasn't playing with Beth's affections in order to make his shift as hostage-holder less tedious than the usual hole-up. And she really hoped he wasn't lying to Allie in order to lure her to her possible death. It was so hard to know who people really were past their shiny hair and toothy faces. Or, in Rosie's case, past their tumbling words.

"Hey," a second man grunted. His voice was like gravel.

"Hey. Did you see my dad?"

"Saw him, said hey and left. Just bring the blow back. It's all cool."

"Okay. Can I talk to Beth?"

"She and Rosie are in the bedroom doing it again. They do it ten, twelve, fourteen times a day."

Of course, Allie thought. At the moment, in her druggy-love-dream, Beth was about as helpful to Allie as Penny had been. But unlike with her mother, Allie saw Beth as her responsibility. She was the one who sluiced Beth into this, after all. "Okay, well, I'm going to drive back now. So I'll see you in seven hours or so. Sound good?"

"Take Highway 5 and I'll see you in six hours. Don't take 101. And whatever the fuck you do, don't take the Pacific Coast Highway."

"All right. See you in six hours." Allie hung up and stared at the phone. She deeply wanted to believe that everything would, in fact, be okay. But could you ever really trust a drug dealer? Or three of them?

Allie dialed her father's number. He picked up right away.

"Dad, are you okay?"

"I'm watching my show," Frank said. "What do you need?" He was back to his laconic ways. There was no way Vice Versa was still holding a gun to his head.

"We're coming over now," Allie said.

"Good," Frank said, and he hung up.

Allie drove the Prelude with Hans beside her, his gun out on his lap. Jorge and Luis were in the van. Topher was rolling around the trunk or kicking it with his bound merman feet. He was making a constant ruckus that was often so forceful Allie could feel the car rocking. "At least we know Topher's not suffocating back there," she said to Hans.

"Would be more quiet if he was," Hans said noncommittally.

"Have you ever killed someone?" Allie asked. She was following Jorge, who had claimed he knew exactly where the address that Allie had written on the magazine subscription card was. They were going about thirty miles an hour down strip-mall streets filled with karate studios and nail salons. Everything looked grimy and faded.

"Luis and I have been working for Roger for six years and in that time we've never had to kill anyone."

"Are you guys lovers?" Allie asked.

"Who? Me and Roger?"

"No, you and Luis."

"He's my twin," Hans said.

"Seriously? But other than your hair and how you dress, you don't look alike. And your names are so dissimilar."

"You think?"

"Well, yeah. If I had one kid named Hans I'd name the other Piet or something."

"Never thought of that," Hans said.

A police siren wailed behind them. Allie pulled the car over and waited. The banging from the trunk increased to an earthquake-like fury. Once the police had passed, Allie pulled out into the road again and searched for the van. Jorge had pulled over with his hazard lights on, waiting for her. They realigned and moved back into traffic.

"Where'd you guys grow up?" Allie asked.

"The valley. Our mother worked for Roger before we were born. She doesn't know who our dad is."

"Oh! Was she a porn star?!" Allie loved this. Finally, someone who had a mother who seemed more far-out than her own mother, the tambourine girl.

"Well, I don't know if she was a star. But she was a porn actress. Roger sort of took us in while she kept working. He sent us to college in Fresno, and when we graduated he hired us and we moved back in with him."

They had pulled up in front of a row of Spanish-style condos. The units looked brand-new. Each had a red tile roof, orangey-red stucco, and a long arched window beside the front door. The yards were a glowing green with flowers planted along the edges of each walkway. It was definitely the nicest place Frank had lived since their house in Pasadena when Allie was small. His last apartment had had bars over the windows and a refrigerator in the bathroom.

Allie and Hans got out of the car and stood with Luis and Jorge in the driveway. Then, without speaking, as if they already knew the plan, Luis and Jorge walked around the side toward the back and Allie went to the front door while Hans crouched down just to the right of the door, away from the window.

Allie knocked. The door opened, and there was Frank, his massive thick body filling the door frame. His hair was shaved against his head, just like Jonas's, but with speckles of gray. His eyelashes were so thick they looked wet. Allie thought her father had never been more handsome than this moment when he was standing there staring at her, one hundred percent alive.

"What happened to your forehead?" Frank said.

"Oh, Dad!" Allie stepped in and tried to hug him. He held her back with one hand, pulled out a napkin that was tucked into his polo shirt, wiped his mouth, and then hugged Allie in a way he never had before. He even kissed the top of her head. And then they pulled apart.

"Did a person do that to you?" Frank pointed at the lump.

"No," Allie said. "I was on the 405 and—"

"And where in the world have you been?!" he asked in his usual barking voice. "I have been waiting for you for two days!"

"Can my friend come in, Dad?" Allie looked over to Hans, who stood up. Frank nodded at Hans, who nodded back. Frank stepped away from the door so they could enter.

"Let me watch the showcase finale," Frank said, "and then we'll talk and you can tell me about that thing growing out of your head."

The TV was on in the living room, and there was a plate of couscous with asparagus sitting on the coffee table. Frank sat, tucked his napkin into his shirt, looked up at *The Price Is Right*, and continued eating. Allie sat beside him. Hans walked to the window and waved at either Jorge or Luis.

"Dad," Allie said. She felt buoyant, relieved. It seemed that Rosie had told her the truth and they were all fine now. "I've got a couple friends in the back. Can they come in, too?"

"Leave them," Hans said to Allie. "They'll make sure no one else shows up."

"I don't think that's a problem anymore," Allie said. She turned to Frank. "Dad, can you just tell me if Vice Versa stopped by?"

"He did." Frank picked up the pad of paper and pen that sat on the coffee table and started writing down numbers as each item in the final showcase was being shown.

"I love this part of the show," Hans said, and he stepped into the center of the room so as to better see the TV. "Is this the first or the second showcase?"

"Second," Frank said. "The first was before you got here."

"I say eighteen thousand," Hans said.

"Twenty-two thousand, three hundred and nine," Frank said, and he looked toward Hans.

"Thirty-two thousand," the egg-shaped woman on TV said,

"nine hundred and thirteen dollars and seven cents!" The audience screamed at her. Bob Barker held his microphone and laughed.

"Now, Darlene," he said. "You told me you're a fan of the show, so you should know that we don't do cents here." The audience howled.

"You're way over, Darlene," Frank said.

"Way, way over, Darlene," Hans said.

They both stared at the TV until it went to a commercial break.

"What did Vice Versa say, Dad?" Allie asked. "Did he have a gun?"

"Allie," Frank said. "I'm eating my lunch and enjoying my show. When the show is over we can talk." He forked up more couscous. Allie and Hans both watched him eat.

"Is that Moroccan or Israeli couscous?" Hans asked.

"They only sell one kind at Ralph's," Frank said.

"The Israeli takes longer to cook but it's worth it," Hans said.

"Are you hungry?" Frank asked, without looking away from the TV.

"I'm not," Allie said. Consuela's breakfast was still warm in her belly.

"I'm a little peckish," Hans said, as he eyed the couscous.

"Pot in the kitchen," Frank said, and he nudged his shoulder behind him toward the kitchen.

"You cooked at home?" Allie asked.

"Well I haven't been able to make it into the restaurant," Frank said, staring at the TV.

Hans returned with a filled plate just as the first showcase's actual retail value was revealed as $16,982. Frank looked down at his pad and then pumped his fist. "You see that," he said, pointing at a number on the pad, "I was within twelve hundred dollars."

Next Darlene's showcase's value was revealed at $22,619.

"She's ten thousand dollars over," Hans said. He was delicately feeding himself couscous and asparagus as if he were in a candlelit restaurant on a date.

"Yeah, but you're four thousand dollars under. Look at this." Frank held up the pad with his estimate. "Only three hundred and ten dollars under. That's almost unheard of on this show!"

"Do you watch this often, Dad?" Allie couldn't remember her father ever being home in the middle of the day.

"It's a terrific show, Allie, and you should watch it, too." Frank put down his fork, picked up the remote control, and clicked off the big, boxy TV. He pulled out his napkin, turned on the green couch so he was facing Allie and Hans, and crossed his legs. "Are you helping my daughter or holding her prisoner?" he asked Hans.

"He's helping me, Dad. He's on my side."

"And what, pray tell, did you do, Allie, that requires you to show up here with this man *on your side?*"

Allie figured since Vice Versa had already appeared, there was a good chance her father knew exactly why Hans was sitting beside her. It seemed foolish at this point to give anything but the entire truth. Wai Po had often said, *HALF-TRUTH IS LIKE WHOLE LIE.*

"I stole a Wonder Bread bag full of cocaine," Allie confessed, and she started crying. Suddenly she felt like she was ten again.

"Get yourself together, Allie," Frank said. "If you're old enough to steal a bag of cocaine then you're old enough to deal with the consequences."

Allie sucked in her breath, sat up straight, and started from the beginning. She told Frank the whole story, including the visit with her mother and Jet, the bird, and the lump on her head. She left out any mention of the fact that she lifted her shirt for Jonas (she doubted her father would want to hear that truth) or hung out with Billy Idol. (Frank had no interest in rock stars or celebrities. When they came into his restaurant, he didn't give them special service and admonished any of the staff who did.)

When she had finished, Frank straightened himself on the couch again. He moved his head from side to side as if he were getting ready to do something physical. "Jonas," he said.

"Yeah," Allie said. "That's the guy's name."

"I know his name, Allie. I've known him for thirty-three years."

Allie shook her head. "No, Jonas was the dealer I was working for at the clothing store."

"Allie, do you think that job just fell in your lap? When I sent out holiday cards last year, I wrote on Jonas's card that you were in the Bay Area and would be a good employee for him. Then he called one day in June and said that he had met you in a restaurant and had hired you. I didn't say anything to you because I wanted you to feel like you got that job on your own. I thought it would be a good confidence booster."

Allie was silent for a moment. She tried to rearrange the events of the past four days in her brain with this added knowledge. The only thing she could think to say was, "Dad, you send out Christmas cards?"

"I send out holiday cards."

"Why didn't you send one to me?"

"Because I sign them from me and you, so it would be like you sending yourself a card."

"I never knew you sent out holiday cards. I didn't think we were a family who did that sort of thing."

"I guess you don't know everything, now, do you." Frank nodded his head as if to put a period at the end of the sentence.

"Can I see the card you sent?"

"Go to the second drawer in my desk and lift up the bills. The cards are there."

Hans looked up from his plate and watched as Allie went to the desk pushed against the window in the living room. Frank placed his desk by a window wherever he lived. Allie opened the second drawer, lifted the bills, then pulled out a stack of holiday cards. The one on the top had a picture of Allie and her father standing together at the hostess podium in his restaurant. The photo had been taken last summer by a waitress who had been working for her father for as long as Allie could remember. In the photo, Allie was looking straight at the camera, while her father, upright and enormous beside her, appeared to be staring off toward the kitchen.

A warm flooding snaked through Allie's arms into her center. Maybe her father did love her more than his restaurant. She shifted through the rest of the cards. All of them were photos taken at the restaurant by the staff. She put the cards back and returned to the couch. Frank was watching Hans eat his couscous.

"So how do you know Jonas?" Allie asked.

"He's the little brother of my childhood friend Lionel."

"I remember Lionel!" Allie had always liked Lionel. He smiled and had brought Allie little gifts when he came to visit, things like ladybug pen and pencil sets, or necklaces with perfume lockets on them.

"He lives in San Francisco now," Frank said. "And I guarantee he'll be spitting fire when he hears what his brother is really doing over there in that shop."

"So I guess Jonas recognized me from the Christmas card." Allie was starting to put it all together.

"I guess he did," Frank conceded.

"And then he did you a favor and hired me," Allie said. She had never thought of herself as one of those girls whose fathers could call in favors on their behalf. Beth was one of those girls. She had told Allie that everything in her life was a series of favors paid to her father through her: the car she drove, the clothes she wore, the expensive haircuts she got when she was home in Nevada. Allie often wondered if Beth's father was in the mob, but she had only asked once, when they were both drunk, and Beth had just laughed at the suggestion.

"And after Jonas hired you he showed you his genitals," Frank said, very matter-of-factly.

"Yes," Allie said, matching her tone to his.

"And now I'm going to kill him." Frank looked at Hans. Hans continued eating.

"Dad," Allie said. "What happened with Vice Versa?"

"First of all, he wasn't black, so you can readjust your racist thoughts on that."

"He is, too, black. I talked to him on the phone this morning."

"How do you know he's black from his voice?" Hans said.

"You can't tell a black man's voice?" Allie asked.

"I'm afraid my daughter has fallen into some very small-minded thinking," Frank said to Hans.

"Dad, please! *You* sound like a black man."

"And do you sound like a black girl?"

"No, but that's because Mom's Chinese *plus* I was always in schools with white kids."

"Your mother's Chinese?" Hans asked.

"Yeah, and her father is Jewish," Allie said, and suddenly she realized why Jonas seemed to know this about her without her ever having told him.

"Allie, Vice Versa is here," Frank interrupted.

"He's here now?" Allie looked around the room. Could she have somehow missed seeing Jonas's henchman? "When did he show up?"

"Two days ago when you called me from that restaurant."

"Wait, so is that why you stopped answering the phone?"

"In fact, it is."

"Have you just been hanging out with Vice Versa for two days?"

"Allie, that man broke into my house at gunpoint. He was holding me hostage until about three hours ago, when I overtook him."

Hans nodded, as if he were impressed. "How'd you manage that?"

"Swiftly and carefully," Frank said.

Allie's insides felt swirly and confused. Had Beth and Rosie deliberately lied to her about Vice Versa being in Berkeley? Or was there more than one Vice Versa? Was it a team, a squad, an underground organization like Mossad? "So where are you hiding him?"

Frank pointed to the ceiling, then stood and headed toward the stairs. Hans followed Frank, carrying his plate of food. Allie hurried behind.

They entered the master bedroom. The only furniture was a king-size bed with white sheets and a green blanket. There was nothing on the walls and no curtains on the windows. The room was sunny and wide.

"This is a great place, Dad," Allie said.

"Sublet. I'm getting it for half the market price." Frank went to the double closet and opened the doors. Squatting on the carpeted closet floor was a duct-tape-bound man with straight, choppy black hair. He was batting his eyes and squealing behind his sealed mouth. He smelled of urine and there appeared to be a small puddle of wetness seeping out his blue jeans. Four white button-down shirts and four polo shirts hung above him. Beside the shirts were folded, pressed jeans and two pairs of dress slacks.

"Vice Versa?" Allie asked. The squealing intensified. It sounded like the condor after it crashed into the Prelude.

"That's him," Frank said. "And you can see that he's not black. In fact, he's Filipino."

Hans took a bite of couscous, then tipped his head down and inspected the bindings on Vice Versa. "Where'd you learn to do that so efficiently?" he asked.

"ROTC," Frank said.

"Did he tell you about the stolen cocaine?" Allie asked.

"I suppose he told me something like that," Frank said. Allie was relieved she had confessed the truth.

Allie, Frank, and Hans examined Vice Versa as if he were a museum artifact. Vice Versa continued squealing.

"Wow, Dad. I can't believe you have a hostage in your closet," Allie said. This entire messed-up situation was getting curiouser and curiouser.

"Admirable," Hans said, and he sat on the bed and continued his meal.

"Allie, take that tape off his mouth," Frank said. "Let's give him some air."

Vice Versa stopped squealing when Allie leaned over and untaped his mouth. He panted for a while, licked his lips, and then dropped his head as if resting. Allie turned to her father and saw that he had a gun out.

"Is that Vice Versa's gun?" Allie asked.

"I only trust my own weapons," Frank said.

"Dad! Since when do you carry a gun?" This was even more startling than the Christmas card.

"I have always owned a gun. I am a businessman. Businessmen need to be armed." Frank's voice was calm and firm.

"I agree," Hans said, cutting a piece of asparagus with his fork.

"Allie," Frank said, "go in your bedroom and get the gun that's under your mattress. *That's* Vice Versa's gun."

"I have a bedroom?" Allie asked. "I've never been here before!"

"Yes, you have a bedroom!" Frank said. "This is your home! Now go get the gun!"

Allie walked down the hall past a white-tiled bathroom and into a yellow bedroom with a single bed with pretty floral sheets and a yellow blanket. She lifted up the mattress. Sure enough, there was a gun there.

Allie returned to the master bedroom with the gun dangling from her first two fingers like a dirty diaper. Vice Versa sat up straight and watched her.

"That's your gun now," Frank said. "Keep it in your purse."

"I don't need a gun. I've got the lucky rabbit foot Wai Po gave me." Allie wasn't joking, but she smiled as if she were.

Hans laughed. "I've got my St. Jude medallion," he said. "And I'm still carrying a gun."

"Keep the gun, Allie," Frank said firmly.

"Are you sure this is really Vice Versa?" Allie asked.

"Of course I'm Vice Versa! You dumb rabbit-foot-believing girl!" Vice Versa's voice clanged like a fork against a tin pot. "What happened to your head? That thing's fucking ugly!"

"Please don't use profanity in my home!" Frank boomed, and he shut the closet doors.

14

Hans and Luis wanted to stuff Vice Versa in the trunk with Topher. Frank, Jorge, and Allie agreed that it would be inhumane to pack two grown men into one trunk with a dead condor. Besides, although they learned through Vice Versa that he had been sent to Los Angeles to retrieve the cocaine *by any means necessary*, he hadn't, in fact, harmed any of them. Even Frank, who had been his prisoner for two nights. Vice Versa was sequestered in the locked van while they opened the trunk of the Prelude. The bird was laid out over Topher's quaking body and examined, bald head to razor claw, by Frank.

"And you're saying it just crashed through your windshield?" Frank said.

"Yeah," Allie said. "I was sitting in traffic and it crashed."

"I can maybe see it going through the windshield if the car was moving. In that case you'd have the velocity of the car versus the velocity of the bird, which certainly would be enough force to break the windshield. But a stopped car?" He paused. "Well, maybe if it weighs enough." Frank lifted the bird and bounced it up and down, assessing the weight. Then he placed it back on top of Topher and said, "I guess that thing's at least twenty-five or thirty pounds. And if it were diving straight down from five hundred feet up, going fifty miles an hour, at thirty pounds, then, yeah, that would break your windshield. Amazing." He looked at Topher, who was crouching and silent, and poked him in the shoulder.

"He claims he lost the address for the guy with the coke," Luis said.

"I only met him a week ago," Topher said.

"You committed a crime with a guy you met last week?" Frank asked.

"I just fucking moved here from Laguna Beach. He was like the first fucking friend I've made!"

"Language, please!" Frank said.

"I think he's lying," Allie said.

"Are you actually dumb enough to lie so that you can protect some infantile surfer boy who had the nerve to steal a bag of already stolen cocaine from my temporarily imbecilic daughter?"

"I got mostly As in school last semester," Allie said, but no one seemed to hear. They were all peering down at Topher, whose dull eyes reminded Allie of a goat or a cow. He shook his head no.

"No, you're not lying?"

"I swear, man! We plotted the whole thing at Tommy's Burgers at, like, three in the morning. He gave me his address on a fucking index card. I mean who uses index cards? I thought it was in my pocket but—"

"Enough!" Frank stepped back and slammed the trunk shut.

Frank knew almost every street in every neighborhood in Los Angeles. So when Allie told him she had met Mike at the gas station across from the In-N-Out Burger with the palm tree that looked like it was bowing toward the ground, he knew exactly where they should go.

Allie got in the driver's seat of the Prelude, her father sat in front with his gun on his lap, and Hans sat in the back. Jorge and Luis were in the van, with Vice Versa.

Allie had never driven with her father as a passenger before and was not prepared for the detailed instructions he gave her. Frank told her when to put on the blinker, when to change lanes, how fast to go, where to center herself in the lane, and how to turn hand over hand rather than keeping her hands in one place. By the time she pulled into the gas station, Allie was exhausted from the concentration it took to respond to each of her father's directions. She pulled up against the fence that bordered the gas station, cut the engine, and leaned back in her seat.

"Do you see him?" Frank asked.

Allie looked out the back window. "No," she said.

"Go out and find him." Frank nudged his chin toward Allie. There was a boom and the car shook as Topher jolted around in the trunk.

Allie got out of the car just as the van pulled in beside them. Jorge was driving. "You find out where he is?" Jorge asked. The van bounced a bit and Allie leaned in and watched Luis push Vice Versa down to the floor.

"We need to tie him to something," Jorge said. "He's been hurling himself all over like a bouncing ball."

"Tape him to the floor," Allie said, and she laughed at the idea of a man being taped to the floor of a van. Then she shuddered and wondered if this experience was eroding her respect for humanity and life. "On second thought, don't tape him to the floor!" she said, and she walked off, with her purse hiked up on her shoulder, in search of Mike's friend Jimmy.

Jimmy's uncle, the owner of the gas station, was working. "Jimmy don't work till tomorrow," he said in a rich Southern accent. His front eyeteeth were missing and he was as bluish-white as skim milk. He was definitely not from California.

"Do you have Jimmy's phone number?" Allie asked. "I need to call him." She burrowed into her purse for a scrap of paper, saw

Vice Versa's gun nestled there, and immediately yanked out her hand.

"Who're y'all again?" the uncle asked. His accent was so thick that at first Allie thought he had said *whore*.

"I'm his girlfriend," Allie lied smoothly in a way that she knew would have saddened Wai Po.

The old man squinted at her. "If you're his girlfriend, why don't you have the number already?"

"New girlfriend," Allie improvised. "We started dating two days ago. I met him here."

"He didn't give you that lump in the bean, did he?" The old man put his hand up above his eyebrow. Allie mirrored him and felt her forehead. She had forgotten about her bump in spite of the fact that each new person she saw seemed to mention it.

"Oh, no!" she said. "I opened a jam-packed closet and something fell on me."

The old man seemed to accept her explanation. "Like in the cartoons," he said.

"Yeah, like in Bugs Bunny or something."

"Okay, well, come in the office and I'll let you use the phone," he said.

Allie followed him inside. The office was the size of a phone booth and smelled like tobacco and gasoline. "I'll dial," the old man said, and he put his crooked white finger in the rotary and dialed as Allie held the phone. "Is it ringing?" he asked.

"It's ringing," Allie said.

"Good," the man said, and he went outside, leaving Allie alone.

Jimmy answered on the fifth ring.

"Jimmy?" Allie said.

"Katie?"

"No, it's Allie."

"Allie?" His voice sounded worried. Allie imagined him panicking over not remembering who Allie was.

"I met you a couple days ago when I got gas but I didn't have enough money to pay and so you called your friend Mike, who, uh . . ." Allie looked around. No one could hear her, yet she still felt uncomfortable mentioning cocaine on the phone.

"Oh, yeah, I remember you! How'd you get my number?"

"Your uncle."

"My uncle? Bart?"

"I guess. The guy with the funny accent."

"Yeah, that's Bart! He's been in California for like thirty years. Can you believe he still talks like that?"

"Not really," Allie said. She looked out the window and saw her father standing next to the trunk of the Prelude. His face was as stern as a hammer. "Listen, can you tell me where I can find Mike? I was supposed to meet him here to give him some more of that stuff, you know, but he's not here and he already gave me the money for it so I want to be sure to get it to him."

"Did you try his house?" Jimmy asked.

"I lost the address," Allie said.

"He lives in that apartment building next to the In-N-Out," Jimmy said, and Allie's eyes immediately landed on the three-story, green stucco building. "But if he's not there, check Zuma. I heard the waves were good today."

"But if he lives across the street, why did he drive over to meet me last time?" Allie asked. She couldn't look away from the apartment building. She feared Mike would walk out any second.

"He always drives over—he loves that truck."

"Which apartment is his?"

"Across the street!"

"No, what's his apartment number?"

"Oh, man, I don't know. I've only been there once. Maybe second floor? Like I told you before, the guy parties a lot and I just don't party."

"You study," Allie said.

"Yeah, for now. I study and work."

Allie stood by the car in front of her father, her back to the apartment building.

"Look behind me," she whispered.

"What?" Frank asked.

"Behind me." Allie was almost hissing. "Mike lives in that green stucco building."

"Why are you talking like that?"

"Dad! What if he's watching us?"

"Well he certainly can't hear us from there! Do you see how many cars are between us and that building? It would be like trying to hear over the Mississippi in a rain storm."

Hans and Luis approached Allie and Frank. "Well?" Hans said.

"He lives in the green apartment building right there." Frank nodded his head. Hans and Luis both turned and looked at the same moment, like synchronized dogs. Allie could see the twinness in them.

"Let's go," Hans said, and he went to the van while Luis slipped into the backseat of the Prelude.

It took four full minutes to pull onto the road and make a left turn into the driveway of Mike's apartment building. Allie could see why he might drive over—it would be hard to dodge through the traffic and there wasn't a crosswalk in sight.

"Pull to the back of the building," Frank said, and Allie obeyed.

Mike's truck wasn't anywhere to be seen. "I'll go knock on some doors and ask people if they know which apartment is Mike's," Allie said.

"Absolutely not," Frank said. "You will wait in the car."

"Dad, come on. No one's going to open the door to any of you guys. People are afraid of men who come around apartments in the middle of the day."

"She's right," Luis said. "Our mother never opened the door if a man was on the other side."

Frank leaned back in his seat and thought for a moment. "Fine. But Luis goes with you. He has blond hair—people aren't afraid of blond hair. Hans, Jorge, and I will be three steps behind you, hiding out."

"That's fine." Allie got out of the car and Luis walked with her. Hans and Jorge caught up with Frank and the three of them followed, just as Frank had said.

The apartment building had exterior hallways with rickety iron rails. There were no people around. Allie and Luis stopped on 2B and knocked. No one answered. They moved down one more, to 2C, and knocked again. It wasn't until they had gone halfway around the square and knocked on apartment 2K that they got lucky: a woman with blond hair that was matted into a nest on top of her head opened the door. She was about thirty years old, with a pink rabbit-looking nose, and was wearing ski boots, underwear, and a T-shirt with an iron-on teapot decal.

"Hey!" she said, as if she and Allie knew each other.

"Oh, sorry, I thought this was Mike's place." Allie couldn't help but notice how easily the lies were now swimming out of her mouth. Was lying like having affairs? What difference did it make if you had one or seven—either way, you were an adulterer.

"Surfer Mike or Musician Mike?"

"Surfer Mike."

"Next door. Two L."

"Oh, that's right. Sorry to bother you," Allie said. "Thanks so much!"

"Okay," the woman said, and she shut the door.

Luis motioned to Frank, Jorge, and Hans, who were peering in from around the corner. They jogged to catch up, Frank in front. Allie had never seen her father move so quickly. He seemed younger, livelier.

The men separated, two on either side of the door. Allie knocked. There was no answer. Allie knocked and knocked and knocked.

"Move aside," Frank said.

There was a loud, snapping crack, like a giant branch breaking off a tree, as Frank kicked down the door. Allie was starting to believe that there was nothing her father couldn't do. Frank had disarmed Vice Versa, given her a gun for her purse, and guessed the final showcase value within $310. What was next?

The group stood back and waited for something to charge out of the apartment. But nothing did. The woman in 2K didn't even open her door.

One by one, they filed in, Allie in the rear. The kitchen was at the back of the room, the living room in front, all of it open. An array of surfing magazines sat on a brown wooden coffee table in front of a long, green couch. There was an orange crochet throw blanket draped over one arm of the couch. Nothing hung on any wall, and the only thing on the kitchen counter was an un-bagged loaf of sliced white bread. The green shag rug in the living room appeared to have been vacuumed and the air smelled of Windex. Allie was surprised that someone with such a crusty, soiled interior would be so tidy.

Hans and Luis explored a small hallway off to the left that led to what Allie assumed were the bedroom and bathroom. "All clear," Hans shouted after a few seconds. He and his brother returned to the living room.

Frank sat on the couch as Allie and Jorge searched in the living room, coat closet, and kitchen. It only took a few minutes to see that the coke was not there.

Luis went to the kitchen and opened the refrigerator. Allie stood beside him and looked at the contents: one Heineken, a roll of salami, two apples, and a small brick of extra-sharp cheddar. The shelves were so spotless they looked almost new.

"Well, at least he's clean," Allie said.

Luis opened the cupboard and grabbed a box of Ritz crackers. Allie took the box from him, pulled out a cracker and ate it.

"Anyone want cheese and crackers?" Luis shouted out.

"Is it domestic cheese?" Hans asked. He was on the couch next to Frank now.

"Yes." Luis rolled his eyes, then whispered to Allie, "He won't eat domestic cheeses."

"I'll have some," Jorge said. He was standing in the middle of the living room, rotating as if something might suddenly appear through the broken front door.

Luis sliced the cheddar and arranged Ritz crackers on a white plastic dinner plate. He took the plate to the living room and set it down on the coffee table. Allie pulled a middle slice from the loaf of bread on the counter.

"This tastes like Wonder Bread," she said, and she grabbed another piece, then sat on the couch between Hans and her father. Frank leaned forward and took a cracker and slice of cheese.

"We've got to figure out what to do with our two hostages," Frank said, before biting into his cracker.

"Trade them for the coke?" Allie said.

"We have to find the man with the coke to trade them for it," Frank said.

"I'd like to beat the shit out of that mouthy surfer," Luis said.

"Sweetheart, no violence, please," Jorge said, and he took a cracker and some cheese from the plate.

"Has anyone fed the hostages?" Hans asked.

"They can go without food, but we do have to give them water," Frank said.

"Why don't we water the hostages and leave them here while we go to Zuma beach and find Mike. His gas-station friend said that that's his beach," Allie said.

"Would be safer than keeping them in the cars," Jorge said. "If we got pulled over there could be big trouble"

"Yeah," Luis said, "a Mexican with a taped-up Filipino in his van would not look good to the police."

"I think the black dude with the taped-up surfer in his trunk looks even worse," Hans said.

"I believe you're right about that," Frank said, and his shoulders lifted and fell as he took a deep breath.

"Can we dump the bird here with them?" Allie asked. "The smell's starting to seep toward the front seat."

"Of course," Frank said, and he surprised Allie by patting her on the head.

Allie went to Mike's bedroom and yanked off the pilly green blanket that was tucked into his bed. She looked at the pale blue sheets, perfectly folded and cornered military-style at the ends of the bed. They were probably clean but there was a softness about them, a shininess, that made Allie think of the oils in Mike's skin, his shedding hair, the beach tar that was probably stuck on the bottom of his feet. To touch these remnants of Mike felt the same to Allie as touching Mike himself. And after everything he'd done to her (dumping her in the restroom alcove at Tambor's, holding her up at gunpoint, stealing the bag of coke), Allie did not want to touch Mike in any form.

Allie reached down anyway, and pulled off the sheets as quickly as possible while keeping her head pulled back as if something sharp and evil would fly off of them. She wrapped the sheets in the blanket and carried the whole laundry-load-size ball into the living room. Frank was waiting by the broken door.

"Should we get rid of our fingerprints?" Allie asked. "In case he calls the police?"

"The advantage of dealing with dishonest, degenerate druggies," Frank said, "is that you never have to worry about them calling the police. Now move along." He put his hand on Allie's back and escorted her, like a bodyguard, along the rickety rail.

"Dad, what am I supposed to do with that gun you gave me?"

"Nothing. I'll teach you to use it as soon as we get a chance."

"What if it goes off and—"

"Allie! Forget about it. At the moment it's no more dangerous than your lucky rabbit foot."

Frank carried a jerking, jolting green-blanket-bound Vice Versa into the apartment, then into Mike's closet, where he dropped him. Allie watched the tiny blanketed man gyrating below the three hanging wetsuits and the polyester pale-blue tuxedo Mike must have bought to wear to someone's wedding.

Hans and Luis together carried Topher, wrapped in the soft blue sheets, up to the apartment. Like Vice Versa, Topher was squirming.

"Why don't you put him under the couch?" Allie suggested.

"It's not a bad idea," Jorge said. He went to one end of the couch, Allie went to the other, and they lifted it and moved it back a couple feet. Where the couch had been were dimes, pencils, a few Cheerios, and several floaty, cloud-like dust balls. Allie was somehow relieved to discover that Mike wasn't clean enough to vacuum under the couch.

Hans and Luis picked up either end of herky-jerky Topher and placed him on the dusty outline, then Allie and Jorge put the couch on top of him. Topher's body was bulky. The couch teetered forward. Frank looked down and shook his head.

"The bird!" Allie said, and she grabbed the throw blanket from the couch and ran down to the car. She opened the trunk and looked at the bird. It was stiff and boney, more like a contraption than an animal. "I'm sorry," she whispered, and then she wrapped the bird in the blanket and picked it up. It felt like a load of weighted, folded yardsticks—all angles, claws, and bones. The mucky, oceany smell reminded Allie of the six crates of rotten oysters once delivered to her father's restaurant at the end of the night and left to ferment until morning. Allie was thirteen that year and happy to spend her Saturday morning hanging out with the kitchen crew as they tried to Lysol away the stink.

Allie humped the heavy, jagged bird up the steps, where Hans was waiting for her, on the lookout. Back in the apartment, she placed the bird on the couch. She cranked out each wing. They opened like stiff shuttered doors on hinges. Allie tilted the bird's bald head up, so that its hook-nose beak looked menacing and ready to hammer down on something. Then she stood back and admired it. "I wish I had a camera," she said.

"I saw a camera in the bedroom," Hans said.

"Really?!" Allie ran off to the bedroom. Sure enough, a camera was sitting with some coins on top of Mike's plain wooden dresser. Allie grabbed it and returned to the bird. She clicked off four pictures, each one getting closer and closer to the bird's scabby head.

"Let me take a picture of you guys," Allie said, and Hans and Luis each took a step in, toward Frank. Jorge stood beside Hans and threw his arm around him. Hans threw his arm around Frank, and then Luis did, too. Allie snapped a couple of shots.

"Now you get in," Hans said, and he stepped out of the lineup and took the camera from Allie while she slipped in beside Frank. She put her arm around her father and could feel the tension in his back. Hans shot off a couple of photos.

"Now just Allie and her dad," Hans said, and he waved one arm so Luis and Jorge would move away.

"For goodness sakes," Frank said. "Do we really have time for this?"

"Come on, Dad," Allie said. "One quick shot."

Allie and Frank put their arms around each other, the bird on the tilted couch behind them, while Hans stood poised in front of them with the camera. He fiddled with the focus, turning the wheel around the lens in, and then out, and then in again.

"Let's hurry this up," Frank said.

"Smile, Dad," Allie said. "You can use this for the Christmas card next year."

Frank looked down at Allie and smiled just as Hans hit the button.

Allie and Frank were alone in the Prelude, following Jorge and Luis in the van.

They were on their way to Zuma beach, with a quick stopover at the hospital. Allie wanted to update Roger on their progress and Luis wanted to pick up the switchblade he had left tucked in the bag of Roger's personal goods. Everyone agreed that with the crowds at Zuma, a switchblade would be much stealthier than a pistol. Hans had stayed behind in Mike's apartment to guard the hostages and deal with Mike, were he to show up.

"You know I saw Mom in Santa Barbara," Allie said.

"I know," Frank said. "You told me. And that little turd showed you his private parts."

"Yeah, that's right, I forgot I told you." Allie wanted to laugh. She'd never heard her dad say "turd."

"How was your mom?" Frank looked out the window, as if he were checking out the scenery.

"She seems to have married that turd." Allie looked at her father, and he looked back for just a second before pointing at the road ahead of them.

"Change to the left lane," Frank said. "And put on your signal."

Allie did as she was told. There was silence in the Prelude for a minute, and then she said, "Dad, do you have nothing to say about the fact that Mom and that turd are married? I mean, you're not even divorced."

"We aren't divorced," Frank agreed. "We were never married."

"You never got married? Why didn't I know that?"

"No reason for you to know it. We didn't want you to feel ashamed," Frank said.

"I can't believe I'm just finding this out now," Allie said.

"We assumed you'd eventually figure it out. Have you ever heard about a wedding or seen a wedding picture? Get in the center of the lane. You're too close to the yellow line."

"Why didn't you ever get married?" Allie asked.

Frank took a deep breath, looked at Allie for a moment, then stared back out the window again. "Wai Po wouldn't let your mother marry me. She didn't like *the blacks*."

Allie could feel the conflicting truths shifting against each other like tectonic plates in her brain: Wai Po was a great woman, Wai Po was a racist. Allie felt older with this knowledge, saddened by it, but also enlightened. The *pretend you are white* instructions made even more sense now. "She always seemed to like me," Allie said.

"Oh yes, she loved you. She loved you more than she loved Penny."

"You don't think she loved Mom?"

"Your mother disappointed her. Wai Po gave up on her."

"Did Mom disappoint you?"

"A long, long time ago," Frank said. "But I'm over that now."

"So you don't care that she's married to the turd?"

"Nah." Frank smiled. "They deserve each other. Couple of twerps."

15

Allie stepped into the hospital room first, her father right behind her, Luis and Jorge behind Frank. Mike was sitting on the plastic mold-form chair next to Roger's bed, his arm tucked behind Roger's back as if he were almost holding him. Roger began trumpeting up and down, his pointer landing on the letter G. G for gun, Allie assumed.

"You must be Mike," Frank said, and Allie could feel the men positioning themselves around the room, circling in on Mike.

"What are you doing here?" Allie asked.

"Well, Lumpy, for one, I'm looking for my man Topher, who didn't show up at my house when he was supposed to. And, two, I want the name and address for your source."

"My source?" Allie asked. She kept her eyes strong on Mike's, as she could feel on the surface of her skin that her job now was to distract him long enough for someone to get to the gun that was being pressed into Roger's back.

"The coke, Lumpy. Where did you get that bag of coke?"

"Oakland, I told you."

"I want a name and an address. I want more of that coke." Mike's head bounced with emphasis.

"Don't you want Topher?"

"Do you have Topher? If you have him, I'll take him. But first I want your source."

"Okay, fine," Allie said, and she slouched on the end of Roger's bed. Everyone was quiet around her. "Do you have a piece of paper where I can write it down?"

Mike patted his left hand on his shorts, then looked toward his pocket for a slice of a second. And in that tiny moment, Frank dove on Mike, swiping him to the ground the way a bear might paw down a raccoon from a tree.

All was silent as everyone took in the scene: Frank's massive body completely covering a writhing Mike, Mike's gun lying menacingly on the floor near his head, Luis with his pistol out pointing at Mike, Jorge guarding the door, Allie on the bed, and Roger trumpeting in the air.

Allie called Beth's house while Mike's hands were being bound with the duct tape Jorge had retrieved from the van. His feet remained free so as not to draw any attention from the nurses or doctors.

The phone was picked up on the first ring. "Hello?" It was Jonas. Allie was surprised by how much his voice rattled her interior. She hung up. "Jonas," she said to the group.

Roger tapped on the C, then A-L-L.

"Call back?" Allie asked.

"I'll call back," Frank said, and he hit the intercom button so he wouldn't have to hold the receiver against his ear. Allie dialed.

"Jonas," Frank said, when Jonas answered the phone.

"Who the fuck is this?" Jonas said.

"It's Frank Dodgson." His voice was stern.

"Frank!" Jonas sounded jovial, friendly. "How's it goin', man?"

"Jonas, you didn't pay my daughter for the hours she served hawking garments in your shop. Additionally, you showed her your genitalia when you were supposed to be showing her how to run a business."

"She was showing me her bits and I was showing her mine. It was tit for tat, get it?" Jonas started laughing. "TIT for—" The idea that her father might find out that what Jonas was saying was more or less true made Allie feel like her blood was made of nails.

"Jonas, you are putting me in a mind to actually murder you," Frank said calmly.

"Yeah, yeah, you always were a thug, weren't you, Frank? Running off to hard-core-nasty-badass college—" Jonas interrupted himself with laughter. "Where's my man Vice Versa, anyway? Only took him, what? Five minutes to find you in L.A.!" Jonas laughed again.

"Vice Versa is resting comfortably in an apartment next to an In-N-Out Burger," Frank said.

"Topher's there, too," Allie added, looking at Mike.

"Are they in *my* apartment?" Mike asked and Luis waved the duct tape in front of his mouth. Mike rolled his eyes like he wasn't afraid of anything, even a man in a sport coat holding duct tape. But he did shut up.

"Now listen, Jonas," Frank said. "We are bringing back your bag of cocaine. You will take the bag and you will never contact my daughter again."

"Why don't you listen to me, Frank," Jonas said. "I have Allie's friend Beth with me, and if you aren't here at Beth's apartment with my coke in six hours, the girl will be dead. After I kill Beth, you have one more hour to show up here before I send my entire motherfucking fuck-you-up-army down there to kill your daughter. Then, if I still don't have my bag of coke, you're next. I don't give a fuck if we grew up three blocks apart. And I don't give a fuck if you and my brother were best friends. I SO don't give a fuck that I'd even seek out that chinky-chink so-called wife of yours and kill her, too, just for the fun of it."

Frank hung up the phone.

"He knows Mom?" Allie asked. Was there anything about her life that Jonas didn't already know?

"Everyone knows your mother." Frank's forehead held a deep vertical line of worry. His hairline glistened with sweat.

Roger trumpeted to get the room's attention, then began tapping out a long narrative about gangsters being all about hype and bravado. Before he could finish this thought, there was a knock and the door opened.

Two perfumed women walked in. They both had white-blond hair. One had dark brown skin. Allie found it hard to look away from their breasts: bulbous, shiny, protruding orbs bubbling out of open cardigans, then cantilevered over identical skin-tight, acid-washed jean shorts.

Luis approached the women and kissed each one on the cheek. "Allie, Frank," he said, "This is Jessie, also known as Juicy Blue, and this is Tracy, also known as Trixie Wallets."

Frank didn't say anything as he shook each girl's hand. He barely looked at them—it was clear his mind and energy were elsewhere. Mike, however, had his mouth hanging loose from its hinges like a kid with a stuffed-up nose. His boney, square chin followed the women's every movement: shaking Allie's hand, kissing Jorge on the cheek, and kissing Roger on the lips.

"You going to be working for Roger?" Jessie asked Allie. Her dark skin was dewy-looking. Allie could understand how people would want to touch her, look at her, rub against her.

"Oh, no!" Allie imagined herself as a squat rectangle compared to these long, linear creatures.

"But you're so pretty. Well, except for that bump. But it will go away, won't it?" Jessie asked.

"Allie is in school," Frank said sharply. "She'll be doing schoolwork and if she gets another job it will be in a library where she cannot get herself in trouble."

"I'm in school, too," Tracy said, in a whispery feather of a voice. She then peeled off her cardigan and dumped it on the counter with her purse. Jessie did the same. Together they climbed onto Roger's bed. Tracy straddled Roger's lap. Her long, shimmering calves reached almost to the end of the bed. Jessie sat by Roger's head with her tank-topped breasts jutting into his hanging cheeks. They chattered with him while stroking his shiny face.

Allie clicked her gaze back and forth between the women with Roger and her father. Frank was patting down Mike and removing everything from his pockets: car keys, a parking receipt from the hospital garage, five In-N-Out Burger receipts, some loose change, a tiny white shell with glittering pink nacre, and thirty-three dollars.

"You shouldn't eat so much In-N-Out," Frank said. "Not good for you."

"Hans says it's not even real food," Luis said. "But I think it's the best stuff out there."

"Now where's the coke," Frank said to Mike.

"You have coke?" Tracy asked.

"It's under the seat of my truck," Mike said. "You can fucking take it, just let me go."

"Where's the truck?" Frank asked.

"In the parking lot."

"Can we have some coke?" Jessie asked. No one answered except Roger, who was pointing out a word that Allie couldn't see through the noodle-limbed bodies on his bed.

"It's a red truck with a red toolbox attached to it," Allie said. "I can find it."

"What section are you parked in?" Frank asked.

"Three-B," Mike grunted.

Luis went with Allie to get the truck. They found it immediately. Allie opened the driver's-side door, then climbed in and unlocked the passenger door for Luis.

Luis leaned in and searched under the seat. "Got it," he said, pulling out a Wonder Bread bag.

Allie looked at it, tilted her head, and looked again. The smeared telephone number was there, a little more blurred now.

"Open it," Allie said.

"This shit'll mess you up," Luis said. "Look where it got you."

"I don't want to do it, I just want to see it," Allie said. "Make sure he didn't fill it up with something different."

Luis untwisted the twisty tie, opened the bag, and stuck in a delicate pinky. He pulled out a little white heap of powder.

"What do you think?" he asked.

"Looks right," Allie said. "Taste it."

"My brother would kill me if I tried this. He's Mister I'm So Pure I Only Eat Whole Grains." Luis lowered his voice to mimic Hans, although he sounded nothing like Hans. The girliness in his tone still pushed through.

"All those years with Roger and you guys never did coke? Doesn't he do it every night?"

"He does it every night. Man can't get a boner, he does so much coke."

"So he can get boners when he's not on coke? In his condition?"

"Oh yeah." Luis laughed. "You wouldn't believe what he can do in his condition."

They both looked down at the coke on Luis's fingertip. Allie thought of her father. She thought of Wai Po. Even though it *needed* to be checked, she would not disappoint them and be the one who checked it. Her coke days, or day rather, was entirely behind her. "Rub a bit on your gums and see if they go numb," she suggested.

"Why not," Luis said. "I'm sick of my goody-two-shoes brother." He rubbed the powder on his gums. They both sat quietly for a minute. Then Luis ran his tongue around the inside of his mouth. "It's numb," he said. "Like Novocain or something."

"Good," Allie said. "Can we not give any to the hookers? I really want to return the bag to Jonas with as little missing as possible." Allie started up the truck and pulled out of the parking space. It felt clunky and heavy compared to the Prelude.

"They're actresses, not hookers," Luis said.

"Sorry," Allie said, and she blushed, remembering that Luis's mother had been an actress, too.

"No problem," Luis said. "Common mistake."

They drove out of the parking lot and circled around to the hospital entrance.

Allie waited with the engine running while Luis went to gather the others. As Roger had pointed out in the hospital room, the shorter distance they had to transport Mike, the less likely they were to arouse suspicion.

Luis, Frank, Jorge, and Mike walked out of the hospital together. Mike was wearing a pink cardigan, buttoned at the neck and hanging over his shoulders cape-style to hide his hands taped behind his back. Tracy's sweater, Allie realized. Frank got in the cab while the others climbed into the bed of the truck, Mike wedged between Jorge and Luis, their backs against the toolbox. Allie carefully drove back into the parking lot to where the van and the Prelude were parked.

Allie and Frank got out of the truck and waited by the Prelude as Jorge and Luis wrangled Mike from the bed and brought
him to the car. Allie squeezed her lucky rabbit foot once, then
clicked the button on the car key and unlocked the trunk of the
Prelude. The smell of rotten bird and scared grown man darted
out like a bad wind.

"Gross," Mike said. "What do you keep in there?" Jorge and
Luis pushed him down into the trunk. Jorge held Mike's feet
while Luis wrapped a few layers of tape around his ankles. As a
final touch, Luis put one thick piece of tape over Mike's mouth,
and then he quietly shut the trunk. Allie turned in a full circle
to check if anyone had noticed them. There were brake lights
on, a few aisles away, too far for anyone to have seen.

"It really does smell in there," Jorge said.

"I guess the condor baked a little," Allie said. "It's been a
pretty sunny day."

"Decomposition is a fetid process," Frank said, and he took
the keys to the truck from Allie and handed them to Luis.

"Allie, if I don't see you again, take care," Luis said, and he
leaned in and hugged Allie.

"What do you mean *if I don't see you again?*" Allie pulled away
from the hug. "Why wouldn't I see you again?"

"We're going to pick up my brother and then head out to
Oakland to deal with your boss," Luis said.

"He's not her boss," Frank said to Luis. Then he turned to
Allie and said, "You go to Jorge and Consuela's and wait there for
me to get you."

"Consuela is making food for you right now, sweetheart,"
Jorge said. "I called her from Roger's room."

"Why are you taking the van *and* the truck?" Allie asked.
"Shouldn't you just leave Mike's truck here?"

"You know how it goes, sweetheart," Jorge said. "One of us might have to be at Beth's house while some of us go to Jonas's work or his house."

"Isn't Chez Panisse in Berkeley?" Luis asked. "My brother has been talking about going to Chez Panisse for years."

"It's right near Beth's house," Allie said. "But I want to go with you guys!"

"You're staying in Los Angeles," Frank said, and his voice was so forbidding that Luis and Jorge slinked away—Luis to the truck and Jorge to the van.

"I don't understand," Allie said to her dad. "What am I supposed to do with Mike? Why don't you drop him off at his apartment when you pick up Hans?"

"Some boys who work for Roger will get him at Consuela and Jorge's house. Now, I'll see you later." Frank got into the passenger side of the van. Allie followed him and knocked on the window, which her father rolled down.

"I don't know how to get to Consuela and Jorge's house." Allie wasn't sure if she could find her way back to any of the places she'd been the last couple of days.

"Oh, sweetheart, I forgot!" Jorge said. Frank turned in his seat and impatiently watched Jorge fish out a folded depression brochure from his back pocket. "I wrote down directions." Jorge handed Allie the brochure. His tidy, block handwriting was in the white margins.

"Dad, will you call me when you get to Oakland?" Allie asked. "Will you let me know when it's all worked out?"

"We'll call," Frank said. He pointed at the ignition key, as if to move things along. Jorge started the engine.

"But Dad," Allie said. "You never call. You never called me at school. And when I call you, you only sometimes answer the phone."

"Jorge will call the house," Frank said. "And I'll meet you there first thing tomorrow morning."

"Promise?" Allie asked.

"See you tomorrow, Allie." Frank adjusted the rearview mirror, then rolled up his window as the van pulled out of the lot. Luis followed in the truck. He gave a fluttery wave out the open window. Allie waved back and then, finally, got in the Prelude.

All this time, the past four days, Allie had been waiting, hoping, praying for someone—her mother, her father, Marc, her rabbit foot even!—to step in and save her from this quagmire. But now that she had gotten what she wanted, it didn't feel as good as she had imagined it would. In fact, Allie felt defeated and depleted. Maybe this was a sign, Allie thought, that she should grow up and clean up her own mess. Be her own guardian.

Allie sat up straight and held the depression pamphlet in the center of the steering wheel. The words looked scattered and abstract—a pile of pick-up sticks. Allie focused in. *Turn right after you come out of the parking lot,* she read. Allie drove out of the parking lot. And turned left.

16

S he only got lost once, and when she did, Allie pulled into a gas station, filled up the Prelude, and was re-pointed by a woman with a bandana tied around her neck the way a golden retriever might wear one.

Allie's heart beat faster when she finally saw a sign for the 405 to the 5. She figured that was the route her father and the others were taking. Depending on how long it took to pick up Hans, she was maybe ten minutes behind them. But she already had gas, and if she didn't stop to go to the bathroom and they *did*, Allie might be able to catch up.

Mike was silent most of the drive, but every now and then a barrage of bouncing thumps would erupt as if he were mule-kicking his bound feet against the inside top of the trunk. He gave a particularly startling kick just as Allie was accelerating into the fast lane of the 5. Allie turned on the radio as loud as she could take it in order to drown out the sounds of her prisoner.

The first three stations she hit were playing Mexican music. And then, on the fourth station, Allie heard Mighty Zamboni. The song was "Weency Willie," a ballad her mother and Jet had written together years ago about a tiny maimed boy who brings homemade potpies to a Native American tribe, which, in turn, brings peace between the tribe and the white townspeople. Jet always claimed Penny's voice wasn't strong enough to do anything but backup, so they hired Olivia Newton-John to sing the harmony and a couple of phrases on the song. Even as a little kid, Allie always wondered if the reason Jet wanted Olivia Newton-John instead of Penny was simply that he had a crush on her.

Allie listened to the song. Each time a spray of tambourine came on, she imagined her mother slapping that instrument against her hip, wearing the single-feather headband she liked to wear when they performed "Weency Willie." During concerts, of course, Olivia Newton-John was never there and Penny took the front-center of the stage beside Jet. Allie could barely tell the differences between the Olivia version and her mother's.

The song ended and a female DJ, whose voice reminded Allie of whispery Tracy, said, "Now there's a blast from the past! Mighty Zamboni singing 'Weency Willie' with Olivia Newton-John. One of my favorite Zamboni classics for sure. The Mighty Zamboni were here at the Hollywood Bowl just last week and will be performing at the Cow Palace in San Francisco tonight, opening for the amazing Billy Idol. Tickets are still available, so if you missed them in L.A., catch a People Express flight to San Francisco—fifty bucks round trip. I flew up last week for the Eddie Money concert—"

Allie punched the button back to Mexican radio. She thought of Consuela. Allie hoped Consuela wouldn't worry about her too much or wouldn't be angry that Allie wasn't there to eat the food she'd prepared. She'd hate to bring any bad feelings into that warm, peaceful household.

Six hours later, Allie was in Oakland, then Berkeley. Her intention was to go straight to Beth's, but, almost without meaning to, she bypassed the exit and instead went to Emeryville, where Marc lived. She drove past the mudflats, where artists, or anyone who claimed to be an artist, had constructed hundreds of sculptures made from trash, tires, wood, shingles, anything. Allie loved looking at the mudflats art. There was a sheet-metal-and-plank-wood woman rising up from the muck. She wore a pleated skirt of two-by-fours and looked as high as a house, her arms reaching toward the sky, head thrown back. Other sculptures stuck out haphazardly from the marshy, silty soil like aliens emerging from the ooze.

Marc hated the mudflats. He claimed the only reason he bought his loft in Emeryville was because one day the mudflats would be filled in, bulldozed, and developed, and then his piece of real estate would be worth as much as a place in San Francisco or the Berkeley hills.

Allie parked the Prelude in the lot outside Marc's building. Mike gave a resounding kick just as Allie was walking away from the car. Allie went to the trunk and slammed her fist onto it, then glanced around to see if anyone had seen. There were two guys getting into a car three spaces away, but they didn't even turn their heads.

The *Trapper John, M.D.* theme song was playing behind Marc's door. *Trapper John* was his favorite show; he wouldn't go out on Sunday night until after it was over.

Allie knocked three times. The volume on the TV went down. Seconds later, Marc was standing in front of Allie. He stepped into the doorway and pulled the door back against himself, as if he didn't want Allie to peek in.

"Hey!" Marc said, with more cheer than was natural for him. His face seemed to redden slightly. Allie could see his eyes focusing on the lump on her forehead.

"Hey," Allie said.

"What happened to your head?"

"Can I come in?" Allie tried to peer over his massive shoulders but Marc stepped out into the hall and firmly shut the door.

"I kinda have someone over," he said.

"Oh." Allie felt a small punch in her gut. "I don't care," she lied.

"You don't care?"

"No. I don't," Allie said, even as the punch expanded into an open palm trying to find its way out of her body.

"So, we're, like, friends?" Marc asked.

"Something like that," Allie said. "You owe me money. You need to pay me back."

"Yeah, did Beth tell you I called? I sold the bar but—"

"Let's not talk about it out here," Allie said, and she pushed past Marc, opened the door, and slid inside.

On the couch was a tiny girl with long blond hair and enormous brown eyes. She looked like a puppet or a doll. Allie thought she was beautiful, and this made the feeling in her gut even worse.

"Hey," Allie said.

"Hey!" the girl stood, went to the TV, and turned it off. She was wearing a red dress and red pumps, as if she had an event to go to. Marc was in jeans and a green T-shirt that had a hole at the corner of the breast pocket. Together they looked like Barbie and an underdressed Ken.

"Cute dress," Allie said, eying the girl's impossibly tiny waist.

"Regan, this is Allie. Allie, Regan." Marc spoke as if he wanted to get this meeting over with. "So what's up with your forehead?" he asked Allie.

"Something fell on me," Allie said, fingering the lump. The true story sounded too unbelievable to be told. Allie sat on the couch. Regan sat, too.

"Must have hurt," Regan said.

"Are you Reagan spelled like our president?" Allie asked.

"No, Regan like in *The Exorcist*."

"Oh," Allie said. "Never saw it."

"Seriously?" Marc asked. He was still standing. "Who hasn't seen *The Exorcist?*"

"Me," Allie said. "My dad wouldn't let me go."

"What about your mom?" Regan asked.

Marc laughed. "Allie's mom is a head case!" Allie wanted to pick up the blown-glass plate on his coffee table and discus-throw it toward his neck. Yes, Penny was a head case, but that was for Allie to say, not Marc. And how had Marc come to that conclusion anyway? Allie had told him only two facts about her mother: (1) tambourine girl, (2) lived in no specific place (obviously, because she traveled with the band).

"She's Chinese," Allie said. "Chinese people don't see those kind of movies." Allie had no idea why she said that. It was entirely untrue.

"Your mom's Chinese?" Marc asked. "How come you never told me?"

"Wow," Regan said. "I had no idea the Chinese were like that."

"I need your help," Allie said to Marc. "I need you to pay me back the money you owe me, so I can pay my rent."

"How much do you owe her?" Regan asked.

"Not much," Marc said to her. He turned back to Allie. "How come you don't look Chinese?"

"I just don't," Allie said. "So if it's not much to you, can you give me a check now?"

"Well, how much is it?" Regan asked.

"Seven thousand dollars," Allie said.

"Seven thousand dollars!" Regan whipped her head toward Marc. "You didn't tell me you owed seven thousand dollars!"

"I have it!" Marc said. "It's not a problem!"

"Not a problem for you!" Regan said.

"Why is it a problem for you?" Allie asked.

"We moved in together," Regan said. "I live here now. We're getting a joint checking account."

For a second, Allie felt like she had to vomit. Then she blinked, changed the channel in her head, and looked down at Regan, in her little red dress and high-heeled shoes. "Is this how you dress when you're just hanging around the house?"

"No!" Regan said. "I sell cosmetics at I. Magnin in the city. I went out with friends after work and just got home."

"Oh. Cool." Allie had always wanted to work in San Francisco. It seemed glamorous and grown-up.

"Where are you getting seven thousand dollars?" Regan asked Marc.

"I have it from the sale of the bar," Marc said.

"But I thought that was going into our joint savings?!" Regan's voice sounded stretched and taut.

"I'm about to get kicked out of school for not paying tuition and I was evicted from my apartment because I couldn't pay rent," Allie said to Regan. "He's owed me this money since December."

"So where are you living?" Regan asked.

"In a car, lately," Allie said. "How long have you two been dating?"

"It's been a while now," Regan said.

"Six months," Marc said.

"It hasn't been six months!" Regan said. "More like two years!"

"You've been dating for two years?" A fire burned behind Allie's eyelids and spread down her spine.

"Well, let's see, I had just started at I. Magnin's and he was still in school then so, yeah, I guess it was two years last month." Regan looked up at Marc.

Allie stared at Marc, too. Marc turned his head away. Allie could feel things shifting in her mind. It was like her thoughts about Marc had been tilted at the wrong angle and her brain was suddenly, desperately, trying to refit these thoughts into the right place. Marc had been with Regan the entire time he was dating Allie. No wonder his schedule had been so limited. They never saw each other more than two nights in a single week, Marc always claimed he had work obligations. And often they'd go days without speaking as Marc would leave messages for Allie with Beth, and Allie would call back to a phone that was never answered. While she had been living in a fantasy, he had been juggling two realities. Even her love for him had been a fantasy—no more based on a truth than her love for John Travolta in *Saturday Night Fever*. Allie had the same feeling she'd had as a kid, when her father showed her a series of optical illusions, one of which was a picture of an old woman hidden in the picture of a young woman. Once the old woman had been revealed, Allie was unable not to see her.

"Give me the check now," Allie said. "I need the money now." Her voice was like stone, like Frank's voice when he had said that Allie wouldn't be working for Roger.

Marc went into the other room. Regan looked at Allie. "I'm sorry," she said. "I didn't know he owed money."

"Not your fault," Allie said. She looked around the room as if waiting for something to happen, a light show on the walls, or fireworks out the window, anything to distract her from having to make conversation. Out of the corner of her eye she could see Regan doing the same.

Marc returned and held out a check. Allie took it and tucked it deep into her jeans pocket. "I need you to help me with something in my trunk," she told Marc. "Consider it the interest you owe me."

"It's the least you could do, Marc," Regan said, and Allie could tell from her voice that he was going to have a rough few hours with her tonight. She was tiny. And very blond. But Allie could see how fierce she was. Allie was going to take that from her, carry it with her like a contagious disease. Allie was going to be fierce, too.

"Come on," Allie said, and she walked toward the door. Marc followed behind.

"Isn't that Beth's car?" Marc asked, as they approached the Prelude.

"Yup. She's CAL GIRL, not me."

"She's a cowgirl?"

"CAL GIRL. The license plate. Haven't you ever noticed it?" Thirty minutes ago Allie would have been shocked that Marc hadn't ever noticed Beth's license plate, but now that she knew about Regan she figured Marc had probably always had a lot on his mind when he was around Allie, and therefore Beth and Beth's Prelude.

Marc leaned back and looked at the license plate. "Could be call girl, too," he said.

"Yeah, whatever," Allie said. She clicked the unlock button. "Get in. This will only take a minute."

"What?" Marc stood at the door.

"I need you to dump the thing in my trunk into the mudflats."

Marc laughed and got in the car. "What? Did you make a sculpture? Express yourself?"

"Yeah," Allie said. She started the Prelude and rolled out of the parking lot. "I expressed myself. It's a sculpture of you."

"Me? Seriously?"

"No. But it represents you. It's an artist's rendering of you."

"And you're the artist?" Marc was smirking. Allie ignored him.

It only took three minutes to get to the mudflats. Allie parked the car along the desolate road. The sculptures were eerie in the moonlit darkness. Giant phantoms frozen, halted, standing by.

Allie walked to the back of the car and waited for Marc. When he came around to the trunk, she popped it open.

Marc jumped back. "What the fuck?!"

"That's the other guy who owed me money," Allie said. "Help me get him out."

Mike, with his taped-shut mouth, looked defeated. He stared quietly at Allie and Marc. Allie bent closer to him and he blinked. Even though Mike had been nothing but mean, racist, and downright dangerous, Allie was happy he hadn't suffocated.

"We're setting you free here," Allie said to Mike.

Mike blinked. Allie could feel his gratitude in the flicker.

"This is fucked up," Marc said. He was standing beside the trunk, running both hands through his thick hair, his eyes marbled out, mouth open.

"It's reality," Allie said. "Deal with it."

"Deal with it?! I could end up in jail!"

"This guy is a coke thief and dealer," Allie said. "He won't call the police. He won't know where to find you. He doesn't even know where he is."

Mike blinked rapidly as if to agree.

"That fucking trunk stinks!" Marc said. "Did he shit his pants?! I'm not going near some dude who shit his pants."

"There was a dead bird back here," Allie said. "It isn't the dude. I swear." Allie went to Mike's feet, took off his flip-flops, threw them into the trunk, and picked up Mike's bound ankles. "Get his upper body," she said to Marc.

"Fuuuuck!" Marc said.

"Listen!" Allie said. "If you don't help me, I'm going to go back to Regan and tell her everything that happened between us. Also, I'm going to give this guy your name, address, and place of work and if Regan hasn't killed you already, he will. So get his upper body *now*."

Marc shot Allie a look she'd never seen. Slit eyes, hard mouth. It was the kind of look that made Allie glad their relationship was over. He took Mike's upper body and together they hoisted Mike out of the trunk.

"Over there." Allie nodded with her head toward the giant metal-and-wood woman with the plank-pleated skirt.

Marc moved faster than Allie. She had to hurry her steps to catch up. It was hard to walk in high heels in the soft, squirmy soil, and Mike was heavier than she would have imagined. When they reached the plank-skirted woman, Allie let Mike's feet drop. Marc abruptly placed the rest of him down.

"Also," Allie said, patting her jeans pocket, "if this check's no good, same deal: I tell Regan and I send Mr. Hitman after you."

"Oh, please." Marc rolled his eyes as if Allie were being childish.

"Please what?" Allie said.

"Would I give you a bad check?! You know me better than that!"

"Yeah," Allie said. "I know you, and now I know that you would give me a bad check. And I also know that I could send someone mean and dangerous after you."

Marc shook his head as if he were dealing with a ridiculous, paranoid, and jealous lover.

"Let's go," Allie said, and she turned and walked toward the car, glancing back once at Mike. He had rolled to his side and was watching them. Allie figured he'd be okay for the night. Fresh air, soft dew. By morning, someone would see him and undo the binds. Probably a homeless person. There were a couple of tent cities nearby.

Allie opened the door and got into the Prelude. Marc got in, too.

"Did I ever tell you I'm black?" Allie asked.

"You just told me your mother's Chinese."

"And my dad's black."

"You don't look like either of those things," Marc said.

"So what?" Allie said.

"Yeah, so what," Marc said. "Why are you telling me this now?"

"I don't know," Allie said. "Just trying to be real. Be genuine, you know."

"What-the-fuck-ever," Marc said.

Marc looked out the window for the entire ride to his loft. When they pulled into the parking lot, he got out of the car without saying a word. Allie pushed the button and let the window glide down.

"Hey Marc!" she called out. Marc looked back with his head dropped at an angle, as if he just couldn't give her his full attention. Allie reached into her purse, pulled out the tiny bong she'd been carrying around for months, and threw it out the window. It bounced slightly on the blacktop.

"What is that?" Marc asked. He didn't move toward it.

"Your favorite bong that you left at my apartment," Allie said.

"You can keep it," Marc said, and he turned and walked into the building.

Allie drove the car slowly over the bong until it made a satisfying pop. She backed up, then drove forward once more just to make sure it was entirely smashed.

17

Mike's truck was parked in front of Beth's apartment, under a glaring streetlight, next to a fire hydrant. Allie guessed no one cared if it were towed. The van was parked in a too-short spot—the front wheels and bumper jutted into a private driveway. Marc once told Allie that he would never live in Berkeley, because there were only three parking places for every four cars. Apparently, Jorge had grown frustrated looking for a right-size spot.

There was a coded keypad to lift the long, yellow, wooden arm to the garage of Beth's apartment. Allie punched in 1122, the code she had memorized when driving Beth's car home for her after Beth had had too much to drink, or had done too much coke, or just didn't feel like driving.

So little time had passed since Allie had driven out of the garage, but she felt like a different version of herself: a little dirtier, a bit more feral. She parked slowly, gingerly, looking all around to make sure no one with a weapon was waiting. Once all seemed clear, she got out of the car and opened the trunk with the key button. Better let it air out before Beth drove again.

Allie took off her Candie's and dropped them into the trunk next to Mike's flip-flops. If she had to run, it would be easier barefoot. She put the rabbit-foot key chain into her purse, then strapped the purse across her chest so it wouldn't slip off her shoulder. As she walked up the exterior staircase in the courtyard, Allie was aware of how quiet she was. She remembered studying Indians in elementary school, before they were called

Native Americans. Her class had taken a barefoot walk along a hard dirt path in a city park. They were supposed to see if they could be as quiet as Indians who were hunting bears, or cougars, or bobcats, all of which still roamed the mountains edging California.

The door to Beth's apartment was locked. Allie leaned her head in close and tried to listen to what was going on. All she heard was music, Pat Benatar, loud. This was a good sign. Beth loved Pat Benatar. She wanted to *be* Pat Benatar.

The next-door neighbor, a slim man wearing an Izod Lacoste shirt and white shorts, came out of his apartment with a leashed, fuzzy dog. One tooth jutted up toward the dog's nose and its eyes were like giant gooey marbles. It was one of the ugliest creatures Allie had ever seen. The dog began circling the man in a cartoonish way. Allie smiled.

"I showed her *101 Dalmatians*," the guy said, "and she's been practicing this move ever since!" He smiled with teeth that were long, like planks. He hadn't locked the door behind him, Allie noticed.

"You really took her to the movies?" Allie asked.

"I'm kidding," the man said, and he stepped out of the leash lasso, untangled it, then picked up the dog.

"Have a nice walk," Allie said.

"If she'll walk," he said. "She likes to be carried half the way."

Allie leaned in toward her purse and pretended to look for something while she watched him go down the hall and descend the tile steps. Once he was out of sight, she opened his apartment door. She suspected she didn't have a lot of time.

The apartment was dark and crowded with thick Persian rugs and gold-framed pictures covering all the wall space. It felt like an old woman's home, but the layout was the same as Beth's.

Allie raced straight to where she knew the balcony would be and stepped outside. She surveyed the three feet of black air between where she stood and Beth's balcony. There were no streetlights in the back and no one had their patio light on, so it was too dark to see what was below her.

Allie climbed onto the thin wrought-iron rail, holding herself steady with both hands against the stucco wall. She reached one bare foot out toward Beth's rail and touched down. Just then she heard a noise from inside the man's apartment. He was back.

Allie stayed where she was, splayed like a starfish with one foot on either balcony. The man was chatting to his dog, telling it about a play he was working on. The dog slipped outside and looked at Allie with its runny eyes. She felt sorry for it.

"Where'd you go?" the man said, and he reached down and plucked up the dog without noticing Allie splattered against the wall. He went inside and shut the door most of the way. If she could look at herself in a mirror, Allie thought, she just might be able to see the movement of her heart as it clanged in her chest.

And with the power of that fear, Allie heaved herself off the rail and tumbled silently onto the hard terra-cotta tile on Beth's balcony. She lay on the ground for a moment, waiting for her heartbeat to slow, and made a quick inventory of her body. She might have a few bruises and scrapes but nothing felt broken or sprained.

Allie scooted to the French doors, staying low to the ground. The lights were on inside, so she could see directly into the kitchen. "Hell Is for Children" was playing. That was Beth's least favorite Pat Benatar song, it depressed her, and she always skipped it if she were near the stereo. Allie waited for the song to stop, a sign that Beth was in the living room, moving the needle to "Little Paradise."

But "Hell Is for Children" continued. Allie reached an arm up, opened one of the doors, and crawled in along the floor. Thumping-loud music crowded the apartment. The sweet smell of fried bacon made the space feel even more closed-in.

Allie scooted toward the living room, hiding herself behind the kitchen counter. She poked her head around and looked into the room. What she saw next seemed so odd that at first her brain couldn't quite process what was there: Frank and Jonas were side-by-side on the couch with Hans and Luis on either side of them, also on the couch. Jorge was in a floral wing chair pulled up to the round glass coffee table. An enormous man sat in the other wing chair—Beth was on the floor, nestled in the nook between his tree-trunk legs. His hand was on her head and he stroked her hair, pulling out long, brown hunks of it that he slid between his fingers as if he were running his palm through water. Allie assumed this was Rosie.

They seemed to be playing Scrabble. There were a few beer bottles and four mostly empty plates on the coffee table. One plate had bread crusts on it. Beth must have made bacon sandwiches. It was what she always made late at night, the thing she craved when she had been drinking. Jonas was speaking, but Allie couldn't hear anything over the music. Beth was smiling, and then they were all laughing. Even Frank, who only seemed to laugh at movies like *Animal House*, which Allie saw with him when she was fifteen.

Allie sensed someone behind her. She flipped around as quickly as a cat and looked up. Lionel, her father's old friend, was standing in the kitchen staring down at her with a grin like a lemon slice sitting across his face. "Allie, what are you doing down there?" Lionel reached a hand toward Allie as if to pull her up. Allie motioned for him to come to her.

Lionel laughed and went down on all fours beside Allie. "What happened to your head?" he asked.

"It's nothing," Allie said. "But is your brother going to kill me?"

"Nah, everything's been worked out," Lionel said, and he stood up and waved his hand in a come-hither motion. "Don't worry. I'm the older one. Jonas is afraid of me."

Allie stood and looked over the counter. No one noticed her. Everyone was staring intently at the board. She followed Lionel into the living room.

Beth looked up, leaped out from between Rosie's legs, and ran to Allie. "Oh my god!" she said, hugging Allie for a moment, before pulling her head back and shouting, "Like, what's up with that gnarly lump?!"

Jonas got up and turned off the music. Everyone stared at Allie.

"Allie," Frank said. He was holding a Scrabble tile in his hand. "What are you doing here? And where are your shoes?"

"I better call Consuela! She's probably worrying about why you haven't shown up!" Jorge got up and went to the phone in the kitchen.

"So you guys didn't already call me like you said you would?" Allie asked. She was hurt that they hadn't followed through on the promise.

"We only got here thirty minutes ago." Frank's thick brow was furrowed into angry rolling ridges. "Now please explain yourself!"

"I just—" Allie didn't know what to say. Everything seemed fine. What *was* she doing?

"I'm so excited I got to meet your dad!" Beth said. "But wait, seriously, what happened to your head?!"

"Can we go to Chez Panisse now?" Hans asked.

"Chez Panisse?" Jonas laughed. "You think you can drive up here from Los Angeles and just show up at Chez Panisse!"

Lionel and Frank immediately fell into what sounded like an old discussion about Chez Panisse. Frank had strong ideas about prix fixe menus and prices that came close to rent.

"Is this game over?" Luis said. "We've only got shitty vowels and no consonants. I want out."

"Are you playing teams?" Allie asked.

"Girl, you are lucky your father got you out of this mess," Jonas said. "Dang, you took me for a ride! And capturing my man, Vice Versa, like that? Dang! Did he do that shit to your forehead?"

"Oh my god, Allie, this is Rosie!" Beth pointed to the basement-freezer-size man. "Oh my god, you guys are, like, so going to love each other?"

Rosie hoisted himself up as if a crane were pulling him from his spine. Allie shook his hand. He had a sweet smile. Gentle golden-brown eyes. Beth was probably right about him being a good guy.

Allie leaned in close to Rosie and Beth so the others couldn't hear, although no one appeared to be listening. (Jonas had joined the Chez Panisse discussion with Lionel and Frank—the three of them sounded like tired old roosters—and Jorge was on the phone with Consuela. Hans and Luis were still studying the Scrabble board.)

"So since Vice Versa was in L.A. the whole time," Allie said, "did you both know that that guy you had put on the phone with me wasn't the real Vice Versa?" This question had been picking at Allie like a too-deep splinter since the moment she met Vice Versa in her father's closet.

"I must apologize to you for that," Rosie said. "I was misled by you-know-who and I believed him. As soon as I have caught up on my sleep and have completely sobered up I'm going to re-evaluate my relationship with—" Rosie nudged his head in the direction of Jonas.

"We were, like, so high for so many days? And I think we were a little vulnerable and stupid?" Beth said.

"Okay, this game is officially over," Luis said loudly, turning the attention toward the coffee table. He dumped his tiles on the board.

"Fine, fine, fine," Jonas groaned. "All I wanted was one quick game before you took off. Seemed like the least you could do to pay me back for my troubles."

"He's been, like, trying to get us to play the last two days and, like, no one has wanted to play?" Beth said. "I told him that you were the best at Scrabble, Allie."

Jorge hung up the phone on the kitchen counter, then said, "*Vamos!* I've got to get back to my family." Everyone was standing and shifting. It was like the end of a party with people patting their pockets for their keys, saying good-bye, wrapping up.

Hans, Luis, and Jorge took off in the van for Los Angeles. Hans had been promised that they would stop somewhere for food but it'd have to be a twenty-four-hour place as it was already ten p.m. Jonas left with the bag of coke and less the money he owed Allie (Lionel had insisted that Jonas not deduct from Allie's paycheck the money she earned from selling the coke or money owed for coke that was missing from the bag). Lionel left, too. Frank and Allie planned to stay with him tonight and he was on his way to the grocery store so that there would be food for his guests for breakfast tomorrow. It was just Allie, Frank, Beth, and Rosie, sitting at Beth's counter. Allie told them how she got the lump on her head, what had happened with Marc, and where she'd dumped Mike.

"That is, like, the best bad-boyfriend revenge ever!" Beth said.

Frank stood, took Allie's arm, and helped her off the stool. "Let's not make Lionel wait up for us all night."

"Why don't you take my car," Beth said, "instead of that nasty surfer dude's truck."

"I think we'll take you up on that offer," Frank said.

"Just take the car key off, though and leave my house keys? Allie, do you realize I couldn't leave the apartment for four days because my house keys are, like, on the set of keys I gave you?"

"Weren't you being held hostage anyway?" Allie asked.

"Only for a few hours," Rosie said, and he leaned down and kissed Beth on the top of her head.

Allie pulled out the ring of keys. She was tired and bleary-eyed and couldn't manage to get the key off.

"Let me have that," Frank said, and he worked it off in a few seconds, then handed the key ring to Beth and whisked Allie out of there.

18

rank was driving and Allie was looking out the window. She was wearing the Candie's again as Frank did not believe that people should ever go barefoot. Just as they approached the end of Beth's street, Allie remembered her battered, once-white rabbit foot.

"Dad," Allie said, "we have to go back to Beth's. I left my lucky rabbit foot on Beth's keychain."

"You are twenty years old," Frank said. "You can go one night without your rabbit foot." Frank turned the wheel hand over hand as he had shown Allie earlier.

"I know it's stupid, and I know it probably doesn't really bring me luck. But I haven't gone a night without it since the day Wai Po gave it to me."

"Don't bother me with this nonsense." Frank's brow lowered over his eyes like an awning. In his repertoire of expressions, this was the one that usually preceded anger.

"Dad, please," Allie said. "I've always thought of it as a way to have Wai Po with me. I mean, Mom's been gone forever and you're always at work."

Frank pulled over. His face looked dark and shadowy. Each time a car drove by, a sheet of light passed over his eyes like a mask.

"Listen up," Frank said, his voice as steely as a gun. "I'll go back, but you have to promise me there will be no more of this *poor me* business ever again. Yes, your mother left, yes, I spend most of my time at work. But we're alive, you're healthy, and you're going to cash Marc's and Jonas's checks and pay your tuition tomorrow morning. If you don't mess up like this again, there'll be a great big future waiting for you when you're done with school."

"Okay," Allie said. "No more poor me."

Frank pulled the car out from the curb, slowly turned around, and drove back to Beth's apartment building. He parked in the private driveway next door. Allie and Frank watched out the window as an acne-stricken, skinny man hooked up Mike's truck to a towing wench.

"Oops," Allie said, and she laughed.

"You know, I should get those tools out of that toolbox before he drags that thing away," Frank said.

"You want Mike's tools?" Allie asked.

"Tools are expensive," Frank said. "And if I don't take them out of there now, you can pretty much guarantee someone in the tow yard will take them before they ever track down that slimy no-goodnik surfer."

Frank clicked on the hazards. He and Allie both got out of the car.

"Don't leave your purse," Frank said.

"But you're right here and you can lock the car," Allie said.

"Anyone can break a window," Frank said. "Take the darn purse."

Allie reached into the car, got the purse, and strapped it across her body.

"Hurry back," Frank said, as he walked toward the tow truck, the keys to Mike's truck in his hands.

Just as Allie reached Beth's door, she heard heavy footsteps behind her.

Allie turned and there was Jonas, smiling.

"Did you forget something?" Allie asked.

"Sure as hell did." Jonas yanked Allie toward himself, his elbow wrapped around her neck, one hand over her mouth. Allie kicked her legs up and around but couldn't land them against anything that made noise.

"Who the fuck do you think I am?" Jonas whispered. "You think I don't know the difference between pure coke, which is what you drove away from here with, and small-time-corner-dealer-shit that's half-laxatives?" Jonas was spitting, hissing. Allie expected burning oil to flicker out of his pores.

Jonas dragged Allie backward down the hallway. He pulled her past the stairway that led to the front of the building where Frank was. Allie thrashed her legs under Jonas's grip. She was terrified. But even more than that, she was infuriated. Allie had survived so much the past four days that to lose it all now seemed simply wrong. With one giant surge, Allie put every bit of her might into pushing Jonas off herself.

And then Allie came to. She was in Jonas's tiny, teardrop-shaped, red convertible, zooming across the Bay Bridge. The cold wind was whipping Allie's hair into a wiry frenzy.

"You're alive!" Jonas said, and he laughed.

Allie touched her neck. It felt as if barbed wire had been run down her throat, then swirled against her tendons. "Did you knock me out?" She felt nauseous, dazed, boneless. There was no energy left for fear.

"You knocked yourself out against the crook of my arm. Time for you to take responsibility for your actions, girl!"

"Where are we going?" It hurt to talk. Allie could feel each individual vocal cord.

"My motherfucking big-brother's house."

"Why?"

"Because the stupid-ass-do-good-cocksucking piece-of-shit-fuck got me into this bullshit. I wanted my men to handle things the way they should be handled. But no, Lionel jumps in and thinks he can make peace between you, me, and Frank. And what the fuck did that get me?!" Jonas looked at Allie.

"What?" Allie asked, because that's what it seemed he was pausing for.

"A fucking bread bag full of laxatives!" Jonas thumped his fist in the center of the steering wheel.

"I thought that was the real coke," Allie said. "I swear." Her purse was still strapped across her shoulder. Allie shifted it in her lap, looked down, and remembered the gun.

The exit for Yerba Buena, a tiny island that connected the two sides of the Bay Bridge, was approaching. Without putting any more thought into it, Allie stuck her hand into her purse and pulled out the gun. She pushed it into the side of Jonas's round head. The wind blew Allie's curls into her eyes, she could barely see, but she could feel Jonas's flesh pressing into the tip of the pistol.

"The fuck!" Jonas said. "Put that thing down!"

"Pull onto the island or I shoot," Allie said. It was a left exit and they already were in the left lane.

Jonas put on his blinker and pulled onto the island. "You know you're in a convertible and people can see you with that gun? Or are you suffering brain damage from when I knocked you out?!" Jonas laughed, but it was restrained.

"I thought you said I knocked myself out," Allie said. "Drive to the top."

The island was woodsy and wild with thick towering trees and giant, craggy boulders. There was a Coast Guard station somewhere, but Allie had never seen it the few times she'd gone to Yerba Buena with friends. As far as she knew, she could fire the gun and no one would hear. If she actually had the nerve to fire the gun. Allie put her left hand under her right upper arm to steady her aim. Reality was rushing up her body and she could feel a shake coming on.

"Park over there," Allie said. They had reached the hilly peak of the island. Black water filled the view with the glittery outline of San Francisco in the distance.

Jonas parked.

"Give me the keys," Allie said.

"Give it up, Allie," Jonas said, but he didn't turn his head. "You know you're too afraid to shoot that thing."

The funny thing was, Allie *was* too afraid to shoot it. But because Jonas didn't turn his head, didn't laugh or mock her, Allie knew that he wasn't certain of this fact. And this small amount of faith that Jonas had in Allie's badass abilities gave her the courage it took to maintain the gun against Jonas's head.

"Hand me the keys, open the door, and get out slowly," Allie said. "I'm coming out right beside you."

Jonas put the keys in Allie's left hand; she shoved them down her front pocket without moving her eyes from the point on his head where the gun rested. Carefully, she climbed over the driver's seat and got out of the car beside Jonas. The wind was whipping around as much as when they were driving in the convertible. Hair was in Allie's mouth, eyes, nose.

"Stand against that rock and face me," Allie said.

Jonas walked to a massive rock wall, turned, and faced Allie. "Can we stop this bullshit? You put down the gun and I won't kick your fucking ass for giving me that shitty-ass laxative-cut shit."

"I didn't know it wasn't the real stuff," Allie said. "Now show me your tits."

"What?" Jonas laughed, just a little.

"Show me your tits." Allie steadied her arm again and peered down the nose of the gun.

"Are you fucking serious?!"

"JONAS!" Allie yelled, and she could feel everything pouring out of her: shame, fear, fury. "TAKE OFF YOUR SHIRT AND SHOW ME YOUR TITS!" Her throat throbbed from the force, but it was a good throb, like a heartbeat that was keeping her alive.

Jonas unbuttoned his dress shirt and took it off. He lifted up his undershirt and took that off, too. He looked at Allie, smiling. "Wanna see my dick now?"

"Yup," Allie said. "Take off your pants, your shoes, everything."

"It's cold out here with this wind," Jonas said, "so the size thing isn't going to be happening."

"Take it all off," Allie said, nudging the gun in a sideways motion.

Jonas lifted his feet, one at a time, and removed his burgundy dress shoes. He took off his slacks and folded them on top of the shoes. He removed his underpants and held them in his hands in front of his crotch. All that remained were his burgundy dress socks.

"Don't you want me to see it?" Allie asked.

"I told you, girl, it's cold out here!" Jonas's voice was stretched and strained.

"Grab your bundle of clothes and throw them down the hill," Allie said, and she waved the gun to the right as if to point in the direction of the hill.

"They're not going to land in the water. Too many damn trees and rocks on this slope for that." Jonas bent over, picked up the bundle, and held it all against his crotch.

"Just throw them as hard as you can," Allie said, and he did. It was too dark out to see how far they went but Allie heard his shoes clattering on the way down.

"Now what?" Jonas asked. "You finally going to do the dirty with me?" Jonas grinned in a forced way.

"Get in the street and start running." Allie pointed with the gun toward the road they'd come up.

"Run?" Jonas asked. "Girl, I don't run. I strut."

"Jonas, FUCKING RUN!" Allie hollered and Jonas took off. "RUN, RUN, RUN!" she screamed until her stretched voice crackled into silence and she could no longer make out Jonas's form on the dimly lit street.

Allie got in Jonas's car, started up the engine, and drove in the opposite direction. She needed to come out of the island driving toward Oakland, not San Francisco. She placed the gun on her lap then cruised down the hill as rapidly as she could without crashing into any looming redwoods or jutting rocks.

Just before the exit off the island there was a culvert with a roaring flow of water. Allie stopped, shifted into neutral, pulled up the emergency brake, and got out of the car. She dangled the gun over the water, then let it drop. Allie got back in the car, released the emergency brake, shifted into first, and pressed the toe of her pointy high heel onto the gas pedal. But instead of accelerating, the convertible sputtered and lurched. Allie looked down at the circular dials in the dashboard. The car was out of gas.

19

There are few places more difficult to catch a ride than in the middle of the Bay Bridge. But Allie was trying. Her thumb was out, her purse was strapped across her chest, the wind was slapping her face so hard that she could feel the pressure on her forehead lump.

A tiny silver Honda pulled over in the nook where the road from the island merged onto the bridge. If the car had been any bigger it wouldn't have fit. Two guys were in the front seat. They each wore a baseball cap. The driver had a blond mustache. *Trouble*, Allie thought. She approached the car. The window was down.

"Where you goin'?" the guy asked. He looked to be in his twenties. A knot of muscle bulged from his upper arm.

"North Berkeley," Allie said.

"Us, too," he said. "I'm Mike."

Allie looked from the driver to his friend. The friend nodded his chin upward. "I'm Mark," he said.

"Mike and Mark?" Allie asked. "Seriously?" Allie felt like she was hallucinating again. How could it be that the only people who pulled over to give her a ride had the same names as two people who had created tremendous trouble for her?

"Get in, we'll take you," Mike said. Allie didn't move. She stared from Mike to Mark and back again. She remembered Wai Po saying, *DEEP DOUBT, DEEP WISDOM; LITTLE DOUBT, LITTLE WISDOM.* Allie's doubts were enormous. She wished there were some magic light that appeared on people's foreheads that would tell you if they were good or not so good.

"We're safe," Mark said.

"I can't tell you how bad my judgment's been lately," Allie said.

"Well if you were my daughter," Mike said, "I'd tell you to stay away from two jocky-looking guys in a Honda. So, I totally understand if you don't want to get in."

"Yeah," Allie said. "You look nice but I think I better stick to, I don't know, old women with gray hair driving '63 Cadillacs or something."

"Totally get it," Mike said, and he removed his baseball cap and ran his hands through his thick blond hair.

"Thanks anyway," Allie said, and she took a step back from the window.

"Do you want us to wait here with you until you get a proper ride?" Mike asked. "Just seems like, I don't know, not a great place to hitch."

"Nah, I'm fine," Allie said. "Really. You guys are nice but lately everyone I think is cool turns out to be some raving lunatic who eventually wants to kill me."

The guys laughed. "All right, well, I hope the gray-haired lady in the twenty-year-old Cadillac shows up soon," Mike said, and he turned his attention to the road, waiting for a break in the traffic so he could pull onto the bridge.

The moment that break came, as the silver Honda slipped into the never-ending weave of cars, Allie turned and saw Jonas, naked except for his socks, running toward her.

Allie stepped out of her Candie's and took off barefoot into the traffic. Cars were on either side of Allie—their energy and heat pulsed against her. She could sense Jonas running behind her. The hairs on her arms knew he was there. The searing pain in her thighs, as she pumped her legs faster than she ever had in her life, also knew he was there.

Allie was choking for air when she finally turned and saw Jonas, who was only a few paces back and gaining on her. She looked ahead. The Honda was stopped in the center lane— hazard lights on, the back door open.

Allie gulped at the wind, pushed herself farther, and jumped into the backseat, pulling the door shut. "Go, go!" she said, looking out the back window. Jonas leaped for the Honda just as it jolted forward. There was a nerve-jangling squeal of brakes. Horns honked. Jonas popped up, body intact, his two hands held high like a fuck-you-finger Jack-in-the-box. Mike zoomed ahead.

"That was fucking crazy!" Mike said, laughing. After the weekend she had just had, Allie understood the laugh. It was the exhilaration of having escaped something treacherous.

Allie leaned over her knees trying to catch her breath.

"You okay?" Mark asked.

Allie nodded and took in giant, scraping, lungfuls of air.

"Was he one of the raving lunatics who wanted to kill you?" Mike asked.

Allie nodded.

"The guy was totally naked, right?" Mark asked.

"He had on dress socks," Allie said. And then the exhilaration hit her and she started laughing, a raspy cackle that was just an exhale away from sobbing.

Frank looked like he actually might cry. He grabbed Allie, pulled her into Beth's apartment, and clasped her against his chest. Allie could feel his lungs pumping in and out like slowly flapping wings.

"Oh my god!" Beth said. "Your neck, like, has bruises around it?"

"Matches my lump," Allie said.

They moved to the kitchen. Beth stood on the stove side of the counter and Allie, Frank, and Rosie sat on stools across from her. Allie relayed the story of Jonas abducting her, from beginning to end. She took particular joy in telling them that Jonas was naked except his socks, although no one else seemed intrigued by this detail.

"Let me see your feet," Beth said, and Allie lifted one foot as high as the counter so Beth could look at the blackened, scraped bottom.

"I was too scared to feel any pain," Allie said. "But my soles feel sort of sunburned now."

"No more high heels," Frank said. "From now on, only sensible shoes."

"Oh my god, your rabbit foot?" Beth plucked the little paw from the bowl that held her keys and handed it to Allie. Allie rubbed the rabbit foot, then shoved it down her pocket. That's when she noticed the Wonder Bread bag on the counter.

"Is that actual bread?" Allie pointed to the bag. It was fresh, new-looking. There was no smeared number on the side.

"That's the pure stuff," Rosie said. "I'll return it to Jonas as soon as I find him."

"It was in Mike's toolbox," Frank said.

"So what was the deal with the bag of laxatives?" Allie asked.

"I assume it was a decoy made especially for us," Frank said.

Beth and Allie went into the bathroom to wash Allie's battered feet. Beth owned a pair of loafers but Allie couldn't bring herself to wear them—they looked wrong with the acid-washed jeans and Flashdance shirts. Allie settled on a pair of flip-flops.

"Do you want to change your top?" Beth said. "I mean, like, haven't you been wearing that for four days?"

Allie looked at herself in Beth's full-length mirror. She liked how worn and filthy the clothes appeared. She felt like a warrior who was coming out on the winning side. "I'll change tomorrow when I get in my room and pick up my stuff," she said. "Do I smell?"

Beth leaned in and sniffed at Allie's neck. "No," she said.

"It's the Chinese in me," Allie said. "Dry ear wax and low body-odor."

"You have Chinese in you?" Beth asked.

"My mom's Chinese. I showed you pictures of her in *People* magazine, remember?"

"I thought she was an Indian," Beth said.

20

"Dad," Allie said, "Mighty Zamboni played at the Cow Palace in San Francisco tonight."

"Oh yeah?" Frank merged into the right lane. For the second time that night Allie was cruising over the Bay Bridge. They were going to Sausalito to check into a hotel that was owned by a Japanese couple who ate at Frank's restaurant every time they were in L.A. Since Jonas had yet to be located, Lionel's house didn't seem safe.

"Should we stop off and see if we can find Mom?"

"Allie, why would you want to see that woman?"

"I dunno. I was almost killed tonight. I've got choke marks on my neck. I mean, I'm happy to be alive and I'm glad both my parents are alive."

"She's not much of a parent," Frank said.

"Wai Po used to say, *IN BROKEN NEST THERE ARE FEW WHOLE EGGS.*" Allie spoke in Wai Po's choppy dialect. It was an imitation she had been doing for her father for as long as she could remember. Usually it made Frank laugh. Tonight he just smiled.

"All right," Frank said. "We'll go see her but you have to take it easy. Rest your throat."

"You can do all the talking," Allie said. "I just want one moment of feeling like a whole egg."

When it was well after midnight, they reached the Cow Palace. A steady stream of cars flowed out of the parking lot as Allie and her father drove in. Frank waited in the Prelude while Allie ran to the steel backstage door and banged with her fist. No one answered. Allie banged again and again.

Frank honked the horn. Allie looked back at him, then bopped her fist against the steel once more, and the door popped open. A guy with a headset on stuck his head out. He was wearing a black T-shirt that said BILLY IDOL. "Yeah?" he said impatiently.

"My mother's in the band and I want to see her," Allie said.

"There are no mothers in Billy Idol's band," the guy said.

"No, Mighty Zamboni," Allie said. "Can you tell the tambourine girl that Allie's here?"

"Zamboni's gone, man," the guy said. "Everyone's gone except a few of us cleaning up." He started to shut the door.

"Do you know where they're staying?" Allie asked quickly.

"No idea," the guy said. His eyes darted between the lump on Allie's head and the cat-paw-looking bruises around her neck. "And if I did I wouldn't tell you."

As they were driving away from the Cow Palace, Allie remembered the beeper number Billy Idol had left her. "Dad, can you pull over at a pay phone?"

"Who you gonna call at this hour?" Frank said.

"I've got Billy Idol's manager's beeper number." Allie dug through her purse and pulled out the piece of Biltmore stationery. "He'll tell me where Zamboni's staying."

"Who's Billy Idol?" Frank asked.

"A rock-and-roll star," Allie said. "His band's playing with Mom's band."

Frank pulled over the car. They were at a dark corner with looming electrical towers and an office park. And there, like a life raft, stood a phone booth.

"Call Beth's house first and see if Rosie's found Jonas," Frank said, and he handed Allie a fistful of change. "And make it quick."

Allie rapidly ran through the last few phone calls she'd made to Beth. Each one had made her feel like there was a bag of shifting sand in her stomach. Now was no different.

Rosie answered the phone.

"Did you find Jonas?" Allie asked.

"He's here," Rosie said. "Everything's fine now."

"So, he's not after me anymore?" Allie asked.

"Shit!" Jonas shouted in the background. "Are you talking to that goody-two-shoes curly-haired pain in my ass?! Is that Allie-fucking-fuck-up-my-weekend?! If I see that college-girl on my side of town I am going to fuck her up, you hear?!"

"Don't listen to him," Rosie said, but Allie couldn't help but tune in to Jonas's rant. "I've got control of the situation."

"Okay." Allie felt vaguely queasy. "I guess I don't have a choice."

"He'll be on to hating someone else within eight hours, I swear. The guy's got so many enemies in this town—"

"My biggest enemy is that daddy's-girl motherfucking—"

"Trust me," Rosie said, and he hung up before Allie could say good-bye.

Another time, Allie thought. She dropped in the rest of the change Frank had given her and hoped it was enough to dial out to the Los Angeles area code of the beeper. The phone rang once, there was a double beep, and then Allie punched in the number for the phone booth. Thirty seconds later, the manager was calling her back.

"Hello?" Allie said.

"You beeped me?" The accent was British, but not Billy Idol. In the background was the layered buzzing of a small crowd.

"Yeah. Billy gave me this number to call in case I'm in trouble and, well, I need to find my mother, who's with Mighty Zamboni, and I was just wondering if you could tell me where Zamboni is staying?"

"What's your name?" the guy asked.

"Allie."

"Allie?"

"Yeah. But Billy was calling me China Blackie."

"Oh, China Blackie!" the guy said. "Billy told me about you. Yeah, your mum's here with us at the pub. Hold on, I'll try to find her." There was a hollow clattering, Allie assumed it was from the receiver being placed on the bar. Allie could see the phone in her head: red, like most bar phones, with a dial rather than a push button on the base. She could hear the *thunk thunk thunk* of shot glasses being slammed down. Music started up, it was George Benson.

After a few minutes, Frank tapped the horn and waved Allie toward the car. She pushed the receiver harder against her ear as if that would bring her mother to the phone sooner. The random titterings in the background folded into group laughter. Very quickly, that laughter increased, thickened, and broadened its range into mass hilarity. And within that dense ruckus, Allie could suss out Penny's laughter, the same way she could hear her mother in the choruses of Mighty Zamboni songs, a single, vibrating thread of sound that Allie knew as well as her own voice.

The passenger-side window glided down and Frank leaned toward it. "Allie!" he shouted. "Enough! Let's get a move on!"

The phone clanked, as if it were being bounced on the bar top, and then Penny was finally there. "Hello?" she said.

Allie found she couldn't speak. There were words in her throat but they felt barricaded behind a trapdoor. She had spent so much of her life waiting for her mother—to come home, to call, to send a postcard, to pick up the phone—Allie knew that she could no longer wait.

"No one's here!" Penny shouted to a rumbling voice beside her. "Hello?!"

"I'm going to go now," Allie finally said, and she waved to her father in the car to let him know she'd only be another moment.

"What?!" Penny was laughing, drunk. "Who is this?!"

"I'm going now," Allie said, and she hung up.

"Jonas has the coke," Allie said. "But he's still raging at me."

"I am certain," Frank said, as he pulled onto the road, "that Jonas fully understands that I will kill him if he touches you." Allie wondered if her father really had it in him to murder someone. He did own a gun, after all.

"Okay then," Allie said. "That's one more thing I'm never going to think about again."

The traffic was as thin as it ever got in San Francisco, so it was only minutes before Allie and Frank were merging onto the Golden Gate Bridge. Just the sight of the bridge made Allie happy. She especially loved traveling over the bridge at night, when it was lit and resembled a giant, unraveled Ferris wheel.

"So that Tommy Idol fellow didn't know where your mother was?" Frank asked.

"No, he knew where she was," Allie said. "But I decided I don't need to see the Queen of Hearts again."

"Good to hear," Frank said firmly.

"I don't think Mom ever loved me," Allie said. She thought she should have cried saying something like that aloud, but it wasn't painful. It just felt like a simple fact.

"She gave you what little she had," Frank said. "It was a type of love."

"I guess," Allie said.

"I wouldn't worry about it too much," Frank said. "You've got me to love you."

"Are you saying you love me, Dad?" Allie nudged her father on the arm, she laughed. Frank had never told Allie he loved her.

"Of course that's what I'm saying." Frank held his gaze ahead.

Allie looked out the window to the sky draped over the bridge all the way down to the inky bay. She felt like she and her father were in a hydroplane bulleting out into the open sea, into an open future. And then she remembered her favorite Wai Po saying: *EVERYTHING IN PAST DIED YESTERDAY, EVERYTHING IN FUTURE BORN TODAY.*

Here I go, Allie thought.

Acknowledgments

Enormous thanks to everyone who read and commented on early drafts of this book: Geoff Becker, Michael Downs, Kit Given, Michael Kimball, Deborah Reed, Cheryl Hogue Smith, Ron Tanner, Stacy Thal, and Marion Winik. I am indebted to the Evergreen Café writing group and appreciate the support of Jane Delury, Larry Doyle, and James Magruder. Molly Peck at Blu Dot in SoHo must be thanked for selling me the most comfortable couch in the world in a year when I didn't have time to shop. Thanks go to David Piltch for helping me with the County Bowl details. Thank you to my family and my children: Madeline Tavis, Ella Grossbach, Bonnie Blau, Sheridan Blau, Rebecca Summers, Josh Blau, Alex Suarez, Satchel and Shiloh Summers, Sonia Blau Siegal, Morgan Ortiz, and Jillian and Jenna Grossbach. I am immensely grateful to all the smart and talented people at HarperCollins, especially Amy Baker, Julie Hersh, Olga Gardner, Mandy Kain, Cal Morgan, Mary Sasso, Margaux Weisman, and Martin Wilson. I wish there were bigger, greater, more powerful words than *thank you*. If there were, I'd save those words for Katherine Nintzel, Gail Hochman, and Joanne Brownstein Jarvi.

About the author

About the book

Read on

Insights,
Interviews
& More . . .

With Dogs

JESSICA WAS BORN IN BOSTON. Her father was a graduate student and her mother stayed home with Jessica and her older sister, Becca. They had a dog named Growlie. Jessica doesn't remember Growlie. They also had an old Chevy that Jessica's parents had bought for twenty-five dollars. The Chevy had a hole the size of a teacup saucer in the floor. Jessica doesn't remember the car or the hole, but she thinks about that hole every now and then—how cool it would be to look down and see the road swooshing by like a fast-moving stream.

When the family moved to Southern California (Jessica now had a little brother, Josh), they adopted a dog named Mitzi. Mitzi was old and gray. She looked like a woman who would hang out in a bar, drink whiskey, and chain-smoke unfiltered cigarettes. Certainly she'd have a raspy, barking laugh that would disintegrate into a phlegmy cough. Mitzi gave birth to a litter of pups. They were all black except one, Gumba, who grew to resemble a matted, orange shag rug. Josh carried Gumba around whenever he could, and he often dropped her on her head. This is why, the family thinks, Gumba was so dumb. Gumba was like the girl in the neighborhood who would do anything you told her to do. If you told her to eat a snail off the sidewalk, she'd pop that snail in her mouth and then follow you down the street chomping the shell, which made noises louder than potato chips. Mitzi ran off into the lemon orchard behind Jessica's house sometime after Gumba was born. It was assumed she died there. Gumba died of old age when Jessica was in college. This was very sad for everyone. Even though Gumba was a very dumb girl, she was a lovable dumb girl.

Before Gumba died, Jessica and a boyfriend impulsively got a dog named Fritz, who looked like a dwarf German shepherd. Fritz was a girl, but they liked the name. They took Fritz to the Lake of the Ozarks in Missouri, where they were camp counselors for the summer. When they returned, they give Fritz to Jessica's mother, who loved her until her death of dog old age.

Just after college, Jessica and her new husband (who were living in Berkeley) got a black lab named Giusi. The dog's name was inspired by a guy they had met in Italy who had a daughter named Giusi. Giusi galloped around the house like a wild mustang, slept on the white couch, where she left behind fallen needles of black hair, and chewed furniture. When Jessica and her husband moved to Toronto, they gave the dog to an uncle in Ventura to keep until they found a house. The dog ran away before they found the house, and neither Jessica nor her husband were too sad about it (although they both hoped the dog was happily frolicking on the beach, chewing driftwood).

In Canada, before she made friends, Jessica was exceedingly lonely. To alleviate her loneliness, she went to the Humane Society and adopted a black dog that she named Moses. Moses was leggy and sleek, and had a hound's ▶

yowl. Jessica loved Moses in spite of the fact that he chewed the legs of the kitchen chairs and once gnawed through a seatbelt and a headrest in the car. Moses was the fastest runner in Withrow Park in Toronto. Every time a group of dog owners stood at the top of the hill for dog races, each owner throwing a ball for their dog, Moses would win. (There are other dogs and dog owners who would disagree with this, but this isn't their bio page—whoever types it first gets the last word.) When Jessica had a baby, she and her husband gave Moses to a man who ran every morning and wanted a running partner in dog form. The other dog owners in the park thought it was creepy that Jessica and her husband traded in the dog for a baby. Some of them gossiped about it. Jessica ignored the gossip because she knew Moses would be happier with the running man than at home with Jessica and the nursing baby.

While living in Baltimore with her second husband, David, Jessica thought it was time for a new dog. Two friends (who had just given birth to triplets) gave her their giant, horsey black lab named Jordan. Jessica's younger daughter looked at Jordan and said in her tiny baby voice, "You're not Jordan, you're Georgie." Georgie was faithful and kind and let the kid who named her ride on her back and slide across the hardwood floor while hanging on to her tail. Georgie was old when the family adopted her, and very old when

she died on her favorite down sleeping
bag in the middle of the living room
where she had insisted on spending her
final days. Before Georgie died, Jessica
wanted a transitional dog for Georgie
to train. She figured the new dog would
behave as Georgie did, and Georgie was
a perfectly polished lady. David did
not want a new dog, but on Hanukkah,
David's brother gave Jessica a small,
white toy poodle named Pippa. The
whole family, including Georgie but
not including David, fell in love with her.
David didn't like her because he thought
poodles were showy and embarrassing.
After Pippa's first haircut, she and Jessica
were frolicking on the front lawn when
David pulled up in the car. He glanced
at the pink bows in Pippa's hair and the
puffy shaved cotton balls of hair on her
legs, and quickly backed up and drove
away. Pippa has never had a haircut like
that since. When Georgie died, David
grew to love Pippa like a daughter. Or
not quite a daughter. Maybe the way
you'd love your best friend's daughter.

One Christmas, Jessica's mother's
dog—an overly muscled rottweiler-
shepherd mix   took a bite out of Pippa's
head and punctured her eye, which now
looks like a foggy blue marble. Pippa
has become increasingly neurotic since
losing the eye. The list of things she
won't do has grown to this: Won't walk
up or down the stairs. Won't walk past
anything shiny or reflective (like the
kitchen trash can). Won't walk over
sewer grates. Won't let strange men ▶

With Dogs *(continued)*

pet her. Won't let big dogs sniff her butt. Jessica doesn't think the butt-sniff is much of a loss, but she finds it terribly inconvenient to carry the dog up and down the steps. Jessica hopes one day to get one of those old-lady chairs that ride the stairs. It would have to be nonreflective and not resemble a sewer grate, a strange man, or a big dog, so that Pippa would be willing to use it. ◡

Chinese Proverbs

I love Chinese proverbs because they can reveal monumental truths in the most economical and succinct way. It was great fun finding these proverbs for the character of Wai Po, who, I imagined, lived by most of them. Here are some of my favorites that didn't make it into the book.

How to Live Your Life

Keeping company with the wicked is like living in a fish market: one becomes used to the foul odor.

Be not afraid of growing slowly; be afraid only of standing still.

If you are patient in one moment of anger, you will escape a hundred days of sorrow.

If the first words fail, ten thousand will not avail.

The wise person listens to his mind; the fool listens to the mob.

A book is like a garden carried in the pocket.

Relationships/Love

Oh eggs, don't fight with rocks!

Curse your wife at evening, sleep alone at night.

Do not employ handsome servants.

In bed be wife and husband; in the hall be each other's honored guests.

He who strikes the first blow admits he's lost the argument.

Do not hasten to rejoice at someone's departure until you see his replacement. ▶

Chinese Proverbs *(continued)*

Family/Children

It is easier to rule a nation than a child.

Govern a family as you would cook a small fish: very gently.

If you want your dinner, don't insult the cook.

The house with an old grandparent harbors a jewel.

Parents who are afraid to put their foot down usually have children who step on their toes.

Work

Be the first to the field and the last to the couch.

The poor are those without talents; the weak are those without aspirations.

To rise high, conceal ambition.

A goal without a deadline is only a wish; a dream with a deadline becomes a goal.

If you get up one more time than you fall, you will make it through.

To read more Chinese proverbs you can go to:

http://www.quotationspage.com/quotes/ Chinese_Proverb/

http://www.sonoma.edu/users/d/ daniels/chinaproverbs.html

http://www.sacu.org/proverbs.html

http://www.chinese-traditions-and -culture.com/chinese-proverbs .html ∾

An Excerpt from *Drinking Closer to Home*

THE YEAR ANNA WAS ELEVEN, Portia was eight, and Emery was three, Louise decided she quit being a housewife. Anna was playing Parcheesi with her sister on the family room floor when Louise told them.

"Portia, Anna," Louise said, and she began searching through the little piles of papers, mail, phone books, and pencils that covered from end to end the white tile counter that separated the kitchen from the family room.

"Yeah?" Portia asked. Anna looked at her freckle-faced sister, her white, hairless flesh, her wispy brown hair that shone like corn silk. As much as she often hated her, she could understand why her parents were always pawing at her with hugs and kisses: the girl was like a pastry or a sweet. She looked edible.

Anna was as small as Portia. But she was all muscle and sinew, as if she were made of telephone cables. No one ever wanted to pinch telephone cables. She rolled the dice and ignored her mother.

"Come here," Louise said. She continued to shift things around. Portia pushed her doughy rump up and went to the counter. She moved aside an empty box that had held ten Hot Wheels racing cars and handed her mother the pack of unfiltered Camel cigarettes she was most likely looking for.

"I quit." Louise tapped out a ▶

9

cigarette, then lit it from the pack of matches she kept tucked in the cellophane wrapper. She had grown her hair long at a time when mothers didn't have long hair. And she didn't wear makeup—a habit that made her look fresher and more alive than the other mothers. Anna hated it when Portia said that their mother looked like a movie star—she hated that her sister couldn't see the drop-out anarchist mentality their mother conveyed through her hippie clothes. And it really drove Anna crazy when she witnessed Louise opening the front door to the Fuller Brush Man or the Avon Lady and they asked Louise, "Is your mother home?" What kind of a mother didn't look like a mother?! One like Louise, Anna supposed, who only wore wide, drapey bell-bottoms, cork platform shoes, and flowing silk shirts with no bra. In her ears were always two gold hoops that hung almost to her shoulders. Anna knew that people in other parts of town dressed like Louise. But no one in their neighborhood did. They lived in a place of pantsuits, helmets of hair, waxy lipstick, sensible sneakers. Anna didn't know any mother who worked, or did art. At least her parents weren't divorced, Anna thought. The only person she knew who had divorced parents was Molly Linkle, a girl who was so fat she wore bras that made her breasts look like cones and shopped in the Ladies' Department at Robinson's.

"What do you mean you quit?" Portia climbed onto the orange stool. Anna wondered when her sister would stop asking questions.

"Your turn," Anna said. She looked toward her sister's back and watched as her mother pursed her lips and let out a slow stream of smoke.

"I quit being a housewife." Louise shook her hair and smiled.

"Can you do that?" Portia asked.

Anna was going to pretend she wasn't listening. There was something inside her that often led her to believe that if she ignored certain things they would cease to exist. She turned the Parcheesi board over and dumped the pieces on the rug.

"Of course I can. I just did. I quit!" Louise took another drag off her cigarette.

"Anna!"

Anna knew Portia was staring at her but she refused to look up. "Mom quit!"

"I heard," Anna said. She could feel her face darkening, like a mercury thermometer.

"Does Dad know?" Anna asked. She crossed her legs and glared at her mother.

"I told him last night."

"What about Emery?" The idea that her mother wouldn't have the same occupation as her friends' mothers enraged Anna. Who would have the nerve to give birth to children, move them into a house, and then declare that she wasn't going to take care of them? A drug-addicted hippie, Anna decided, that's who.

"You girls are in charge of Emery now."

"Really?!" Portia's cheerful voice made Anna want to knock her off the stool. Portia was such a wannabe mother, she coddled Emery as if she owned him. In fact the only thing Portia had ever claimed she wanted to be when she grew up was a mother. She had a doll, Peaches, with whom she slept every night. When the family traveled, Portia always packed Peaches first in the bottom of her white, satin-lined suitcase. The current Peaches was actually the second Peaches, as the first Peaches had devolved into a repellent floppy, dirty thing with a body like a lumpy mattress and arms and legs that were four different colors from dirt and stains. She'd gone bald from Portia's carrying her by her hair, and she smelled like spit. Anna didn't even like being in the same room with old Peaches. When Portia was seven, Louise had sewn Peaches a pink satin retirement gown with a matching satin-and-lace cap, and gave Portia a new, fresh Peaches who smelled like plastic and who, Anna thought, wasn't the embarrassing rag that was old Peaches.

"Yeah, Emery's yours," Louise said.

"Can he be mine alone?" Portia asked Anna.

Anna couldn't believe that her sister felt compelled to ask this question. It was like asking if Anna wanted to share old Peaches.

"What do you say, Anna?" Louise asked.

"I don't want him," Anna said. "He's dirty and he smells."

"He's adorable!" Portia said.

"Are we getting a maid?" Anna asked. Her friends' mothers ▶

cleaned their houses, but people on TV, characters with apartments and homes that seemed much smaller than theirs, had maids.

"No!" Louise snorted. "There are enough people hanging around here between your and your sister's friends. Besides. We don't have that kind of money."

"So who's going to cook dinner?" Portia asked.

"Anna will cook."

"Fine." Anna stood up and joined her sister at the counter. She could feel rage inside her like a team of insects crawling through her veins.

"And what about everything else?" Portia asked, although to Anna she didn't seem particularly concerned. And why should she be concerned? Other than giving Emery an occasional bath, Anna couldn't really name the things Louise did as a housewife. By all appearances, their mother did little other than swim naked in the pool and write poems or paint in her studio. On the rare day when Anna's friends came over (despite Louise's claims of frequency, Anna always tried to steer them to someone else's house), she had them wait on the porch on the pretense of having to ask her mother if it was okay if they came in when, really, she was checking to see that Louise was dressed. Anna preferred to hang out at her friends' houses, as even when Louise was dressed, she was an embarrassment. ∾